Shiloh

Until the Day
Breaks,

Helena Forrest

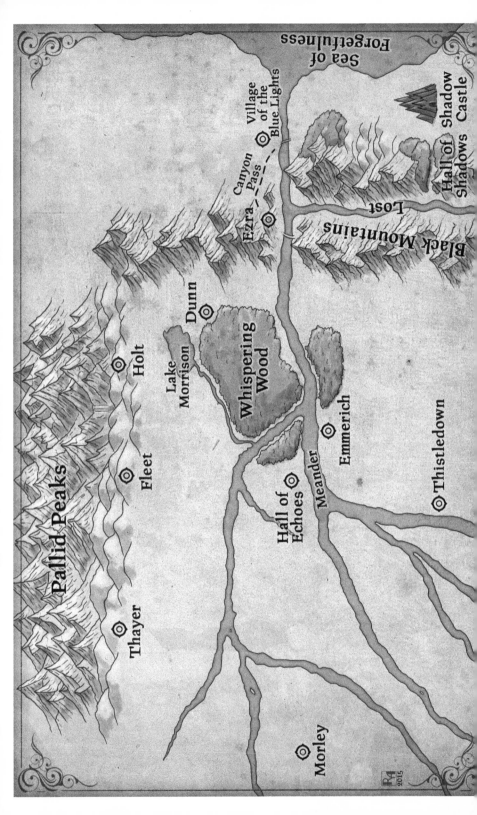

THE SHILOH SERIES
BOOK ONE

SHILOH

HELENA SORENSEN

Contents

Prologue

In the beginning, there was Ram. He was alone and apart from everything, and he was great and joyful and immensely strong and good. To begin, he created the sun, round and red and gold, and he loved its brightness and its warmth. But the sun shone down on an empty world, and Ram was grieved. He looked at the void and longed to fill it with color and life.

So Ram created other creators to help him fill the emptiness. Three sons and three daughters burst into being from the soil of Ram's thought. Leander, Rurik, and Vali were fierce, daring, brave. Petra, Callista, and Riannon were strong, beautiful, wildly free. These sons and daughters of Ram, like their father, were not bound by flesh. They could see into one another and discern one another's minds. And whenever one of the immortals (for so they came to be called) saw in another immortal an image that matched something in his own mind, that image came to life. Leander and Riannon shared many visions of wild creatures, and it was not long before the world was filled with soaring birds and creeping beasts. Vali and Petra shaped the mountains, great windswept peaks tipped with snow, and Riannon and Callista formed the flowers, soft purple heather, and delicate wild roses.

In this way Shiloh was filled with life, and the immortals at times even created other immortals to share in their work. At the birth of Linden, trees spread over the land, gathering into forests and hedging the meadows, their great branches stretching toward the sky. Some of the trees were touched by Ram, and they took on a spark of the life of the immortals. At Maya's birth, rivers cut through earth and stone, laughing and rollicking their way across the land. Ram was so delighted that he filled the waters with nymphs, shimmering creatures whose eyes sparkled in the light of the sun.

But Rurik, as yet, had taken no part in creation. He went to his brothers, Leander and Vali, searching their minds for some vision that matched his own. It was not to be found. He went to his sisters, but neither Petra nor Callista shared any thought with him. Rurik was angry at this, for his brothers and sisters shared in their father's work and their father's glory, but he did not. He wished, in fact, that he might create alone, bringing into existence the thoughts of his own mind as only Ram could. It was not until Rurik went to Riannon that he discovered some trace of himself, for Riannon was the wildest of Ram's children and she, too, longed to be free of the immortals' one restraint. In her heart, as in her brother's, a dark sliver of rebellion resided. Riannon was neither cruel nor wicked, but, like the wind, she could not be contained, and she hardly knew what she did when she stood face to face with her brother and brought into being the *Shadow*.

One

amos was no more than seven when he killed a Shadow Wolf, in the dark of the Whispering Wood, no less, where wolves were as thick as the undergrowth. The story spread like wildfire. It was rehearsed in every cottage, alehouse, and market from the Pallid Peaks to the southern moors until there was hardly a person in Shiloh who didn't know the tale by heart.

"He was huntin' with his da," one man would say.

"Aye," another would say, "and 'e wasn't even watchin' out fer danger, though 'is father warned 'im of it time and again."

"Amos was born without the fear," a third would interject. "He strolls through the dark o' the Whisperin' Wood, whistlin' . . . as if it was nothin' more than the lane outside his cottage."

"'Twas crouched in the thicket," the first man would continue, eager to reclaim the role of storyteller. "He saw the flash o' the wolf's eyes and heard a growl like distant thunder."

"That's when 'e came alive!" the second would say. "In the flickerin' of a candle, 'e pulled an arrow from 'is quiver and *breathed on it*."

"And the arrow was set ablaze," the third would interrupt. "He marked his prey and shot straight and true inta the Shadow."

At this point in the story, a boy would inevitably burst in on the gathering, brandishing his bow and arrow and shouting the words Amos had spoken to the wolf. "You're no more than shadow and smoke, beast! Be gone!"

Then the men would laugh, shooing the boy back to his play, and finish the tale, their voices hushed with wonder. "And the demon blew away like vapor on the wind."

It was not unheard of for a man's breath to set something alight. For that matter, it was not unheard of for any number of extraordinary things to happen in Shiloh. It was just rare. And as year followed year, in an endless line of unbroken darkness, it had become increasingly rare. Nearly fifteen hundred years had passed since Hammond had learned the secret of fire and wielded it in battle against the Shadow Wolves. He had founded the Fire Clan, but, despite its name, the clan could boast no more than a handful of men and women in its long history who shared Hammond's gift. That is why Amos was special.

He would have been openly revered by his clansmen, would doubtless have risen to become the Light of the Clan, if it weren't for the stories. If only he and his father didn't speak so often of what lay beyond the Shadow. There was nothing but darkness in Shiloh. In the Shadow they lived and moved and breathed. It was the sky above them, the night enclosing them, the darkness blinding them, and the power hunting them. It was what they had always known, all they had ever known. And only the most foolish had ever dreamed that anything lay beyond it.

Wynn finished mending the gray, woolen tunic and folded it neatly, laying it on the cot in the corner. She sat down at the kitchen table, its wood surface worn smooth from years of use, and began to chop the potatoes that waited in a basket on the floor nearby. Other than the cots and the table where Wynn sat, there was little furniture in the stone cottage. A wooden trunk, bound with iron and bearing the sign of the Fire Clan, sat against the wall, and two chairs rested on a woven rug near the fireplace. No curtains covered the windows, for light was scarce in Shiloh, and the candles and the fire did little to brighten the interior of the cottage.

Outside, gray sheep grazed in their fold. Across the lane, night-blooming jasmine hung thick over the fence that bordered the meadow. On warm days its fragrance was heady and sweet. Wynn loved it above all things, and she often wove its flowers into her daughter's hair.

Her eyes filled when she thought of Phebe, and she cut her hand with the knife. "Curse it!" she said.

"Ya alright, Ma?" A girl of four, dark-haired and dark-eyed, sat on the rug near the fire and played with a little rag doll.

"I'm alright, little bird. Just clumsy is all," Wynn answered, her eyes hardly grazing Phebe's face. It was still too new. Only a few months had passed since the attack, and the angry red gash stretching from the girl's forehead to her jaw line was still too much of a shock. *What if Amos hadn't been there?* The question haunted Wynn in the quiet of the night, when visions of green eyes and cold fangs and the echo of her daughter's screams drove away the sweet oblivion of sleep and awakened older, darker terrors.

Amos walked into the cottage with an armload of firewood, and his sister jumped to greet him. He set his load by the hearth and scooped her up, placing her in his lap as he sat on the bench next to his mother. Playfully, he tugged at strands of Phebe's dark hair. Wynn looked him over. His tunic and trousers were stained, as usual, his red-brown hair awry. Though he hadn't been hunting that day, his arm guard was firmly in place, and his quiver and bow leaned against the wall beside the door, ready at a moment's notice.

The cat's claw hung around his neck on a leather cord. Wynn didn't like to look at it. *What if he hadn't been there?*

"Couldn't ya use another candle, Ma? How can ya see ta do yer cookin'?"

"I can see just fine, Amos." She reached over to smooth the boy's hair and pinch his chin. "You work on yer arrows fer a while, and dinner'll be ready soon."

Phebe went back to her rag doll, and Amos sat cross-legged on the floor, pulling stalks of river cane from a nearby basket. He notched the ends of the cane stalks with his knife, then fitted them with small pointed stones. He was just beginning to wrap the ends of the arrows with sinew when Abner came through the door.

"Good evenin', m' dear ones," Abner greeted. His wife was the only one to notice when his eyes reached Phebe and his smile faltered. He placed a small quail on the table. Wynn took the tiny bird, plucked and cleaned it, and stirred it into the kettle with the potatoes and a handful of herbs. As she worked, she listened to the chatter of her children and exchanged meaning glances with her husband.

"And what song do ya have fer me today, little nightingale?"

Phebe sat on her father's knee and smiled up at him. It was not her old smile. This one was smaller, favoring the wound that still pained her. But she sat up straight and tall and proudly announced, "I've learned a new one, Da."

"Aye? Well, ya must sing it fer me then."

The little girl opened her mouth, and when the first clear note rang out, everything else in the room seemed to dim.

She sang:

"Far, far away
In the crystal teardrops
Hangin' from the branches o' the silent trees
Gone, gone away
Ta the Hall o' Shadows

Peerin' through the mist with eyes that cannot see
Shine, shine away
Keep the lights a' burnin'
Never let the embers o' the flame go out
Run, run away
For the Shadow Weavers
Come ta take a trophy ta their Master's house"

When she finished, the cottage felt colder. Wynn resumed her work, wondering how it was that children could make a playful sing-song out of such a dark reality. It chilled her blood to think of it.

"Where did ya hear that song, Phebe?" Abner asked.

"The children in the village were singin' it," she said, "last time we took the vegetables ta market."

"Don't sing it anymore, little bird, alright?"

"She doesn't know what it means, Da," Amos chimed in.

"Still," Abner said, looking his son in the eye. "Still, I'd rather she didn't."

Phebe's eyes grew large, and her chin quivered. "I didn't mean to, Da. I won't sing it no more. I swear it."

Abner wrapped her in both his arms and stroked her hair. "Hush, now, little one. It's alright."

The cottage filled with the smoky-green smell of herbs and potatoes, and the family sat down to a dinner of bread and cheese and rich stew. They spoke of their day's adventures and misadventures, of the progress of the garden and the health of the flock, and soon Wynn was clearing the dishes and tucking the children into their cots.

"What will I dream of tonight, Ma?" Phebe asked. She had been captured of late by the tale of Maeve, who dreamed of a great light in the sky.

Wynn kissed her cheek tenderly, careful to avoid the angry scar.

"Well, little bird, perhaps you'll dream the meadow is filled with wildflowers in colors you've never even imagined."

Amos sat up in his cot. "I'm goin' ta dream o' the Pallid Peaks. I'll be huntin' fer Sirius, the great black dragon."

Amos, Wielder of Fire, Wynn thought to herself. She bent to kiss his forehead, resting a hand on his wayward hair. *There's no end to the boy's ambition, no limit to his courage.* Her mother's heart twisted with pride and pain.

Of course, none of them dreamed, and that was a mercy. Dreaming was strange, a rare gift. Dreamers were treated with suspicion and fear, and they often came to bad ends. No mother would wish dreaming on her children.

Phebe's small, clear voice broke the silence, bidding goodnight with the familiar phrase.

"May the light shine upon you."

"And you," they each replied.

T w o

The mighty River Meander was the heart of Shiloh, and most villages were situated on one of its many branches. From its headwaters on the eastern side of the Black Mountains, the river's main channel flowed due west, bending south toward the moors when it passed the western limit of the Whispering Wood. Nestled in that crook of the Meander, less than an hour's walk from the cottage, was the village of Emmerich.

Amos would have liked to go to the village more often. He would have liked to play with the other boys, who wrestled with each other, spent hours practicing their marksmanship, and swam in the black water of the river. He would have liked, at the very least, to gather the shiny, black stones that littered the riverbank. Those stones made the best arrowheads. But the river was strictly forbidden. Abner would have none of it.

"There's evil in that water, Amos," he would say. "I'll not have ya goin' anywhere near the river."

Amos had argued the restriction just once with his father, and Abner's stern reply, with his brow furrowed and his jaw set, had told

Amos that he had no chance of changing his father's mind.

"It makes ya forget, Amos," Abner had said, "and ya mustn't ever forget."

"Forget what, Da?" Amos had asked.

"Who ya are, and what lies beyond," his father had answered.

"I won't forget, Da. Never." Amos had not asked to go to the river again.

This morning, they traveled north toward Emmerich, through fields and meadows dotted with dark trees. Wynn walked with a sack strapped to her back, and Abner carried Phebe on his shoulders while Amos led the way, holding aloft an iron lantern to light the path. It was midmorning. Just a few hours would pass before Shiloh lay in full daylight, but even then, lanterns and candles were a necessity, for the Shadow lay like a dense and suffocating blanket over all that country. Its misty fingers stretched from behind the Black Mountains in the east to the very ends of the western horizon, and the brightest light of noonday was no more than a gasp in the breathless darkness.

Amos knew they were nearing the village not because of any clear view of its cottages or stables. It was the lights that distinguished Emmerich from the land around it. There, lanterns hung from iron hooks in dozens of doorways and along the path that led to Market Circle. The flickering glows of many fires lit the village still more, shining from cottage hearths and from the blacksmith's furnace. Best of all was the open fire just behind the brewer's shop where he cooked, in an enormous iron kettle, the potatoes and cherries and huckleberries he used to make his beer and ale. Amos loved the smells that came from that great pot, and he loved the lights of the village. He puffed out the lantern's flame as he led the family past stables and a few outlying cottages into the heart of the village.

Men and women bustled about, buying roots and herbs from the apothecary, having their jugs filled with ale, or commissioning work from the town's craftsmen. Many stopped to stare at Abner and his family, their eyes drawn first to Amos and then to the girl with the scarred face. Orin, the blacksmith, stopped his work to nod in Abner's direction. His was the first shop on the street, and this morning he was hammering away at a horseshoe. Abner nodded in return just as Caedmon, the carpenter, spoke.

"And what brings the Clan o' the Madman ta the village today?"

A cackle sounded from across the street, where Lark leaned in the doorway of her shop. These two gave them no respite. The broad, hairy carpenter had a special loathing for Abner, and the chandler was no better, though her malice was more often directed toward the rest of the family.

"What? The whole clan's 'ere? You've even brought the girl?"

Amos took a step forward, his hands clenching into tight fists, but his father raised a hand to his chest and stopped his advance. Caedmon's mocking grin faded as Phebe's face came into view.

"Careful," Abner said. "You'll not speak o' my daughter again." It was not a request, and the carpenter knew it. He kept silent and turned back to his work.

"I'll take 'er ta see Darby," Wynn whispered to her husband. He nodded once, and Wynn and Phebe hurried off to the weaver's shop.

"Amos, can ya wait here a while?"

"Where ya goin', Da? I'll go with ya."

Abner sighed, his shoulders sinking. "I'm goin' ta the apothecary's shop ta see about somethin' fer Phebe. Can ya wait here, just fer a bit?"

"Aye." Amos looked around Market Circle as his father moved away. Today was not market day, and the few stalls that surrounded the circle stood empty and forlorn in the dim light. Beneath Amos's feet a wide stone mosaic marked the village as belonging to the Fire Clan. Its three tongues of flame, laid out in black stone, stretched inward from the edges of the circle. There they met and twisted around a smoothly polished chunk of edanna, which glowed red-gold in the light of the lanterns. Across from the circle, near the river, stood the magistrate's hall. Amos listened for the sound of the latest village dispute, but the voices he heard came from the southern corner of the hall, a poorly lit portion of town out of sight of the villagers' cottages. He moved in quietly, eyes and ears alert.

A frail boy stood against the wall. His hair and skin were so pale, they looked almost white, and his eyes, wide with fear, were the lightest of blues. This is what Amos noticed first. The second thing he noticed was that the boy's arms were tied behind him with a coarse rope. His ankles were bound as well. And not a dozen steps away, a larger, darker boy stood with an arrow at the string. His friends stood nearby, shouting instructions.

"Get 'is ear! You can make the shot, Ferlin!"

"Course I can make the shot. I could part 'is hair if I wanted."

"Not 'is ear . . . 'is eye. That's where the danger is. Ya never know. 'E could be a shifter."

"No, 'e couldn't. They've got green eyes, Dorian, ya blockhead. I ought'a kill 'im straight out."

"Don't, Ferlin. They'll take ya ta the magistrate."

"And what if they do? No woman can spill my blood, whatever 'er title be."

"Come on, Ferlin. Let's see what ya can do!"

All this Amos heard as he approached, and before the boys noticed his presence, he could see, even in the meager light, beads of sweat breaking out on the face of the boy against the wall. In a flash, Amos had strung an arrow. He stepped out, blazing with purpose, between the group and the boy.

"Drop yer bow!" he commanded.

Ferlin and the others were taken by surprise. One of the boys slunk back into the shadows, but to Ferlin's credit, he stood his ground.

"Out o' the way," he said. "This is not yer fight."

"I told ya ta drop yer bow," Amos repeated. He drew the string along his jaw, closed one eye, and prepared to loose the arrow.

"You're askin' fer trouble. I'm the best shot in the village, and everyone knows it," Ferlin fired back.

"Aye. It takes a great marksman ta hit a bound target." At this, one of Ferlin's friends snickered. "Why not try huntin' somethin' that fights back? Then we'll see what kind o' shot ya really are."

Ferlin, whose rage and injured pride had almost driven him to release his arrow, finally realized the identity of the intruder. His mouth went slack, and his bow sank to his side. This was Amos. He had killed a Shadow Wolf in the deep dark of the Whispering Wood. It was a feat that many boys in the village dreamed of accomplishing. Some even boasted that they had done it. But here, in the flesh, stood a mere boy of seven who had actually killed the most feared predator in all Shiloh. This boy was a legend . . . already. And if he could shoot a Shadow Wolf in the blackness of the wood, he could shoot a boy on the edge of the village. Ferlin threw a quick glance at his remaining friends before turning and melting away into the darkness.

Amos dropped his bow slowly, releasing the muscles held tense during the encounter with Ferlin. Then he slung his bow over his shoulder, and, using the dagger he carried in his belt, cut the ropes of the captive. Now the boy's eyes were wide with awe instead of fear. His mouth was open and tipped up on one side.

"You're Amos," he said.

"Aye. And you're welcome," Amos replied with a broad grin that told the boy he was only teasing.

"I'm Simeon," he said with a shy smile. "Thank you."

"Have they done this before?" Amos asked.

"A few times, but they've never got up the nerve ta shoot me."

"It's a good thing. I'm not in Emmerich enough ta keep an eye on 'em."

"I wish ya were. But I understand. They're none too kind, are they?" Amos's brow furrowed, making him look like his father in miniature.

He wondered what Simeon had heard about his family. Did he, like everyone else, think they were mad?

"What do ya mean by sayin' that?" he snapped.

"Nothin'," Simeon retreated. "Only, they don't take well ta anyone who's different."

Amos looked at the boy carefully. His fair hair and eyes were certainly different. In Shiloh, the overwhelming majority of people had dark hair and dark eyes. The fair ones stuck out. No doubt Simeon had experienced his share of cruelty at the hands of the villagers.

"You're a Dreamer?" Amos asked.

"That's what they say," Simeon answered, "but I've never had a dream."

Amos nodded understanding. "Who's yer da?"

"Don't know." Simeon looked at his feet. "Jada's my ma."

Oh. The magistrate. Simeon's plight seemed more wretched than ever. "Would yer ma let ya come ta our cottage? It's not too far from town."

Abner's voice rang through Market Circle. "Amos!"

"I'll ask," Simeon said.

"Good," Amos replied. He reached out to grasp Simeon's thin forearm, in the usual gesture of greeting and farewell. "May the light shine upon you."

Simeon hesitated, and Amos realized he'd never heard the phrase.

"It's just somethin' we say." And with that, he turned and ran to meet his waiting family.

Somethin' who says? Simeon thought. He stood a long time in that spot, hardly aware of his chaffed wrists and ankles. In the short space of a few moments, his world had changed completely, and his loyalties had been decided forever.

Three

"Tell us a story, Da."

Phebe sat on the edge of the fire, braiding the colored threads Darby had given her during their visit to the village. Amos and Simeon sat nearby on the rug, hungry for one of Abner's tales. The two had become fast friends, spending four of the past five days together, but this was the first evening Simeon had spent at the cottage with Amos's family. He was fidgety. Again and again, Simeon would glance at Wynn, spinning wool on the drop spindle, or Abner, oiling his bow as he sat in a chair by the fire. *So this is what it's like*, he thought.

"What would ya like ta hear, tonight, little bird?" Abner laid his bow aside and leaned back in the chair.

"The Tale o' Grosvenor!" Amos shouted. The story of the great and fearless hunter, Father of the Clan of the White Tree, was one of his favorites.

"No, the trees, Da! Tell about the trees in the Whisperin' Wood!" Phebe pleaded.

But before Abner could respond to either of these requests,

Simeon asked, in a small voice, "What about the *other* stories?" Every eye turned to him.

"What stories do ya mean, Simeon?" Abner asked.

"Well," Simeon hesitated, afraid to spoil his newfound friendship, "in the village they call ya mad because o' the stories ya tell. Caedmon says you're 'mad as Evander.' What does he mean? Do ya think there's a great lantern in the sky . . . somewhere outside the Shadow?" There, he'd said it. He couldn't believe he'd strung so many words together, dangerous words at that, on his first evening with Amos's family.

"'Mad as Evander,' eh?" The creases in Abner's brow smoothed, and he gave Simeon a smile. He liked this boy. "I've been called worse than that, worse by far. 'Tis an honor ta be named with Evander and his Lost Clan." Abner rested his head against the swirling grain of his chair and looked up, thinking. "Perhaps, Simeon, I should begin with the story o' the Cataclysm, when the world was unmade."

"Unmade?" Simeon asked.

"Aye, that's a good one, Da," Amos said. He leaned forward, propping his elbows on his knees. Phebe curled up in Wynn's lap, and Simeon held his breath. For a moment, the only sounds were the crackling of the fire and the soft bleating of the sheep.

Abner closed his eyes and began:

"There are some who say that a High God ruled all Shiloh many, many years ago. Years beyond count. They say that the land was filled with light and color; that even the water sparkled and flashed like a thousand candle flames dancin'. They say that everything was alive and beautiful. And they say that Man and Woman were great and powerful, that their voices moved the world. This was before the comin' o' the Shadow Lord, before the Shadow fell."

"But I thought," Simeon was whispering to Amos, but Abner stopped and waited to hear his question.

"Go ahead, Sim."

"I thought that Shiloh was the Shadow Realm, Ulff's Realm." He spoke the name in a whisper, his eyes darting to and fro as if Ulff himself were present in the cottage.

"It wasn't always so. Shiloh was different once, but that world has been all but forgotten."

"Ya said there was light," Simeon continued, a little more boldly. "Were the lanterns larger, the candles brighter?"

"I don't know. But I think, perhaps, they had no need of lanterns and candles."

"They had great fires, then?"

"No. They had no fire at all."

"But how could they see?" Simeon could not understand.

"Well, Evander's mother dreamed of a great light, brighter and hotter than any candle or fire, hangin' high in the sky. It lit everything in Shiloh, and there was no need of other lights."

Simeon's mouth hung open. He tried to imagine such a light, but his mind refused to create an adequate picture. He had never seen more than twenty paces distant. He could not form an image of even the whole village of Emmerich, much less the whole landscape of Shiloh.

"Tell the rest, Da." Amos had heard the story many times, but his eyes were lit with anticipation.

"Where was I?" Abner muttered to himself as he rubbed the knee of his leather trousers. "Ah, the comin' o' the Shadow Lord . . . yes. Man and Woman were great and powerful, and their voices moved the world . . . until the comin' o' the Shadow Lord." The crackling of the fire stilled, and its light guttered.

"Did 'e wear the darkness like a cloak when 'e came?" Phebe whispered. "No, m' nightingale," Abner replied. "He came robed in shinin' light, beautiful ta behold. Man and Woman were deceived, for they *chose* the Shadow. Ulff lured them inta the heart of 'is realm, and they became 'is captives."

"What happened ta the world then?" Simeon wondered aloud.

"There was a tremblin' and a swellin' and a shakin' that drove the mountains inta the sea. And other mountains were thrust up from the depths o' the earth. The Black Mountains, we call 'em. The waters rushed and foamed and roared. The River Meander, which used ta flow down *inta* the Sea of Forgetfulness now flows down *from* it, so great was that Cataclysm. That's why they say the world was unmade. Did ya know, Simeon —"

"Abner, wait," Wynn interrupted. Her eyes were narrowed, and her head was tilted to one side. Her chair sat nearest to the window at the back of the cottage, so she heard it first. They all stopped, waiting, and then the sound came again, louder and clearer. It was a dreadful sort of screaming bleat.

"The sheep!" Amos shouted, leaping from the floor to grab his bow and quiver. Phebe's eyes followed Amos's every move. She was trembling.

Abner had already reached the door when he turned to his wife. "Keep 'er near the fire!" he said.

Outside the cottage, Abner stepped past his son, whose arrow was already notched, his bowstring tense. They crept around the edge of the house to get a look at the sheepfold. There, south and east of the cottage, their small flock waited, protected only by the torches that burned at each corner of the fence. The fires kept the wolves away, more or less, but only because wolves preferred human prey. The cats would take whatever they could get. They were a constant danger, stealthy and cruel, with slanting green eyes and dagger-sharp claws.

Abner could see sheep stumbling blindly around the fold, bumping into the fences, their eyes streaming blood. Other sheep were bleating and moaning. In the flickering torchlight, it was difficult to see how many of the cats had come. He could make out the shape of one, crouched over the belly of a dead sheep, tearing away at its entrails. Another peered through the grasses outside the fence, ready to pounce.

Abner stepped into the circle of torchlight just a second before his son. He put a hand on the top rail of the fence and vaulted over. He thrust his arrow into the oiled cloth at the base of the torch, catching fat and flame on the tip, and strode toward the feasting cat. Phebe's face flashed before him as he shot the beast through the back of the head.

He turned to see how Amos fared and found him locking eyes with the other cat. Its mottled coat faded almost entirely into the rocks and shrubs of the landscape, but thick tufts of white fur came to sharp points at either side of its mouth, and white showed in its tall, pointed ears. For Amos, they were like the four white corners of a target. The boy blew softly on the end of his arrow, setting it alight with red flame, and sent the shaft straight into the cat's forehead. It disappeared with a scream just as Abner reached him.

All this time, Simeon had stood peeking out from behind the cottage. He couldn't bring himself to stay inside with the women, but he had no weapons to fight with the men. *It makes no difference,* he thought. *Had I the White Bow itself, I couldn't have killed the cats.* He hovered there in the eerie silence following the attack, his forehead beaded with cold sweat, until Abner came back to check on the family. Even then, he could not raise his eyes to look at him.

"It's alright, Sim. Only two this time." Abner rested a hand on the boy's pale hair. "Would ya check on the women while we tend ta the flock?"

Simeon's chest felt tight, his eyes hot. Abner had not been angry, had not shamed him. Instead, he had given him a small task, something that gave him a sense of purpose in his wretchedness. He nodded assent and rushed back into the cottage where Wynn waited by the fire, rocking gently back and forth and stroking Phebe's hair.

27

"Shhhh. 'Twill be alright, little one. The men'll protect us from the Shadow. They'll come back. I'm sure they will. 'Twill be alright. Shhhh."

"It's over," Simeon announced, and Wynn's whole body relaxed. She let out a slow breath and moved Phebe to her knee. Simeon noticed that tears rolled down the girl's cheeks. She made no sound, but the scar on her face stood out in vivid red. Somehow, the room seemed filled with the sound of that scar, of the fear and anguish it held.

He sat down on the bench beside the table, wondering what to do. He wanted to be strong, like Abner and Amos. But what could he possibly do now? A few moments passed in tense silence before it came to him, and he turned to Phebe with a question.

"Amos says ya can sing. Is it so? I've never heard ya."

Simeon's distraction was just what she needed. Phebe's eyes brightened at the challenge, and when her mother nodded she answered.

"I can sing," she said with shy pride. "I know a host o' songs."

"Don't believe ya," Simeon teased. "You're too little."

In defiance, Phebe hopped from her mother's knee, squared her shoulders, and began. Her voice, at first soft and tremulous, steadied and strengthened with every note.

"Come, little nightingale, rest in the willow
Sing me a song through the darkening night
Come as I lay with the shadows my pillow
And sing me a song o' the light

Come, though the darkness around ya is deepenin'
Sing, for yer song is a flame burnin' bright
Come, though the Shadow before ya is creepin'
And sing me a song o' the light

Come, for yer music will ring out the clearer
Brightest when darkness is all but complete
Come when the nightfall would threaten ta take me
Show me the path fer my feet

Come, little nightingale, rest in the willow
Sing me a song through the darkening night
Come as I lay with the shadows my pillow
And sing me a song o' the light
Come, sing me a song o' the light"

Outside, Amos rubbed salve into the gashes of the wounded sheep. Abner cut the gray wool from the dead and gleaned the sinew from their bones before burning their remains. Both tasks were filthy and bloody, and father and son knew better than to relax their guard. As they worked, their ears were alert for the sounds of predators; their weapons were ready. Outside, the darkness was closing in. But inside, the sound of Phebe's voice was like the ringing of bells, and the cottage was filled with a fierce, golden light.

"I helped pick 'em. Did the weedin', too," Phebe announced.

"Many thanks ta you, too, miss," Darby said with a mock bow.

Phebe giggled. She liked it here. The strange milky white of the weaver's eyes did not frighten or disgust her. On the contrary, since the attack, she felt safer here than anywhere else in the village. Darby's eyes never lingered on the red scar that marked her face. Darby never looked at her with pity. Darby never shuffled away from her, clinging to the other side of the street. In this shop, Phebe could sing and laugh and smile. Here, the light of two small lanterns seemed brighter than the brightest bonfire at the largest village celebration.

"Have ya heard about the apron fer Rowan's comin' of age?" Darby directed her question to Wynn, who moved another stool to sit by the weaver. "They say the embroidery covers near half the fabric."

While Darby and her mother talked, Phebe made her usual exploration of the small cottage, lifting her lantern to gaze at the stacks of cloth. Most of it was gray, though some was of a finer weave. A few precious bolts of white wool were displayed on a high shelf. Phebe stared at these, imagining her own coming-of-age celebration. Perhaps she would even wear white on the day she became a wife. White sheep were so rare in Shiloh that their wool was reserved for such occasions. Phebe tried to picture the embroidery that would adorn her own gown. The sign of the Fire Clan would appear in the center of the elaborate border, of course. *And I'd like birds*, she thought, *and jasmine.*

In a large basket, on a table at the back wall, was the most marvelous thing in the weaver's shop. Phebe could have lingered at that basket for hours, fingering the skeins of colored yarn. There were deep blood reds and earthy brown reds. There were mossy greens and bright grass greens. There were rich berry purples and dark eggplant purples. There were rusty orange yellows and clear golden yellows. *So many colors*, Phebe thought, and sighed. She was clothed in gray wool, standing in a dim, gray room in a dim gray world. How she longed for everything to be as lovely as those coils of yarn. She knew already that the yarn was far too expensive to be used on every shift or blanket. Darby bought the colored skeins from a weaver in a larger village some ways to the northwest. Each color was marked with a small carven stone, and in this way, Darby could distinguish the different shades. But the dyes were rare and costly, and they traveled far to reach the little village of Emmerich. Phebe had little hope of buying any of the colored yarn until her seventeenth birthday approached. The little girl sighed again, replacing a coil of purple yarn in the basket, and went to join her mother.

"Ya mustn't be so melancholy, little one, or the night weavers will come fer ya." The soft sounds of Phebe's sighs had not escaped the weaver's keen ears.

"Please, Darby, don't," her mother protested.

"I was only teasin', Phebe. No need ta worry. Come, would ya like ta hear a story?"

"Not today," Wynn answered for her. "The light's goin', and we'd best get back."

Phebe was disappointed. The weaver was the best storyteller in the village.

"Aye. Another time, then, but don't stay away too long." Darby squeezed Wynn's hand and brushed a hand over Phebe's cheek as they moved toward the door. By the time they crossed the threshold, Darby's fingers had resumed their rhythmic work on the loom.

Directly across the street from the weaver's shop was the brewery, where Payne made beer and ale. Though he sold no food and kept no lodgers, his shop did boast a haphazard collection of tables, stools, and benches. Often, villagers who came to buy a mug of huckleberry ale or potato beer would sit to gripe or gossip with one another, and Payne's shop was the best spot in Emmerich for hearing a good story. If you sipped your ale quietly and listened patiently, you might hear about the building of the Hall of Echoes. Or you might hear what the sons of Burke saw from their watchtowers before the Shadow Lord took them. On this particular day, the conversation centered around Abner's family.

"It's a shame about the girl. She was a pretty little 'un . . . before. But I think 'er fool of a father brought it down on 'er 'ead." Caedmon sat on a tall stool, spewing hatred between gulps of potato beer.

"Abner? How do ya mean?" Payne topped off Caedmon's mug for the third time.

"Just think, Payne. Every time some daft fool gets it into 'is 'ead that there's any power in Shiloh but that o' the Shadow Lord," here, he lowered his voice, "somethin' goes awry. 'E brings down 'is own doom. 'E's marked. Just look at Evander. That crazy mother of 'is starts dreamin', and before ya know it, 'e leads 'is whole clan ta their deaths."

"Ah, but ya don't know that. Nobody knows fer sure they died," Payne replied. "Anyway, it's nigh unto a thousand years since Evander went over the Black Mountains."

"Aye? Hundreds o' people just up and disappeared, then, is that it? The shifters got 'em . . . if they were lucky. Or the wolves. But I've no doubt they were dead before the first night fell. And 'ere's this wee girl, just gatherin' a bit o' firewood, and suddenly the cats are on 'er. The Shadow's huntin' 'er. Huntin' all of 'em, I'd say." Caedmon set his mug on the table, his knuckles white as he gripped the handle. "It's a shame about the girl, but I say good riddance to 'em. We don't need their kind bringin' the Darkness down on Emmerich."

"And what o' the boy?" Payne refilled the mug that rested in front of him and grabbed another mug for himself. He preferred the cherry ale, when it was in season, but the beer was good, too. Payne knew that beer was Caedmon's preference. He knew also that the man could finish seven or eight mugs when he was in a temper. He'd keep the beer handy until Caedmon had his fill.

"Amos?" Caedmon said, before drinking deeply again. "A strange boy, that."

"Heard he put Lark's boy in his place not so long ago."

"Did 'e? Well, that boy could use it. Filthy brat. Always stealin' dowels from m' shop. Thinks 'e's a great marksman."

Another man stepped into the brewery. He had unusually fair hair and dark eyes. Like Caedmon and Payne, he wore leather trousers and a long wool shirt, but both were partly concealed behind a heavy leather apron. Around his neck hung the sign of the Clan of the Builder. This was Orin, the blacksmith, and the mood in the shop changed with his arrival.

"Just the usual today, Payne," he said, after giving a brief nod to the carpenter. Orin handed the brewer a jug and waited while Payne filled it with huckleberry ale. Apart from the sound of the ale splashing into the earthenware jug, the silence in the room was stiff, and only when Orin had nodded his thanks, paid for his ale, and left the shop did Caedmon continue.

"Like I said, that boy's a strange one. To 'ear some tell it, you'd think 'e was 'ammond 'imself." At that, he slammed his mug on the table and stood. "But if 'e really did kill the Shadow Wolf, then 'e's more dangerous than 'is father . . . much more." He drew several edanna coins from the leather pouch on his belt and tossed them on the counter. "I'd keep an eye on 'im if I were you. 'E'll bring down the doom on us all."

Wynn and Phebe had to pass by the brewery on their way out of the village. It was unwise to travel at the waning of the day, so Wynn had hurried her daughter along, past the stone, toward the southward path that led to their cottage. She had caught only a snatch of the conversation in Payne's shop, but it was enough to put a chill in her blood. And as she walked into the gathering darkness, guided by the feeble light of her lantern, one phrase rang in her ears: *The Shadow's huntin' 'er. Huntin' all of 'em, I'd say.*

Five

Not all the Lost Clan was lost. They kept to themselves, mostly, just a dwindling remnant tucked away in a village called Fleete far to the north. Yet even in the foothills of the Pallid Peaks, they had heard how Amos killed the Shadow Wolf. It was a story Isolde loved to hear, and Rosalyn told it often, but on this night, Rosalyn shared a different tale. "There were some who said ya must be a true daughter o' the Fire Clan, for yer hair was red as flame, yer eyes blue as dragons' breath. But there were others who knew better, who remembered the tales o' Valour, the bride of Evander who led our people inta the Black Mountains."

Rosalyn drew another segment of silken red hair into her fingers and continued the elaborate braid across her half-sister's forehead. They had sat like this, she and Isolde, for as long as Rosalyn could remember, and by now the story almost told itself.

"Fer a thousand years we've waited, this last remnant o' the Sun Clan. We few, cloistered in the foothills o' the Pallid Peaks, could never make up our minds if Evander and Valour were more akin ta heroes or madmen. And so we've waited, frozen by indecision, paralyzed by fear and doubt, as if in some long sleep."

"And it is I who will awaken us." Isolde interrupted, pulling away as Rosalyn tied a cord around the end of the braid.

Rosalyn said nothing.

"Because o' my hair," Isolde sighed. She loved to hear the story of her birth and her birthright. But there were days when she grew weary, when her destiny seemed as distant and unreal as the legend of the sun.

"Yer eyes as well, fair sister. In all the old tales, Valour was described in the same way, with hair as red as flame and eyes as blue as dragons' breath. The midwife knew it only too well. That's why she spoke the prophecy."

Isolde spoke without emotion, absently pulling at her shift and gazing into the fire on the hearth. "'Through ages o' Shadow the tale will be told. Fair daughter o' Valour, I name you Isolde.'" It had been left to the midwife to name her, for her mother's lifeblood had soaked the straw mattress of the cot where Isolde was born. With a cry of agony, that woman had left the world of Shadow forever.

"I once thought the midwife foretold some great triumph, some escape. Now I wonder. What tale will be told, Ros? She never said what sort o' tale."

Rosalyn stirred the venison stew that was simmering in the iron kettle over the fire. "You'll do what Valour failed ta do, Isolde. You'll find a way out. I know it."

"We don't know that Valour failed. She may have found that great lantern, blazin' in the sky."

"Without the glass, I can't imagine how she ever found the sun. Besides, if she'd discovered somethin' beyond the Shadow, she would've come back fer us."

The door of the cottage swung open and smacked against the wall. Their father, a lean, hardened man with dark hair and eyes, stepped over the threshold and tossed a heap of blood and fur on the floor. "Make some use o' yerself, girl," he said to Isolde. He settled himself onto the bench by the table and waited for Rosalyn to serve him while Isolde took the day's kill and hurried out into the gloaming.

She drew a dagger from the leather sheath on her belt. Her mother's dagger. It was beautiful, its wooden handle inlaid with silver, its blade engraved with the sign of the Clan of the White Tree. Her mother's clan. If only the dagger had proven its worth when Sullivan came to carry her away in the night. Isolde sighed again and spoke to the dagger, "You'll serve me better when I get out o' here." She took her time skinning the rabbits, peeling away the gray-brown fur and setting it aside before burying the entrails. She cleaned the blade in the spring, where frigid water bubbled up to bite at her fingers. Then she carried the carcasses to the stable, where she placed each on an iron spit and leaned them against the wall in the corner.

Resisting the pull of the cottage, of her father's silent will, she stepped up to the new foal, Echo, and stroked her neck. Sullivan had traded a large doe for the little foal, hoping she would one day replace his aging stallion. Isolde smiled as Echo shuffled and stamped on her spindly brown legs, and finally pulled away, taking the rabbits inside to roast on the hearth fire.

"It's awfully close ta the Black Mountains, though, Da," Rosalyn was saying, as she ladled another helping of stew into her father's bowl.

"Ya know nothin' of it, girl. Some o' the finest hunters in the north go ta that lake. No end o' bull elk there, they say, grazin' in the meadows and drinkin' from the still water. I'll be leavin' in the mornin'. You'd best pack my things."

"Do ya mean Lake Morrison, Da?" Isolde asked as she settled the spits over the fire. "I've heard stories of hunters disappearin' near the lake, of strange things happenin'. Melburn says it's —"

"Speak the name o' that fool mapmaker once more. Just once."

Sullivan's voice never rose. He spoke with complete calm, complete control. Isolde was tempted to challenge him, and she held his eyes with hers for the space of a single heartbeat. Then the moment passed. She took a bowl of stew and sat down at the table.

"That man preys on ignorant men and silly girls. He draws 'maps' of he knows not what. Any fool can scribble on a parchment. I'd like ta see him brave the Hunter's Paths through the Whisperin' Wood. See what he's made of."

Sullivan finished his stew and set the bowl aside. "I catch ya near his cottage again, Isolde, and you'll be sorry."

The sisters exchanged the briefest of glances. They'd both been sorry before, Isolde more often than her sister. Rosalyn was always finding some way to make herself useful, even invaluable, to their father. But Isolde had never proven her worth.

Before long Sullivan was asleep in his cot, and Rosalyn as well, on the opposite wall. Soft night sounds filled the cottage: the playful crackling of the fire as it died away into embers, the creaking of the cots as sleepers turned and tossed, the roar of the wind coming down from the mountains. Isolde heard none of them. For her, the cottage was filled with a ringing silence. It was oppressive. At times, it was unbearable. On many nights, she snatched a lantern from the hook on the wall and made her way to the only place in the village where she felt she could breathe.

Fleete rested on a hill that, for the most part, rose gently from the surrounding landscape. But cottages, stables, and shops were scattered about in an erratic, disorderly fashion, for the village had no real center. Just before the hill reached its peak, it changed its character, rising steeply to a rocky summit. There, an immense boulder braved the icy winds that whipped down from the white spires of the Pallid Peaks.

It was a hallowed place for Isolde. She loved the precarious climb to the summit, the sting of the wind on her cheeks, the empty, open darkness that lay all around her. A faint golden glow of fires and lanterns floated beneath her in an ocean of inky black. And she was lifted above them, free from the terrible gravity of her tiny world.

As always, Isolde was grateful for Rosalyn's skill with braids. Her hair was tightly wound away from her face, and even this wind could not pull it free. She settled into her usual place and stared out into the void. Once in a great while, there were bursts of blue flame that appeared in the distant mountains. It had been a hundred years at least since any of the dragons had come down into the foothills, but they still lived among the peaks, waiting in snow and Shadow.

I'd risk any fate if only I could go and see the dragons with my own eyes. Or the southern moors, or the western plains. Or the Hall of Echoes, or the Three Bridges. She thought back to the many cheerful afternoons she'd spent in Melburn's cottage, hovering over his shoulder as he drew and redrew his maps of Shiloh. The mapmaker had perfected inks of several different colors, and perhaps it was those that most fired Isolde's imagination. She could still envision the green of the Whispering Wood and the rich blue of the River Meander. At times, when Sullivan had been hunting in some far-distant clime, Isolde had sat with Melburn as he listened to hunters and travelers give accounts of their journeys. He hung on their every word, and he paid them in edanna coins, so they were always willing to share. Melburn had collected hundreds of accounts in the course of his life, and the best of these he had compiled into the Red Maps.

If I had one of the Red Maps, I could search the whole of Shiloh. I could find Valour's Glass. And then ... then ... perhaps ... Her thoughts wandered out of the mapmaker's cottage and up into the Pallid Peaks and down through the Whispering Wood and back through a thousand years to the tale of her forebear. And she envied the wind its freedom and wished that her father might never return from Lake Morrison and imagined all the places in Shiloh where she might roam, until her toes were stiff with cold, and she rose and hurried back to the cottage and the warmth of the fire on the hearth and the softness of her woolen blankets.

Six

Linden Lake looked like a hole in the earth. Those who had seen it often wondered if there was any bottom to it. Its dark depths seemed to have no end. Tall trees surrounded the water, growing up to its very edge. Their branches stretched in every direction, as if in hopes of finding some weak shaft of light to nourish them. Their gnarled roots snaked down into the water, drinking deeply.

Yet Linden Lake was a pleasant, homey place to Abner and his family. It was just a short walk to the south of their cottage. They came here to bathe. They came to haul the water they would use for cooking and cleaning and drinking. And they came to practice. In years past, father and son had spent many a happy hour in a small glade not far from the water's edge, where a target was nailed to a tree. It was just a scrap of leather, marked in the center with a chalky white circle, and it would have been nearly useless were it not for the torches that burned on either side. The torches, made from sturdy branches wrapped in strips of oiled cloth, provided enough light for an archer to perfect his aim from twenty paces or so. As targets go, it wasn't much. But then, in Shiloh, the keenest eye could see no more than twenty paces distant at midday in high summer. If something hunted a man from any greater distance, it would not be his eyes that told him so.

"Just use the tips o' yer fingers, Simeon."

Abner and Amos had invited Simeon to join them for "target practice." They all knew it was a pretense. Abner was a great marksman, a great hunter. He was brave and wise and seasoned, and he'd taught his son all he knew. Within a few years, Amos's strength would match his skill, and he would be as great an archer as his father. The boy was a natural, and there were few who could remember seeing him without his quiver and bow over his shoulder or his leather guard fastened to his left forearm.

Simeon had never had a teacher or a weapon with which to practice. More than once, he'd gone hunting with Abner and Amos, following along empty-handed, looking lost when the time came to make a shot.

"Be sure the white feather is up." Abner reached out and rotated the arrow a bit, then refitted it to the string. He looked down at Simeon's thin, pale arm, shaking under the strain of holding his new bow parallel to the ground, and marveled at the boy's determination. He'd carved Simeon's bow from the branch of a yew tree, being careful to make it as flexible and lightweight as possible. Still, Simeon could hardly keep it in the air long enough to rest an arrow on the string and grip its end with his right hand. But the boy's pale, silver-blue eyes were fixed on the target, and he made no complaint.

"Once more . . . just the tips o' yer fingers . . . that's right. Now bring the string up ta yer nose . . . good —"

Suddenly, the arrow flew from the bow with a twang, sailing far to the left of the target. Simeon hung his head. "I'll never get it right."

"Course ya will, Sim. Just keep yer right hand at yer chin and move it back along yer jaw as ya pluck the string. Then the arrow will fly straight and true. Watch." Abner moved quickly through dozens of tiny steps that flowed together into one graceful, fluid motion. Simeon watched in awe as the arrow sliced through the air and stuck fast in the trunk of the tree.

"You'll get it soon enough, m' boy," Abner said, reaching down to tousle Simeon's yellow-white hair. Simeon beamed back at him. He'd never been called "m' boy" by anyone. He decided to try again.

Slowly, with great care, he picked up the bow and moved through each step just as Abner had shown him. He pulled the string with all his strength, holding the bow as steady as his frail arms could manage, aiming directly between the two torches Abner had set up on either side of the tree. Then he let go. The arrow grazed the left side of the trunk and landed in a bush just beyond it.

From behind Simeon and Abner there was a cheer. "Nice shot, Sim! Wonder what Ferlin would think o' that, eh?"

Simeon laughed softly, knowing Amos could have made a better shot with his eyes closed. Amos, who had slain the wolf; Amos, who breathed fire into the heart of the enemy; Amos, whose tunics were marked with the blood of his kills; Amos, whose neck was adorned with the claw of the Shadow Cat; that Amos was his friend.

Abner guided Simeon to a fallen log and drew an oiled cloth from the leather pouch that hung on his belt. The mark of the Fire Clan was branded into the pouch, though no red-gold edanna sparkled at its center. Unlike the mosaic in Market Circle, these three tongues of flame met only in a charred, black point. The brand on Amos's arm guard looked nearly identical to the one on the pouch.

It was custom in Shiloh for men to wear the sign of their clan at all times. Poorer men branded the sign into belts, pouches, quivers, or arm guards. Wealthier men wore the sign of their clan, delicately shaped in iron, on leather cords around their necks. The heads of the clans, wealthiest and most powerful of men, wore belts fashioned from bright edanna, on which the sign of their clan was worked over and over. That red-gold metal, nearly as valuable as fire itself, flashed like flame whenever it caught the light.

"The oil keeps water from gettin' inta the wood," Abner explained. Simeon nodded, observing Abner's movements as he ran the oiled cloth back and forth along the bow.

"You give it a try." Abner handed over the cloth, and Simeon set to work.

"Abner?" he asked, "Who gave ya that pouch?"

Abner glanced down, lifting the leather pouch slightly from his belt. "'Twas a gift from my father, when I came of age."

Amos approached the fallen log, carrying several recovered arrows in one hand and a torch in the other. He piled the arrows on the ground, then thrust the end of the torch into the dirt a few paces from the log. Simeon caught another glimpse of his arm guard in the flickering firelight as Amos sat down to clean the arrows.

"Why do ya wear the clan sign when ya haven't come of age?" he asked Amos.

"This is Da's guard. He says I need it more than him," Amos responded, glancing at his father with a half smile. "One day my arm will be tough enough I won't need it anymore, like Da."

"Some hunters wear their guards ta their deaths, Amos," Abner said. "It's no sign o' toughness not ta wear one." He winked at his son.

"I bet you'll wear the Fire Sign 'round yer neck, Sim, yer ma bein' magistrate an' all," Amos said.

Simeon stopped his work on the bow, leaning it gently against the log, and contemplated his feet. He was keenly aware that no heirloom would ever come down from his father.

Abner tried to reassure him. "I'm sure yer ma has some family token set aside fer ya. No need ta worry."

The words were no consolation to Simeon. He knew of no such token, and for the first time in his life, he wished his mother had never been. He wished he'd been born to Abner and Wynn. He wished that Amos were his brother and that he, too, wore an arm guard with the clan sign emblazoned so confidently into its surface. More than that, he wished he were strong and tall and dark, with brown hair and eyes, and that he'd never heard of Penelope, Giver of Dreams. He wished he'd been born without the fear, like Amos.

But he hadn't. He could not exchange his yellow-white hair or his pale blue eyes. He could not unmake his fair skin, light as a tallow candle. He would always know the feeling of fear, cold and blue in his belly.

He put on a brave smile and lied, "Perhaps she has." Then, standing and gathering his quiver and bow, he changed the subject. "Is it true Grosvenor's arm guard was made o' dragon skin?"

"Aye! He cut it from Sirius himself!" Amos answered, scooping up his own things and lifting the torch high into the air.

"Nay, boys. I've heard the tale told many ways," Abner broke in. "Some say it was 'is cloak he fashioned out o' the dragon's skin, while others swear it was the handle of 'is bow he wrapped in Sirius's black scales."

"Grosvenor took the dragon's eye as well," Amos added, relishing the gory details of the epic tale. "It glowed blue in 'is hand fer a thousand days." He looked at Simeon with brows raised and eyes wide.

"What did 'e do with the eye?" Simeon asked.

Abner and Amos both paused. They were uncertain about that part of the legend.

Finally, Amos said, "Perhaps 'e passed it down ta yer ma, Sim. That'll be yer heirloom ... the eye o' the dragon!" He punched his friend lightly on the arm, and Simeon laughed.

"Yer mad as they say, Amos ... maybe madder."

Amos pretended offense, taking another swing at Simeon. This time, though, Simeon ducked out of the way and took off running toward the cottage, while Amos followed in hot pursuit. Abner stayed behind, walking at his steady pace and carrying the other torch through the feeble gray light. He watched the boys as they played and fought. He smiled and chuckled at their antics. But all through that journey home, a sense of deep foreboding grew in him. It grew with every stride toward the cottage, sinking cold claws into his heart.

Under his breath, he whispered, "May the light shine upon you both," and even as he repeated the familiar phrase, he knew that it would not.

Seven

ada had heard the story of Riannon's Betrayal more times
than she could count. It was the most ancient tale of their
people, telling how Ulff, Lord of Shadows captured the wild
wind to be his wife, how she betrayed him and fled with their
daughter, Miri, and how Ulff drowned his daughter in the river,
staining the water black with her blood. Riannon, the wild, unpre-
dictable, unfaithful wife, he bound in chains forever.

They never said it as such, but most men of Shiloh believed
that all women were Riannon. They feared the capricious, incon-
stant nature of woman and determined to rule her with a heavy
hand. It was not uncommon for men to capture wives from other
clans. No law forbade the practice, so long as the girl had come of
age. A man need only nail a branch of belladonna over his door and
carry his wife across the threshold to make the marriage binding.
The deadly nightshade sent a clear message: "Death will find you
if you leave this place without consent." Most girls understood this
reality from a very early age. It was not only the beasts of Shadow
that hunted them. For many, men would hunt them as well. And

though no eye could see the chains that bound them, most would waste away in captivity, just like Riannon.

It was not surprising, then, that Jada had never married. As the only child of the former magistrate, she had never feared abduction. No man would dare such a thing, for he would risk war between the clans, and that had not happened in centuries. Jada's unique position, too, provided her with everything she needed. She lived comfortably in the hall, collecting a small tax from the villagers to feed herself and her son. And her word was obeyed, if grudgingly. The role of magistrate had always passed from father to son, and it irked the people of Emmerich that Jada's mother had only borne a daughter.

She let out a weary sigh, sinking into a chair beside the fire. There was some truth in what they said. Surely no woman alive could relish the punishment of liars and slanderers that was written in the four eternal laws of Shiloh. Payment for stealing a man's name was made in flesh, and it was the lash that collected that flesh. Jada's eyes flickered to the hooks above the mantelpiece where the lash was kept. Its iron shaft, wrapped in leather, was suspended horizontally against the gray stones, and the light of the fire flashed off the tiny shards of glass laced into the leather cords that hung from the whip's end. She closed her eyes against the memory of dark blood oozing down flayed backs and placed a hand to her forehead. She rubbed her temples, circling again and again, in hopes of easing the tension that lay always just under the surface of her skin.

"Evenin', Ma."

Jada looked up to see her son standing in the doorway. "Come and sit with me, Sim," she said.

She saw the smile in the boy's eyes as he came to sit in a smaller carven chair beside her. She'd seen that look much more often these days. Simeon seemed to have some newfound radiance, and her relief at her son's happiness was shadowed only by her fear of his choice of friend. *If only it had been another boy*, she thought. *One of Payne's sons, perhaps, or the boy Turner, who lives on the far end of the village. Anyone but Amos.*

"What've ya got there?" she asked, hoping that her face revealed neither her exhaustion nor her fear.

"It's a yew bow," Simeon said with scarcely-concealed delight. "'Twas a gift from Abner. He's teachin' me ta shoot."

Perhaps it was good that Simeon was learning to hunt. Jada could hardly imagine her tender son taking on the role of magistrate. The people wouldn't allow it. To accept the leadership of a woman came hard enough for them. They would never follow the council of a Dreamer. Besides, Simeon was not Jada's natural-born son. Since he had come to her, he'd been the brightest, loveliest thing in her world. She remembered watching him sit with a faraway look in his bright, pale eyes. It was as if the boy had wandered the world in thought and pondered its greatest mysteries from the very moment of his birth. Of course, that was only before he learned to talk. When the boy found his voice, he had no end of questions for his mother. "What's leather, Ma?" "Where does fire come from, Ma?" "Ma, why is the river black?"

Simeon was kind-hearted as well, often bringing her shiny stones from the riverbank or some fragile flower struggling for life on the edge of the village. No, the iron will and flinty determination required of a magistrate were not qualities her gentle boy possessed, and Jada was comforted by the inescapable fact that the office would be taken up by another family at her death.

Jada's eyes took in her son's appearance as he sat oiling his new bow. She noticed that his wool trousers were a bit short at the ankles, and his leather boots showed signs that his toes were pressing against the edges. Even his tunic looked snug at the shoulders.

"You're growin', Simeon . . . taller every day. We'll have ta have ya fitted fer some new clothes."

He looked down with resignation at his thin, frail legs and arms. "I'll never be as tall as Amos," he said.

"Ya don't know that. Ya might grow taller, in the end. You've many years o' growin' still ta do, Sim." She wanted to tell him he would be tall like his father, that his muscles would grow strong and his heart would grow stronger, but she had no such certainties.

"Maybe." Simeon stopped his work on the bow and laid it across his legs. "Ma, do ya think I could have an arm guard?" He hesitated a moment, then rushed on ahead. "It's just that, if I'm goin' ta be shootin' an' all, I need somethin' ta protect my arm. The bowstring can snap pretty hard, see, and . . ." He trailed off and fell silent.

The look that came into his eyes at that moment, the moment when he lost the sparkle of hope and anticipation that had burned in him just seconds before, broke his mother's heart. She had seen that look of resignation far too many times, when the light had died in her son's face, and a veil had seemed to fall over him. In one awful sweeping vision, she saw Simeon pierced with an arrow, attacked by a Shadow Wolf, and bloodied by the claws of a cat. Freezing dread tore at her heart as she imagined her son roaming the vast darkness of the Whispering Wood. *If only it had been another boy,* she thought again. *Any other boy.* And then, she pushed it all aside.

"Aye," she said. "We could get ya an arm guard on the next market day."

A bright smile lit Simeon's face, and his mother's heart ached with joy and pain as he wrapped his thin arms around her neck and kissed her hair.

Jada's throat was too tight to speak, but Simeon whispered, "Love ya, Ma." He lifted his bow and hung it over his shoulder, as if he were embarking on the Great Hunt there and then, and, still grinning, he went to his cot.

&ight

The edges of the Whispering Wood were hardly frightening.
Soft grass spotted with low shrubs carpeted the ground
beneath the cover of numberless scattered trees. Just a few
paces inside the wood, however, the undergrowth rose up to meet
the tightly woven branches of the ancient trees. Vines half as thick
as a man wound their way from earth to sky, crossing over one
another and forming tangled nets of Shadow. Mist rose from who-
knows-where, leaving the hard lines of ground and tree indistinct
and indiscernible from more than a few paces.

There were many legends about the Whispering Wood. It was
here that Grosvenor spoke with the white tree, here that he received
the famed White Bow. Through this wood the Lost Clan had journeyed, and none could tell whether they had ever reached the other
side. Here, too, Mariah was said to have wandered, searching and
mourning for her daughter, Imogen. There were even some who
claimed that shifters waited in the wood, disguised in some form
or another.

Then there were the wolves. The Whispering Wood was thick

with them. They seemed to move in on the mist, silent, stealthy, stalking their prey. They lurked in thickets in a hundred corners of the forest, waiting, waiting, always waiting, their eyes burning like embers. Only the Hunter's Paths provided any hope of venturing into the wood unharmed. The much-traveled trails cut through the gloom from half a dozen entrance points, leading hunters to sheltered meadows in the heart of the wood where deer and elk often grazed.

When he could avoid it, Abner never hunted this deep in the Whispering Wood. But their stews had been thin this winter, more potatoes than anything else, and their supply of candles had been thinner. If Abner could bring home a large kill today, the meat would sustain his family through the spring, and the skin could be traded for a good stock of tallow candles.

Three brilliant flames floated along the Hunter's Path. Abner and Amos carried torches; Simeon, a lantern; and though they could not see far beyond the walls of trees on either side, they could at least see one another and the path clearly.

"How much farther?" Simeon asked. His voice hardly carried. It was eaten up by the walls of night that surrounded them. Their leather boots made no sound on the damp, mossy earth, and even the torches burned in silence.

"Few hundred paces, I think," Amos answered.

"Is it true what they say, that the trees talk ta ya?" Simeon hoped the sound of his own voice might slow the racing of his heart. The further they pressed into the Whispering Wood, the more loudly the blood beat in his ears.

"Don't know," Amos replied. "Maybe only the white ones."

Later in the year, the boys, now twelve, would participate in their first Great Hunt. They would carve new bows, don leather trousers, and set off with the seasoned hunters to prove themselves. For all his practice, Simeon was still awkward under the weight of his bow, still weak on marksmanship. And he was still smaller than

Amos. This hunt should have been a chance to focus, to prepare for the challenges ahead. But Simeon's mind kept drifting to the sons of Burke. Abner had told them the tale around the campfire only the night before.

"They were great builders, the sons o' Burke," Abner had said. "Some say their father could shape stone with naught but 'is hands."

He had sat with one knee up and an arm resting loosely on his trousers. Golden firelight and shadow had moved across his face in a curious dance.

"And though the clan they founded is known fer its skill, these seven were the greatest, the most skilled. It was they who oversaw the buildin' o' the Three Bridges that cross the River Meander and they who built the great watchtowers, fashioned from gray stone, atop their mighty fortresses. They even ventured inta the Black Mountains ta build their towers, for from those heights they could see somewhat o' the land around 'em, and they could better defend their families."

"The Black Mountains?" Simeon could hardly believe it.

"Aye. There was a time when men lived in those mountains, though it's many years since."

"Could they see the wolves movin' in?" Simeon had asked. With the Great Hunt fast approaching, wolves were foremost in his thoughts.

"Perhaps," Abner had responded. "But it wasn't downward or outward that they looked, after a time." He reached to the pile of firewood nearby and chose a handful of thick branches, adding them one by one to the campfire. "None can say when it first happened, or how, but the sons o' Burke began ta see lights in the sky."

"Lights comin' out o' the Shadow?"

"No, Sim." It was Amos who'd answered. "They saw *above* the Shadow. It pulled away like frayed cloth, and they saw lights *beyond* it."

"What kind o' lights?"

"Little ones, like candle flames far, far away."

"What did they do?" Simeon knew some history of Shiloh, but his mother had always been reluctant to share certain tales, and he knew little of Evander or the sons of Burke.

Amos had looked to his father, handing over the telling.

"Fer a time, they waited in their towers," Abner had continued, "watchin', hardly believin' their eyes. Some thought they'd gone mad. But slowly, each came ta tell 'is wife and children what he saw, and soon they told each other. They knew then they could not be mad, not if all seven brothers had seen the same lights. So they spoke of it openly. They even changed the sign o' their clan."

"All o' them?"

"Not all, Sim. Only some took the sign o' the Star Clan. There were many who scoffed, among them at least one traitor. Whether man or woman, none can say, but one o' their clan sent word ta the Lord o' Shadows."

"It could've been a shifter in disguise. One of Ulff's spies," Amos had said. "They mightn't've known 'e was among them."

"True enough, Amos, but it matters little in the end, for Ulff took them."

Though he sat close to the fire, Simeon shivered, and the tongues of the flames flickered blue, just for a moment.

"The Lord o' Shadows took the sons o' Burke and cursed them. He changed their bodies, warpin' and reshapin' 'em inta hideous winged things. He sent them back ta their watchtowers as emissaries o' darkness, and their flight struck terror in the hearts o' their families. Their wives and children fled from the towers forever, and even today, the Clan o' the Builder is dispersed among the other clans, livin' in this village or that, workin' at their trades. The watchtowers remain empty, crumblin' ta ruin. And no man will go ta seek the lights that the sons o' Burke saw, for the towers are guarded by those servants o' the Shadow. The stargazers, they're called."

They had sat in silence for some time, listening to the hissing of the fire as Abner replenished it with branches and the scraping of metal on stone as Amos sharpened his dagger.

"What do they do ta ya? The stargazers, I mean," Simeon had asked.

Abner's gaze had not left the fire. His eyes had glowed strangely in its light.

"It's time you boys got some rest. I'll set up the torches," he had said, and Simeon was left to imagine a hundred monstrous possibilities. Those phantasms had not left him, and now, as they moved deeper into the Whispering Wood, they seemed poised to burst into life. He glanced anxiously back and forth, alert to every breath of wind.

"Amos, are we near the Watchtowers?"

This time Amos didn't answer. He and Simeon had rarely been apart for more than a few days at a time during the last five years. They had chopped wood and carried water for Wynn. They had delivered messages and run errands for Jada. They had practiced their aim, hour upon hour. They had skipped rocks across the glassy black surface of the lake, until the light was so faint that they had to judge their progress by the sound of little popping splashes on the water. And they had hunted together, though never this deep in the wood. Simeon knew his friend. He knew that his questions had begun to irritate Amos. But he couldn't help himself.

"What about the shifters? How can ya tell 'em from the other animals?"

"Hush, Sim! Wait." Abner hissed. He stopped, and the three stood silent, their eyes searching for some break in the impenetrable darkness.

Behind them there was a sound, a low, heavy rolling. It rose gradually, growing and spreading, until they were surrounded by the insatiable thundering growls of many wolves. They had been marked.

The air grew colder and, suddenly, their lights went out. They stood in almost total darkness, isolated for an instant from everything but their own thoughts.

For Abner, that moment was like the coming of doom. His darkest fears had come upon him. They would surely be devoured by the Shadow. He had failed to protect his son and Simeon, and his wife and daughter would be alone, vulnerable. He was overcome with a sinking despair.

For Simeon, the extinguishing of the lights by some nameless dark in the heart of the wood was almost more than his frail heart could bear. Panic overtook him. His pulse raced, and his skin was covered with clammy sweat. He trembled uncontrollably.

But the darkness was not complete. Not quite.

The people of Shiloh were born with a certain incandescence, a certain radiance about them. They shone. Though they did not know it, this light was the last remnant of the glory that belonged to them before the world was unmade. Babes came wet and shining from their mothers' bellies, and they lit their parents' cottages as well as any lantern. But the Shadow took its toll. Children learned too quickly that no shining dawn ever came to that world. Too quickly, they learned that they were hunted, always hunted. They saw the faces of hunger and death. They felt the fear. Their glory faltered and faded and finally vanished.

It was rare indeed to find a child of five or six who radiated any light at all, rarer still to find a man or woman come of age who still possessed some hint of their glorious birthright. But they could be found. Orin's skin glowed faintly when he worked at the forge. Abner's face shone, just slightly, when he marveled at his son's skill with the bow. Wynn was luminous when her husband stepped through the door of the cottage, and Phebe fairly blazed when she sang.

Amos's pulse had quickened too, when the darkness fell, but not from fear. Unlike the others, he felt remarkably *alive*. His mind was clear, his senses acute, his muscles relaxed. He let out a long breath, fixed his eyes on the cold torch in his right hand and spoke one word: "Burn." A red-orange flame shot up from the oiled cloth.

All at once, the menacing growls of the wolves ceased.

The hunter's path was warm and bright. Amos whistled a little tune. "By the gods," Abner swore, turning and staring in awe at his son. Amos burned brighter than the torch, and it was he who filled the wood with radiance. Abner raised a hand to rub his chin, then dropped it again.

"Are we goin' on?" Simeon asked.

"Course we're goin' on. We're almost there, right Da?" Amos replied.

Abner paused a moment before nodding. "Aye. We'll go on." He turned and led the boys down the path. Not half a hundred paces ahead, they came to a broad meadow. Where the trees opened up, the dark was thinner, and the hunters could see a dozen deer, scattered across the tall grass, grazing.

Abner laid aside his cold torch, drew an arrow from his quiver, and fitted it to his bow. Guided more by the gentle rustling of the grasses than the clarity of his vision, he shot an arrow into the meadow and heard the thump of an animal falling to the ground.

One day, I'll be able to make that shot, Amos thought. He didn't yet have the strength to make a sure kill from such a distance, but he knew he would, and he marveled at the easy power with which Abner moved across the meadow, retrieved the deer, and slung it over his shoulder. They wasted no time there, hurrying back to the path with their kill. On the return journey, Abner took up the rear, slowed not at all by the weight of the beast he carried. Simeon traveled ahead of him, full of thoughts and questions. And Amos led the way, carrying the torch high and looking, for all his twelve years, like the warrior he knew he would become.

Nine

As usual, Rosalyn had forgotten nothing. Sullivan's best bow was slung over his shoulder, and his quiver as well. His packs were laden with dried venison and bread, his skins filled with water from the icy spring. He had returned from Lake Morrison that first summer, despite Isolde's secret hopes. He'd made a good haul, good enough to draw him back year after year. On this particular morning, he rode into the gloom without a word, lost from sight in only a moment or two.

"I've a mind ta clean the cottage while he's gone," Rosalyn said as she stepped inside. "It's been an age since I scrubbed the floors."

Isolde groaned. "Oh, please. Will ya leave the cursed cottage and come ride with me? The cherries are ripe." She took Rosalyn's hand and tugged. "We'll make a pie fer supper tonight. *Please* come."

Rosalyn smiled at her, squeezed her hand, and let go. "You go, Isolde. I'll make ya a pie when ya get back. Take Da's other bow and get us somethin' fer a stew as well."

Isolde could see from her expression that Rosalyn would not budge. Sullivan might be gone as much as a week, or as little as a couple of days, and she knew Rosalyn would not risk his returning without her having done something to appease him. Both girls feared their father, but only Rosalyn could bend that fear to Sullivan's will.

"Alright then." Isolde slung the bow and quiver over her shoulder and made her way down into the valley. The branches of the trees hung low, burdened with clusters of fruit that shone faintly red in the dim light. Isolde filled the pouch that hung from her belt before helping herself.

She was leaning against the trunk of a tall tree, her mouth stained a deep blood-red, when she spotted a doe nibbling at the grasses beneath the trees, sniffing out the ripe cherries that had already fallen to the ground. Her white-spotted fawn followed cautiously behind. Isolde shot them in the next breath, loosing two arrows with marvelous speed. *The blessing of the gods must be upon me today*, she thought. *It's enough to feed us for weeks. More than enough.* And then an idea struck her. She struggled up the hill with the animals over her shoulders. She went directly to Melburn's cottage, laid the doe over his table, and said, "I want one o' the Red Maps."

Melburn was a man of many years, with white hair and stooping shoulders. He looked up from his work, his eyes bright with amusement. "Fer the doe?" he asked.

"Aye."

He ignored her, returning his attention to the parchment stretched beneath his hands.

"Ya need the meat, Mel. Ya can't listen ta travelers' stories and sketch on yer parchments if you're dead o' starvation."

Melburn smiled. "I know ya have 'em all memorized by now, Isolde. Why do ya need it?"

Isolde didn't answer. She merely looked back at the old man with her jaw set.

"If yer da finds the map, he'll destroy it." His face and his tone had hardened. "He thinks little o' you and less o' me."

"He'll never know."

"You're leavin', then?"

Again, Isolde gave no answer. They both knew she would . . . one day. Melburn moved to a large cabinet on the back wall of the cottage and opened the door. Inside were dozens of rolled parchments. He pulled one from the top shelf. It was tied with a red cord and marked with red ink. He handed it to Isolde carefully, almost tenderly, his eyes holding it a while before looking away.

"Ya could've at least dressed the doe," he said to Isolde as she left.

She slipped the parchment into her shift and tightened her belt, hardly breathing until she pulled it out and spread it on the table in her own cottage.

Rosalyn shook her head. "If Da finds out, Isolde, he'll —"

But Isolde pushed the words aside, running her hands over the map, taking in every inch. "We're not so far north o' the wood, ya know." Her fingers ran down from the village toward the vast darkness of the Whispering Wood. What if Valour's Glass was there? What if it had lain in wait for a thousand years, just for her?

"Do ya think it's really there?" Isolde asked.

"The glass?"

"The sun."

There was a smile on Rosalyn's lips that never reached her eyes. "A flame in the sky so bright and so strong that it sets all the world ablaze? I hope it's real, Isolde. I hope."

"A fool's hope, some say," Isolde remarked, "but I'd hate ta think our people died fer so little."

"You'll come back fer me, won't ya, Isolde? If ya find the way out?" Rosalyn asked.

"Ya know I will, Ros." There were so many things unspoken between them, years of secret knowing, of intimate understanding. Though born of different mothers, though different in nearly every particular, these two were as dear to one another as life.

Their father returned from Lake Morrison without any strange tales or any meat. He did well enough during the summer months, but before the year was out he was forced to trade his aging stallion for what he hoped was enough food and ale to last the winter. He saw no trace of the map.

Ten

There was something about being twelve that made Amos want to jump out of his skin. His world had gotten smaller, and it chafed.

What he needed was an adventure.

"Sim," Amos said one day as the boys skipped rocks across the lake. "I've been thinkin' about yer family heirloom."

"What?" Simeon had found the perfect stone. It was wide and flat and light. With this stone, he might be able to beat his record of six skips.

"Yer heirloom," Amos went on. "If ya don't have a father ta pass on an heirloom o' yer family, ya can't come of age, can ya?"

"I don't know." Simeon took aim and flung the stone at the perfect angle to the surface of the water. It smacked once, twice, then again and again. After the fifth splash, the rock slipped beneath the dark water and Simeon plopped to the ground with a sigh. "They can't stop me comin' of age, can they? I can't help it I don't have a da."

"I know ya can't, but it's tradition, Sim. The clansmen have done it that way fer centuries. Besides, I've been thinkin'. Remember the lantern we saw at the stone house on the edge o' the wood?"

"'Course I do. Everyone knows about Hadrian's Lantern. What of it?"

"What if that was yer heirloom?" Amos asked, as if it were the simplest answer to all Simeon's problems.

Amos knew nothing of Hadrian, but Simeon and the villagers knew a little. They knew that Hadrian had always lived in a large stone house northeast of Emmerich, just on the edge of the wood. Aspen, the apothecary was the oldest woman in the village, and she could not remember a time before Hadrian had come. Truth be told, Hadrian had waited and watched for many long years before the four eternal laws of Shiloh were carved into the stone. Before the mosaic was laid in Market Circle and the village of Emmerich was founded by the Fire Clan, he had been there. No one thought much about him. He existed on the fringe of the villagers' knowledge and understanding, little more than a shadowy unknown.

Only one thing about Hadrian shone clear in the minds of the people. His lantern. In a world all but drained of light and color, a world where firewood was vital, candles were precious, and lanterns were more precious still, this lantern was a wonder. At its top and base were bands of exquisite edanna filigree. The rest of the lamp was faceted with panes of colored glass in green, gold, and purple. It was lovely to behold, even when the lantern was dark. But when the oiled wick inside was lit, the light of the fire danced through the filigree work and awakened the panes of glass into brilliant color.

It was beautiful, priceless. And it must have been ancient. The art of coloring glass had disappeared with the Lost Clan a thousand years before. If any man had found a way to make it his own, he would have hidden it in the darkest recesses of his cottage. Not Hadrian, however. He hung the lantern on an iron hook outside the door of his great stone house. He was not afraid.

"What're ya talkin' about, Amos? The villagers don't know half the madness in yer head if ya think Hadrian would give us that lantern."

"Never said he'd give it to us, Sim."

"What do ya mean, then?"

Amos looked at Simeon with a mischievous grin. "We could take it. Just borrow it fer a while, 'til ya come of age."

"Ya don't know what yer sayin'. It's against the laws o' Shiloh."

"Ya know there's no great penalty fer stealin'. If it came to it, we'd just give it back. Besides, no one has ta know about it. We'll go at night."

"Hadrian will know!" Simeon stared at Amos in horror. He knew his friend feared nothing, but this . . . this was reckless.

"Ya can come with me or not, Sim. But I'm goin'. Tonight." Amos stood, snatched up the torch he'd driven into the mud, and headed toward the cottage.

Simeon was left in an awful spot. Every bone in his body told him that no good would come of this, but he couldn't let his friend take such a risk on his behalf without helping or at least showing up. Anyway, he was tired of being afraid, tired of leaning on Amos's courage. He decided that twelve years old was old enough to take a risk, and he would go with Amos if it meant he went to his certain doom.

"Wait!" Simeon jumped to catch up with Amos, whose long strides had already taken him far from Linden Lake. He ran to his friend and fell into step beside him, guided only by the light of the torch as it bobbed up and down several feet above the ground.

"I'm goin' with ya," Simeon said. Amos gave him a broad grin in reply, and his face was lit with its own light as he discussed hasty plans with Simeon.

Wynn was huddled over her small candle, trying to mend one of Phebe's shifts in the semi-darkness when the boys returned. She heard Amos sigh in frustration as he looked from the lone candle to the fireplace and back again. She wondered what was bothering him. Of late, he rather reminded her of a wild animal caught in a trap. She watched him plunk his bow and quiver by the front door and sit on the trunk against the wall. Simeon, as usual, was trying to make himself useful. He was stoking the fire, jabbing the metal poker absently into the embers.

I wonder where Phebe's gotten to. She should be back by now. Wynn pushed aside the haunting memories of another little girl who wandered out into the dark and never returned. She willed herself to concentrate on the tear in the shift. One stitch at a time, she forced the panic down, down, deep down, back to its lair.

"Good evenin', m' dear ones," Abner greeted, stepping through the door of the cottage holding three rabbits by the ears. Wynn let out a slow breath when Phebe appeared, close on his heels, hauling a basket of peppers for the soup. She had grown into a willowy girl of nine. The scar, slashing across her face from forehead to jaw line, was still distinct, but its angry red had faded to white. Her dark hair hung loose, whipping around her shoulders as she dumped the peppers onto the table.

"I was startin' ta worry about ya. Both o' ya," Wynn said with mild reproach. One hand swept over her husband's shoulder, and her eyes searched his face, questioning. He looked weary, for all his cheerful words and smiles, but he said nothing. It was Phebe who answered.

"Ya needn't fret about me, Ma. I'm nearly grown now."

Wynn caught the subtle challenge in her daughter's voice. Phebe was not permitted to go to the lake alone. Apart from their trips to the village, Phebe's world extended to the fence across the lane in front of the cottage, the sheepfold in back, and the garden to the side. It was a point of contention in the family, but Wynn chose not to press the issue tonight. Instead, she made preparations for dinner. She laughed at Amos as he teased his sister, pulling strands of her hair whenever she turned her back and ducking out of reach when she swung at him.

Amos and Phebe chattered all through their meal, speculating about their first trip to the Hall of Echoes. Simeon seemed distracted, offering a comment here and there, but never joining in the excitement of the others. Abner was quiet. *It must be the Hunt*, Wynn thought. *He's worried about taking the boys this year.* She was thinking she might veer the conversation in another direction when Amos spoke up.

"Da, I've been thinkin'," he began.

"About what, m' boy?" Abner raised questioning eyebrows as he ladled more stew into his bowl.

"If we split up on our huntin' trips, we could catch twice the game."

"I don't think so, Amos. Too dangerous."

Abner had clearly finished the conversation, but Amos continued. He was burning with plans and ideas.

"I was thinkin' maybe I could get enough skins ta buy Ma a lantern. She can't see well enough ta do her cookin' and sewin', and I could help."

"We'll soon have enough extra meat and skins ta get yer Ma a lantern. I'm strikin' out tomorrow, headin' west. You and Sim can come if ya like."

There was a pause, and Wynn rushed to fill the silence. "You've done well with the garden, Phebe," she said. "I've never seen —"

"But, Da," Amos interrupted, "we could get twice as much if we split up. I'm old enough ta go on my own."

"It's not safe fer ya ta hunt alone." Abner raised his voice ever so slightly.

"I'll be alright, Da. I know what ta do if I run inta danger." Amos's voice rose to meet his father's. If he had looked at his mother or his sister, he would have seen the warning in their eyes.

"I said it's not safe, and that's an end to it."

"I'm not afraid."

"Ya should be afraid!" Abner shouted, slamming his fist on the table.

Tears welled up in Phebe's eyes, and she hid her face in her hands. "Abner?" Wynn said. Something was wrong.

He stood up quietly, walked to the hearth, and knelt down to stoke the fire. It hissed and crackled, little tongues of flame licking up the ends of the logs.

Wynn went to his side, and it was then that she saw streaks of dull brown across the back of his tunic. She lifted the edge of the fabric and gasped at the sight of her husband's wounds. He pulled away from her, moving to his familiar chair, but she had seen all she needed to see. Four parallel gashes. It could only have been a wolf. He must have washed his tunic and bathed in the lake in an attempt to erase all signs of the attack.

"Da, what happened?" Phebe asked.

Abner responded only by saying, "It's not safe fer ya ta hunt in the wood alone, Amos. Don't ask again."

The others finished their meal in silence.

Eleven

The Shadow hung heavy over the cottage that night. It wasn't long before even the faintest hint of light was smothered by inky blackness. To Simeon and Amos it felt like an eternity. Amos, lying in his cot, stared at the dying embers of the fire, exchanging glances with Simeon, who was settled on a pile of blankets in front of the hearth. He waited until he heard Phebe's steady breathing and the soft snores of his parents. When he was sure that sleep had claimed them, he motioned for Simeon to follow, then crept from the house, taking his father's lantern with him.

They moved quickly and silently, Amos just ahead of Simeon. They knew when they neared the village, for a few lanterns still burned outside the doorways of shops and cottages. No one stirred. The fires of the blacksmith's furnace were dark and cold, and the only sound came from the huffing and stamping of the horses in the stables. As they skirted the edge of the village, the dim light of the lantern fell on the stone. It had stood on that spot, warning the people of Emmerich for centuries, and its surface was engraved with these words:

For any who steals a man's goods, payment in kind.
For any who steals a man's name, payment in flesh.
For any who steals a man's life, payment in blood.
For any who steals a man's light, payment in exile.

The boys had seen the stone too many times to think much of it as they passed. But its words and its warning snuck along behind, shadowing their steps as they cut through grasses and over stones, making their way to the edge of the Whispering Wood and the large house that stood on its border.

At last they saw the lantern, suspended high above the ground, its green and gold and purple light flashing on the stark gray stone of the house.

"It's a thing o' beauty, isn't it, Sim?" Amos was surprised at the lantern's power. He was drawn to it. It awakened something in him that he could not quite place.

"Still sure we won't get caught?" Simeon whispered.

"Stop yer worryin'." Questions and limitations were not what Amos wanted. Simeon was starting to sound like his da. "Just keep ta the plan." Simeon nodded assent, and the two stepped softly into the wall of trees. Not far behind the house, a little creek ran through the wood. It must have branched off from the River Meander and wound its way down to this dry, sickly end. Abner had mentioned the wide, flat stones that lined the banks of the creek when they made their way home from their last hunt in the wood. He had thought them perfectly suited for building fences. Amos thought them perfect for stacking, and his impetuous plan hinged upon them.

He and Simeon bent to lift the first stone, carefully placing Abner's lantern on top and using its light to guide them to Hadrian's lantern. The pillar grew, stone by stone, until both boys were covered in a thin layer of sweat. Amos watched with some amusement as every crack of dry branches beneath their feet sent Simeon's pulse racing. At times, Simeon would stop, straining his ears for some hint of movement within the house. It did not come. They finished their task without incident.

"Here goes," Amos said, with a wink at his friend. He wiped the sweat from his face with the sleeve of his tunic and lifted one foot to the top of the pillar, placing a hand against the wall of the house to get his balance. The stones shifted and rocked, making dull cracking sounds, but still, nothing stirred within the house. Carefully, oh, so carefully, Amos shifted his weight forward and lifted himself up. The pillar leaned, stone crunching against stone. He gripped the wall with his fingertips and struggled to steady himself. When the teetering pillar finally stilled, Amos reached up to take the lantern from its hook. His face was bathed in its warm light. He had never seen anything so beautiful in all his life. How he longed to hold it in his hands, to give it to his friend. He tore his eyes from the sparkling glass and looked down at Simeon. His eyes were wide, his mouth slightly open. Amos thought he could almost see Simeon's heart beating through his tunic.

"Sim, why don't ya hide in the trees on the edge o' the wood?"

"No, Amos. I'm stayin'. Just hurry."

"Sim, I don't need the other lantern anymore. As soon as I get this one, I'll meet ya over there."

"I said I'm —" He stopped. He was certain he'd heard something. It was a muffled sound, like wool brushing over stone. He looked at Amos. "Hurry!"

Amos lifted his arms above his head and took the lantern in his hands. He lifted it slightly, moving it along the hook, trying not to scrape the brass against the iron. He inched toward the edge of the pillar. The lantern was nearly free. Every muscle was stretched taut. Then the rocks pitched beneath him. The lantern clanged into the wall. Amos fell to the ground with a thud, and the pillar toppled onto his leg.

Simeon rushed to help him, frantically shoving the rocks aside. Amos helped as best he could, and soon he was free, but neither boy noticed the creaking of the great wooden door as it swung open. Hadrian stared down at them.

"What have we here?"

Simeon froze. Amos thought his friend might faint, for he looked as if he wasn't breathing.

"We came ta see yer lantern," Amos said, standing to his feet and looking Hadrian dead in the face. Around him, a fitful radiance shone.

"Is that so?" Hadrian came closer. He looked at Simeon first, smiling a little. Then he dismissed him altogether. He turned to Amos. "You came to see my lantern in the dead of night?" His eyes moved to the tumbled pile of stones, then returned to Amos. The cold smile never left his face. It seemed etched there, as if in stone.

"I know who you are, boy. You're Abner's son."

"I am," Amos said.

"Amos, Wielder of Fire, the boy who fears nothing, is that right?" Hadrian's eyes narrowed. The light of the lanterns didn't fall on him. It flickered over Amos's face and Simeon's, over the stones of the house and the grasses at their feet. But it never touched Hadrian. He stood cloaked in darkness, and only his eyes and his teeth shone distinctly.

Amos hesitated. "There's nothin' ta fear." His left hand clenched into a fist and relaxed, causing the slightest movement of his arm guard.

"Not even the Shadow?" Hadrian asked.

"There's more than Shadow in this world," Amos replied.

Hadrian laughed. "You're awfully sure of yourself, aren't you?" He looked up to the lantern still swinging on its hook. "My lantern would be a fitting prize for you. I won it long ago from someone afflicted with the same madness as yours."

Hadrian stepped closer, his eyes smoldering with blue flame. "I know what waits for you in the Shadow. You might not fear it yet, boy, but it's coming all the same. It's coming for *you*." He leaned in, his breath reeking. "And it will feast on you before the end."

Lightning streaked and branched across the sky, and there was a deafening crack of thunder. For the first time in his life, Amos's courage failed him. He spun around, grabbing Simeon by the arm, and ran like mad into the depths of the night.

They never spoke of that night.

In the days that followed, a small, nearly imperceptible trembling began in Amos's heart. He wrestled with Hadrian's words, turning them over and over. What could they possibly mean? How could Hadrian possibly know what the future held? He tried to silence the voice that rang in his ears, tried to forget the cold light in Hadrian's eyes. But fear stood at the door, knocking, knocking, begging entrance.

It might have encouraged him to know that he had held Evander's own lantern in his hands. Perhaps. But he did not know it. And he was only just beginning to understand the terror that gnawed at every heart in Shiloh, a terror as constant and inescapable as the darkness. He was only just beginning to feel it, but in Amos's heart, at last, the feasting had begun.

Twelve

Simeon had his first dream on the eve of the Great Hunt. He was draped in a heavy mantle, blinded by its dark folds. He reached to touch the fabric, gave it a tug, and felt the movement of the thick wool brushing over his head. He struggled to breathe, the mantle growing heavier, pressing against his mouth and nose. Its lower folds encircled his legs and arms. He was smothered, choking. He struggled to lift the mantle, straining under its weight. Finally, it gave way. He flung the loose fabric from his body and took a gasping breath of air. As it fell to the ground, the fabric took form. An immense body covered in ragged black fur, four black feet with merciless claws, jagged white fangs, and blazing orange eyes appeared before him. A growl of rage rumbled in the wolf's belly, and without knowing why Simeon screamed, "Abner!"

His eyes shot open. He stared up in confusion, and then turned to see his surroundings. Embers were cooling on the hearth, and his mother stood over his cot.

"Simeon? What is it? What's wrong?"

He didn't know what to tell her. How could he explain what he had just seen? It hadn't happened, wasn't real. Yet, his body had responded as if the wolf crouched in that very room.

"Nothin', Ma. I'm alright," he said. But something had changed; something had begun; something had taken over which he could neither predict nor control. Now, when the villagers stared, he would know. He would know and tremble, for he was a Dreamer.

Three great halls stood in Shiloh, though their designs and purposes could not have been more different. Of the existence of the Bright Hall of the Immortals no man knew, and the Hall of Shadows lived only in whispers and rumors. The Hall of Echoes, however, was known to every man of that country. For more than seven hundred years it had stood at the northwestern corner of the Whispering Wood, its massive walls formed by a series of tall stones standing vertically in a circle. Smaller stones, lying horizontally, connected the gaps at the tops of the larger stones, and the stone floor was inlaid with the signs of the four clans. To the left and west of the raised platform in the center of the Hall of Echoes was the mark of the Clan of the Builder. A black stone watchtower circled by black stones represented the clan responsible for erecting the great hall. To the north was the sign of the white tree, by far the most intricate of the mosaics, with white stones cut in the shapes of leaves and branches and spreading roots. To the east was the sign of the Lost Clan, its twelve sun rays stretching out from a central circle in an odd mixture of short and long, straight and curved lines. To the south, the sign of the Fire Clan was laid out in reddish stones, its three tongues of flame uniting and twisting around a core of beaten edanna.

The Hall of Echoes had no roof and no doors, and it stood gray and cold nearly all the year. Until the first frost. Then the torches, held by iron braces within and without each vertical stone, were lit. A bonfire was built on the central platform, and the Hall of Echoes was transformed into a fiery ring with a fiery heart. The surrounding landscape came alive with light and clamorous activity as thousands came from villages all over Shiloh to celebrate the Great Hunt.

Abner's family, and Simeon with them, had taken the Builder's Bridge across the Meander and traveled north and west, keeping well clear of the wood. To Amos, the journey had felt interminable.

"Why must we bring this cursed cart?" he had complained. "Dried venison and a water skin would've served us just as well."

"Not fer the celebration!" His mother had argued, clearly offended at the suggestion. "It's tradition! There's been feastin' before the start o' the hunt fer centuries."

"But if we'd just left the kettle, Da and I could've carried the rest in packs."

"I'll not send my men inta the wood without a decent meal in their bellies."

Amos had grumbled until they neared their destination, and the sights and sounds of the assembling crowd swept all other thoughts from his mind.

Around the Hall of Echoes, the air crackled with a current of nervous excitement. Torches and lanterns moved in every direction. Boys in gray tunics dueled with wooden daggers. Girls in gray shifts skipped about, carrying rag dolls. Women stirred the contents of their iron kettles, chatting or complaining to one another in a cacophony of voices. Men clustered in groups, discussing the upcoming hunt, their harvests and trades. They boasted about great feats of bravery and rehashed favorite tales.

"I've never seen so many people," Simeon said. He wore leather trousers and carried a new bow, but the trousers hung a bit loose, and, somehow, the bow still seemed an awkward encumbrance. He was taller now, though his fair hair and eyes still drew the attention of many in the crowd.

Amos drew more attention. Men, women, and children gaped or whispered to one another as he passed. They had heard that the famed Wielder of Fire, the true son of Hammond, the boy who killed the Shadow Wolf, had come, and those who recognized his face had wasted no time pointing him out to those who did not. He strode about the campsite, tall and proud in his leather trousers, talking to the boys who got up the nerve to ask their questions, and laughing when they begged him to breathe fire on the spot.

"And here are the two heroes, I see. The great Wielder of Fire and the young Dreamer."

Amos cringed at the sound of the voice. It was Lark, the chandler. "She should've been called Crow," Simeon said, under his breath.

Amos laughed at the joke until Ferlin and a handful of his cronies appeared.

"Goin' ta make yerselves names in the Great Hunt, eh?" Lark continued. She looked pointedly at Amos, taking in his tall, lean frame, his tousled red-brown hair, and the hard set of his jaw. "Ya think ya can best all the wolves in the wood, I suppose? Well, you've got some things ta learn, boy." Lark's husband had been killed on the hunt some years back, and everyone knew it. But it drew no pity from the villagers. She had been a hard, bitter woman long before her husband's death.

"And you," she spat, turning to Simeon. "You'll be hidin' in 'is shadow, won't ya?" She dismissed Simeon with a sneer and turned. "Come on Ferlin. I wouldn't stay too close ta these two. The Shadow's marked 'em already." She stalked off, leaving the two groups to face one another.

Amos's hand clenched into a fist, relaxed, and clenched again. His eyes bored into Ferlin's. He had not the smallest fear of this boy, whose habit of stealing had obviously taken a turn from dowels to casks. He'd grown fat on Payne's beer, most likely. Amos could see the question in his eyes and the uneasy set of his feet. A challenge was never made, no word spoken, but Ferlin turned first, and led his gang away. After a moment, Amos turned as well, and he and Simeon made their way back to their campsite.

The Shadow's marked 'em already. Amos would have liked to dismiss the statement, but Lark's words were too reminiscent of Hadrian's. He remembered Hadrian hovering, shadowlike, above him. He felt cold.

"You boys hungry?" Wynn asked. She passed them both bowls of stew without waiting for an answer. Then, to their great wonder, she handed each a mug of cherry ale. This was a rare treat, for cherries were scarce, and the ale was costly. The boys smiled to one another and set aside the stew, lifting their mugs high and drinking deeply. Amos forgot about Lark and Hadrian.

"Slow down, you two!" Abner's voice surprised them, and Simeon choked on his ale. He coughed and spluttered while Amos laughed and slapped him on the back. "Anyone would think we had barrels o' the stuff at home," Abner teased, tousling Amos's hair, giving Simeon a gentle slap on the back, and seating himself between Phebe and Wynn. He took a steaming bowl from Wynn's hand and dug into his meal with a vengeance.

"When're ya comin' home, Da?" Phebe asked.

"Don't know, m' nightingale." Abner ran a hand over Phebe's hair. In honor of the celebration, Wynn had woven it with night-blooming jasmine. The white flowers stood out in bright contrast to the black hair.

"But I have the boys ta help me this year. We'll bring in a good haul. You'll see."

"Who's Sim goin' with?" Phebe didn't mean to bring up a

sore point, but at her words, Simeon dropped his eyes and fiddled nervously with his belt. He knew, as they all did, that though the hunters would travel in large groups through the wood, every man must also have one partner to look out for him. It was a tradition, and it was a necessity. Two boys of twelve could not be partners, for neither had sufficient experience to help the other in case of difficulty. Amos would be partnered with Abner, and Simeon had no one.

The words had hardly left Phebe's mouth when Orin stepped into the circle of light cast by their fire. He looked strange to them, for his leather apron had been traded for a belt, his hammer and tongs for a bow and quiver.

"Abner," he said. "Wynn." He nodded to each, then turned to Simeon. "Who will you be huntin' with, Simeon?" he asked.

At this Simeon seemed to shrink even farther into the ground. He glanced to Abner for help.

"We weren't sure, Orin. I'd wondered if maybe both boys could partner with me."

"The men'll give ya a hard time about it," Orin replied. "What if the boy hunted with me?"

Simeon's stomach lurched, with hope or dread, he could not tell. Again, he looked to Abner.

"What do ya think, Sim?"

At last, he found his voice. "Aye, sir. Thank you."

"You can call me Orin." He nodded to Simeon. "I'll meet ya here after the ceremony." Orin disappeared into the crowd without another word.

Abner and Wynn knew, though the boys did not, that Orin's story was a sad one. His wife, carrying their firstborn in her belly, had drowned in the River Meander many years ago. Since then, he'd kept to himself, so it wasn't surprising that he had no partner for the hunt. Still, taking a young, frightened boy to watch his back was no small gesture of kindness. Orin was taking a great risk entering the wood with Simeon to look after.

"Well, that's settled," Abner said. He rose just as a loud, melancholy horn sounded, filling the air with a solemn call. It was time. Around the camp, the frenzied motion of lights changed. Torches and lanterns moved toward the Hall of Echoes, as if pulled by invisible ropes.

"You three go on ahead," Wynn urged. "Phebe and I can finish up."

"Please, Ma. Can't I go with 'em? If I wait, I won't be able ta see anything."

Wynn sighed. "Alright. Go with yer da. But don't let go his hand, Phebe. I mean it. Don't let 'im out o' yer sight."

"Don't worry, Ma," Phebe said as her father lifted her to his shoulders. The boys downed their last few drops of ale and followed Abner into the crowd that flowed toward the bright circle of red-gold light. The muddle of anxious voices was silenced by the sound of a single drum pounding out a slow rhythm. It was joined by another drum, then another and another. Each took up the same rhythm, until the Hall of Echoes pulsed with the beat. People's hearts pounded in answer. Gradually, the drums quieted, dropping out one by one until a single drum carried on its rhythm alone. When it too was silent, the crowd held its breath.

A man stepped onto the platform. The bonfire behind him and the torchlight before him gave him a godlike appearance. His features were so bright, so clear. His edanna belt, carved with many signs of the Clan of the White Tree, sparkled in the light of the flames. This was Hale, Father of the Clan of the White Tree. It was his clan that took precedence at the celebration of the Great Hunt, for his was the clan founded by Grosvenor, the Mighty Hunter. Every man longed to display Grosvenor's courage in the coming days. Every man longed to achieve Grosvenor's fame and glory.

From somewhere within the hall, a panpipe began to play, and over its queer, haunting music, Hale began the tale of Grosvenor.

> Hearken, my children, come gather ye 'round
> Ta hear o' the hunter of greatest renown.
> No traveler bolder, no warrior more fell
> Than Grosvenor. List, and fall under the spell.

Amos didn't have to be told. He had long since fallen under the spell of this tale. In his mind, he spoke the words in time with Hale.

> Far from the village o' Thayer he wandered
> No more than a whelp. From father and mother
> He journeyed ta mountains of snow in the north,
> And down from the perilous peaks 'e rode forth

> Ta scour southern moor and search hidden glen,
> Ta comb darkened forest and meadow 'til when,
> As a man of great stature and strength he returned
> Ta village and fam'ly ta find they were burned

> By the wrath o' the dragon, by Sirius slain
> And Grosvenor wept. He remembered the name
> O' the monster and swore that 'e never would rest
> 'Til Sirius' flame was extinguished at last.

By this time, everyone had fallen under the spell. The gentle undulations of the panpipe worked like Darby's hands at her loom, endlessly weaving. The song of the pipe changed; it rose and fell, but never ceased. And Hale's words mingled with the sound.

Then mountin' 'is stallion with arrow and sword
He rode fer revenge through the tenebrous wood
Where waited in darkness 'is rivals of old.
The ambush set Grosvenor's blood runnin' cold.

The Shadow awaited, like darkness crept in.

Amos's mind stopped its dance to the music and the words.
Something had tripped him up, confused his rhythm. It was that
phrase. The words were so like Hadrian's, so like Lark's.

He heard the grim howls o' the wolves on the wind.
The eyes o' the cats glowered down from above,
And behind came the thunder of black Daegan hooves.

Captured 'e was by the night and the dark
When before 'im a tree rose with shimmerin' bark.
A voice drifted down like a rustlin' wind,
"Take shelter, good trav'ler, for I am a friend."

Among the white branches and silvery leaves
Grosvenor took shelter from shadowy fiends.
Ragin' and stampin', they circled their prey,
Repelled by the unearthly light o' the tree.

As if by some magic as ancient as night
The tree gave the hunter a bow of bright white.
"Yer arrow will never fall short of its foe.
With blessings from Linden and Olwen ya go."

So swiftly he fitted an arrow ta string
And inta the ranks of 'is foes it went singin'.
The wolves and the cats fled back inta the night,

And 'is arrows fell thick on the Daegan in flight.

Wolves and cats held no fear for Amos. He had conquered both, and from his neck hung a trophy of just one of his victories. And what of the Daegan? They hunted horses and elk, not men. Was that all that waited for him in the darkness?

'Twas not 'til the nights had grown colder by far
That Grosvenor came ta find Sirius' lair.
In Pallid Peaks layered with blankets of snow
Where only the bravest or foolhardy go,

It waited in darkness, silent in sleep,
Broodin' on sorrows, like treasures ta keep.
Then Sirius woke with a hideous scream,
For a silver-white bow had been hauntin' 'is dreams.

Wings that were torn from the fabric of night
Lifted the dragon ta terrible heights.
From there, like a blot on the canvas of snow,
He spotted the hunter and plunged in the glow

Of 'is ragin' blue flame, burnin' colder than death.
The storm of 'is flight robbed our hero of breath,
But Grosvenor drew back 'is magical bow
And pierced the black heart o' the dragon o' Shadow.

It fell ta the ground with a thunderin' roar,
Blackened the snow on the white mountain's floor.
One talon of sable 'e took fer 'is own,
A trophy o' vengeance fer fam'ly and home.

An eye from the beast 'e cut, still burnin' blue.
From its back, a wide swath of black armor he hewed.
He took the worm's head as the boast of 'is battle
And mounted it high on the walls of 'is castle.

The story of the slaying of Sirius still thrilled Amos. The thought of bringing down a dragon and hacking it to bits before riding home victorious was sweeter to him than the rich flavor of the cherry ale. Still, no dragons roamed the forests. They haunted the northern mountains, and perhaps the land beyond the Black Mountains. No man had ever faced a dragon in the Whispering Wood. *What a fool I am*, he thought to himself. There was nothing to fear in the wood, nothing to fear on the hunt. He squared his shoulders and took a deep breath, shaking off the doubts and questions that had plagued him.

Soon Hunter was husband, and Hunter was father,
But ever and always 'is feet longed ta wander,
Ta scour southern moor and ta search hidden glen,
Ta comb the white mountains fer Sirius' kin,

Ta hunt the Black Mountains, ta roam far and wide.
He's journeying still in the tales of 'is tribe.
The greatest of hunters, the fiercest of men,
Hail, Grosvenor, Father and Light o' the Clan!

The last line of the tale rang out across the plains, for it was as familiar to the people of Shiloh as their own names. Men raised their bows, their daggers, their mugs of ale and shouted the words at the tops of their voices. Women and children shouted and called. Every clan joined in.

As the echo of their cries rang out over the surrounding land, Hale said a few words of warning and blessing over the men. Then the pipe began again. This time it was joined by drums and reed flutes, and the people broke out into a dance. From their tight cluster around the Hall of Echoes they spread, kicking their feet, raising their arms, lifting children off the ground, swinging one another in sweeping arcs. And for a few moments, the grief of the coming departure was laid aside. Abner twirled Phebe until Wynn joined them. Then Amos and Simeon took turns with her, swinging her around and around until the jasmine was flung from her hair, and she laughed with breathless delight. They danced in the bright glow of a thousand lights, arm in arm, full of joy. They could not have known that they danced on the dagger-edge of darkness.

All too soon, the music stopped, and the horn sounded again. This was their warning. The men would say their final farewells and depart.

Abner turned to his wife. He put a hand on each side of her face and kissed her.

"I'll be back before ya know it, m' love."

She looked into his eyes long and hard, trying to hold them in her gaze, trying to hold *him* in her grasp. "May the light shine upon you," was all she could manage.

"And you." Abner kissed her again quickly, squeezed her hands, and let go.

He turned to Phebe, "I'll miss yer singin', little bird."

She threw her arms around his neck and kissed him on the cheek. Abner returned her embrace, then kissed her on the top of the head and hoisted his pack onto his shoulder. Orin appeared, silent and solemn, and Simeon made his way awkwardly over to his side. As the third horn blast pierced the air, Abner smiled a sad smile, picked up his lantern, and joined the fiery procession that wound its way toward the wood. Simeon and Orin joined him.

Amos would have gone, too, but Wynn stopped him. Out of habit, she ran a hand over his hair to smooth it.

In a quavering voice she said, "Take care, my boy, and look after yer da." Amos thought it strange that she had not told Abner to look after him.

"I will, Ma." Amos kissed his mother, pulled a lock of Phebe's hair playfully, and ran to catch the others.

Thirteen

That was how the hunt began. As the women and children cleared their campsites and set off homeward in many directions, leaving the Hall of Echoes gray and cold once more, the men and boys made their way into the Whispering Wood. The company would travel along one of the Hunter's Paths that cut almost due east, through the heart of the wood, across a wide branch of the River Meander, to the grasslands at the base of the Black Mountains. For the boys, it was a grand adventure. For the men, it was a necessary evil, though they still found some pleasure in telling tales around their campfires at night.

"I'm goin' ta bring down the biggest o' the bulls," Amos boasted to Simeon as they sat by their fire after a long day of walking. They had seen nothing but trees on that first day. Even the combined light of hundreds of torches and lanterns could not pierce more than a few paces into the dark of the wood. Now, weary and tense, the company had spread out along the path to rest. Some had even ventured within the first line of trees to make their camps.

"Ya think so?" Simeon said. "I'll be glad if I get in one good shot."

"You'll do better than that, Sim. You'll show Ferlin what a great marksman looks like." He smiled his easy smile and glanced in the direction of Ferlin's camp.

Orin and Abner sat across from the boys in quiet conversation. But beyond them, from the other campfires, Amos and Simeon could hear stories being told. The Tale of Grosvenor was repeated often, and the story of how Hammond rescued his village from an army of Shadow Wolves was another favorite. Hammond, the most ancient hero of Shiloh, had been the first to learn that fire could destroy the wolves. He had built a great trench of flame around his village; he'd shot fiery arrows and thrown balls of fire into their ranks. The hunters boomed as they told the story, as though the sound of their voices would frighten away the beasts that lurked in the undergrowth. They didn't have to wonder. They knew they were being hunted.

Early on the second day, something happened. Simeon, thinking he saw the movement of a deer, had loosed an arrow into a tangle of dark trees. A few of the men nearest him had stopped, asked him to describe what he saw, then hurried on in disgust. Even Orin had thought it unwise to go and check on his "kill." The risk was too great.

"Lousy waste of an arrow," Simeon had said. He'd given the ground a frustrated kick and fallen back into step with the others, not even noticing when Amos slipped off the path.

Amos had seen something as well, something that reflected the light of the passing torches. He moved quickly, silent as shadow, covering twenty paces, thirty, forty. Behind him, the hunters' lights grew dim, but he pressed on until he came to a little rise in the land and something sticking out of the dirt. He knelt to clear away the surrounding soil and unearthed a shining, silver object no longer than his hand. Without stopping to examine it more closely, he tucked it into his trousers, hurried back across the wood, and slipped unnoticed into the line of hunters. Later that day, a man named Ingram disappeared. Whether taken by wolves or cats or merely lost in the wood, even his partner could not say.

On the third day, they crossed the river. There, the northernmost of the Three Bridges spanned the black water. It sloshed and foamed beneath their feet, reflecting in strange, fitful bursts the lights of the lanterns and torches above it. On the fourth day, someone discovered elk tracks. A large herd was moving east, toward the grasslands between the wood and the mountains.

The hunters quickened their pace. Every man and boy in that company longed to be free of the oppressive dark of the wood. Their days and nights were running together. The hours of putting one foot in front of the other, holding torches and lanterns high, peering into the featureless darkness, jumping at every snapping branch or crunching leaf, had worn them down.

But when the thick net of vines and trees came to an abrupt halt, and a wide, grassy land opened up before them, they did not step out. The seasoned hunters knew that if they could sneak up on the herd, they could take down several of the animals before they had time to react. They kept to the forest, veering away from the Hunter's Path to creep through the undergrowth within the shadow of the trees. They used as little light as possible, the large company splitting into smaller groups, each man poised to strike at the first sign of movement from the herd.

Abner walked ahead with Simeon and Orin, bow in hand, arrow at the ready. But Amos hung back. He longed to bring down a bull elk by himself, and he had yet to match his father's strength and skill with the bow. If he wanted a chance at a kill of his own, he would have to move away from the group.

At last, they were spotted. The herd must have been at least a hundred strong. They were grazing quietly in the grasses under the shadow of the mountains. Though the light was faint, Amos could see the bulls' widespreading antlers moving up and down in the grass. He held his breath. And in that moment of perfect silence before the first arrow of the Great Hunt flew, Amos heard something he hadn't expected to hear. Ahead of him and to his left, in a black tangle of trees, there was a menacing growl. Two orange-gold eyes burned through the dusky light, and they were fixed on Abner.

Time slowed to a crawl. Abner's bow was raised, his eyes on the herd. The beast, with fangs bared, leaped into the air. Abner pulled the arrow almost to his nose, closed his left eye, and released the string. Behind him the wolf seemed suspended in midair.

"No!" Amos screamed. He pulled an arrow from his quiver, fitted it to the string, and let it fly. It burst into flame as it covered the ground between Amos and the monster. But it was too late. The wolf had descended on Abner and enveloped him in twilight. Its fangs sank into Abner's neck, its claws into his back. He struggled, thrashed, then shuddered and fell beneath the weight of the beast. By the time the arrow found its mark, Abner's lifeblood was spilling out on the ground.

Amos reached his father just as the fire consumed the Shadow Wolf and it blew away in fume and smoke.

"Da! Da! I'm here."

Abner lay in a heap. His son gently turned him on his side and stared in horror at his ravaged body.

"I'm sorry, Da. I'm so sorry. I should've stayed with ya."

Tears slipped from Amos's eyes. He shook his head in disbelief. He could not understand. In his mind he heard the echo of Hadrian's voice. *I know what waits for you in the Shadow.* It was not the dragons, not the cats, not even the wolves. This was a darkness more vast and deep than any of those small foes.

"No, m' boy. Don't be sorry." Abner's breathing was labored, ragged. "Tell yer ma I love 'er. Tell Phebe never ta stop 'er singin'."

Amos crouched over his father with one hand supporting his

head. The other hand rested on his father's chest. He could feel the feeble beating of his heart. Amos's own heart felt shattered into a thousand bloody pieces.

"Amos," Abner looked his son square in the eyes. "Ya mustn't forget who ya are. There's more than Shadow. Don't forget."

Long ago, Amos had promised that he wouldn't forget. But this time he couldn't speak. With all his remaining strength, Abner placed his hand over his son's and squeezed it lightly. "May the light shine upon you, m' boy," he whispered. His eyes closed, and he was gone.

Amos threw back his head and screamed his agony at the ashen sky. The awful, throbbing pain that racked his body, his mind, was spewed out into the heavens. But there was no answer from the darkness above him. No light broke through the cloud. No stars shone through the night. No help arrived. Nothing happened. Nothing. There was only silence. And the cold indifference of the changeless gray sky.

Fourteen

A midst a blaze of torches, a silent procession made its way
south.

Abner's body, spread out on a makeshift cot, seemed to
float through the twilit country, for he was carried on the shoulders
of four strong hunters. Orin was among them, and nearby were
Simeon and Amos. The soft padding of leather boots on grass and
stone, the faint crackle of the torch fires, and the heavy breathing of
the men were the only sounds that could be heard, but a soundless
scream echoed out from Amos's heart as he made his slow way
home.

He remembered nothing of the journey, only the jolting realization that he had reached the lane leading up to the cottage. To his
right was the split-rail fence, half covered with the dead remains of
the summer jasmine. To his left, looming larger and closer in the
gathering dark, was home. He had always thought of the cottage
as a living thing: a warm, breathing part of his family, but now the
dead dark of his father's eyes spilled ahead of him, spreading down
the lane, threatening to extinguish the fragile glow of the cottage.

There was no way to postpone that meeting, no way to avoid being seen. The women, no doubt waiting anxiously for their return, would be watching the road. When they saw the torches, they would know. Amos felt his muscles tense, his hand working against his will, his jaw set tight. Then he heard it: Phebe's cry. It burst from the open door of the cottage and filled the meadow, clinging like mist to the brown rushes. More terrifying still was his mother's silence. She stood like stone in the doorway, the drop-spindle hanging limp in her hand.

The procession continued. Those men who did not carry the body gathered branches and stones as they passed. A hundred paces south of the cottage, in sight of the windows where light still shone, they set up a mound, piling stone on stone and branch on branch. Even Amos, the blood cold in his veins, lifted wood onto the mound before Orin and the others hoisted Abner's death cot to the top. It was tradition. Someone set fire to the wood. This, too, was tradition in Shiloh. Without pause, without ceremony, the dead were "given back to the light." What light, none could have said. The phrase had lost all meaning, drifting down from some forgotten past.

Simeon wept little boy tears as Abner's body burned; Orin put a hand on his shoulder and squeezed tight. Phebe, too, shed silent tears as her father and protector disappeared in smoke. But Wynn was mute, and Amos as well. He stood thinking about light, about sun and stars and whatever light his father's burning body was being transferred into. It all seemed thin, foolish even, when cold eyes melted in hot flames. His father, his hero, was fading away forever. In moments, only ash would tell the tale of Abner's existence. That man's great strength would be utterly consumed by the power of those relentless yellow-orange flames. Their hunger was never satisfied. They could lick up a man's body and his life and his hope, and still they would keep devouring.

Phebe's voice, small and tremulous, broke the weighty silence with a strange lament.

Whither, whither little maiden?
Whither light and laughter gone?
Wherefore would the
Darkness take thee
From the warmth of Mother's arms?
Inta Shadow
I must follow,
Inta twilight, inta death,
Though immortal gods oppose me,
Though I find no place of rest.
Ever onward,
Never homeward
'Til my heart be whole again.
Whither, whither
Little maiden?
Come ta me, my Imogen.

And that was all. One by one, the hunters scattered, fading into the dark of the countryside. Simeon walked home with Orin's hand still grasping his shoulder. Wynn and Phebe stood long at the pyre before returning to the cottage. But Amos stayed all through that night, in the light of the devouring flame, until the very last ember cooled to black and the fire was gone.

He woke and waited in the quiet, without opening his eyes, allowing his mind to surface slowly from the depths of exhausted sleep. He had a vague memory of stumbling over the threshold, of falling into his cot; and someone must have covered him, for he could feel the weight of wool blankets against his chest. His left hand ached, his fingers clenched around something long and stiff. Then he remembered the belt. One of the men had thought to remove his father's leather belt, the one with the sign of the Fire Clan branded into the pouch, before the pyre was lit. Amos had seen it resting near the mound and brought it inside. *I shouldn't have it*, he thought. *Not yet. It should've been a gift for my coming of age.*

Soon Amos was aware of the sounds in the cottage: the slow, rhythmic creaking of the rocking chair where he knew his mother sat gazing into the fire, the dull thudding of a knife slicing through potatoes into the surface of the table, the groaning joints of his cot when he shifted his weight. It was all so familiar. Except for the void of sound that should have been filled by Abner. There should have been a shuffling as his father carried firewood to pile on the hearth, or perhaps the rough scratching of his father's hand over his stubbly chin. There should have been a smooth rustle of an oiled cloth on a wooden bow, and someone should have been telling tales to his "dear ones" as he rubbed the knee of his leather trousers.

Amos took the risk, the immense risk, of opening his eyes and surveying the cottage. As he had guessed, his mother sat in her chair by the fire, mechanically gathering and hooking tufts of raw wool with one hand. The other hand dropped the spindle with a flick, and wild clouds of gray were twisted and tamed. She dropped the spindle again and again before wrapping up the newly spun yarn and starting over. There was a strange sort of comfort in the work. The rhythm and repetition were like a heartbeat pulsing through the cottage. At the table, Phebe steadily chopped potatoes, long strands of hair spilling over her thin shoulders and arms.

But there was no one else.

"Awake at last, Amos?" Phebe had noticed his movements.

"Aye," he answered, unable to say more when he looked into her red, swollen eyes.

Wynn turned to face him, pausing briefly from her spinning. "We could use more firewood, Amos. Are ya up ta choppin' some today?"

"Aye," he said again, grateful for an excuse to leave. He sat up awkwardly, tucking Abner's belt under his tunic, and made for the door. He ran past the sheepfold and the mound, through the trees to the little glade, where his old target still hung on the tree. When his feet reached the brim of the lake, he pulled his father's belt from beneath his tunic. He touched the worn leather, running his finger over the branding on the pouch. A scrap of wool was caught in the belt. Amos tugged it loose. It was caked with blood.

He roared in rage and grief and hurled his father's belt and the scrap of fabric into the lake. The belt sank. The bloody fabric floated on the surface of the water.

He tossed a stone at the scrap and missed. He tried again and missed. "By Ulff! Sink, ya cursed thing!" he screamed. And the scrap of wool caught fire.

He had never sworn by the Shadow Lord before, and a little nagging voice at the back of his head told him his father would not approve.

His father. Da.

The thought struck him again, hard. Abner was gone. It was as if Hammond had never beaten the wolves, as if Grosvenor had never slain the dragon. The story had gone wrong. The hero had fallen.

The lonely hooting of an owl drifted down from the branches overhead, and Amos turned to go. His foot bumped against something, and looking down, he noticed the silver tube he had slipped into his trousers during the hunt. Like so many other things, it had been forgotten, but now he picked it up and examined it closely. It shone bright and smooth, much like edanna but without the red-gold hue. The tube was no longer than his hand, but it could be extended to more than twice that length. He stretched it to its full span, noticing that each section was smaller than the last. On each end was a circle of glass, and engraved on the side were these words: "Until the day breaks, and the Shadows flee away."

Amos wasn't interested in the origin or the purpose of the glass. He had no heart for it. When he returned to the cottage, he tossed the thing into the trunk against the back wall.

"What o' the firewood, Amos?" Wynn asked.

Phebe stopped her chopping and looked at him carefully. "Are ya alright?"

"Aye," he said to his sister. "I'll get it now, Ma." He hoisted the axe over his shoulder, left the cabin, and set to work, pounding out a desperate rhythm of his own.

Fifteen

Simeon was at the door the next morning, nearly collapsing under the weight of a large slab of meat and a heavy sack.

"Ma sent the bread and potatoes," he explained, emptying the contents of the sack onto the table. "The meat's from Orin. The shop was busy today, or he'd have come." It was a whole side of venison, salted and dried.

Simeon had thought long, on his journey from Emmerich, about what he should say to Amos, or to any of them. The image of the wolf in his dream still haunted him. Its eyes had so resembled those of the monster that killed Abner. He wondered now if he shouldn't have told someone about the dream. Then, it had seemed such a risk. But what if his dream had been sent as a warning? What if he'd been intended to speak up, to warn Abner, to change the dark course of events that had unfolded in the wood?

He sank onto the bench by the familiar wooden table and waited, his eyes flickering from Phebe, who was carding wool in a corner, to Wynn, who worked her spindle silently by the fire, to Amos, who sat on his cot, stripping the bark from a pile of branches. Only

Phebe looked back with a smile. It was pained, but kind.

"Ya must thank them fer us, Sim," she said.

"'Twas kind o' yer ma, Sim, but Orin needn't have bothered." Wynn lifted her eyes from the fire and paused in her spinning to nod in her son's direction. "Amos is as fine a hunter as 'is father."

Amos froze. His dagger waited halfway down the side of what would soon become the shaft of a new arrow. Simeon could see the tremble in his hand, the hesitation. He saw the blank, unfocused eyes, the lips slightly parted. He saw the pulse race in his friend's neck. It stopped him cold. Not in five years of danger and adventure and conflict and darkness had he seen Amos like this. Amos was afraid.

And then, as quickly as it had appeared, the look of fear passed. Simeon watched as Amos's expression changed. His eyes narrowed. His mouth closed, the muscles in his jaw contracting fiercely.

"You'd have me go back inta the Whisperin' Wood, Ma?" he said.

"You could go south," she replied.

"There's not enough large game ta the south, not enough ta feed us through the winter," Amos countered.

"East then." Her words kept time with the creak of the rocking chair.

"Toward the Black Mountains?" The dagger dropped from his hand. "Why not send me ta fetch dragons from the Pallid Peaks? Perhaps I could storm the gates o' Shadow Castle on the journey home? Would that please ya, Ma?!"

Wynn stood up. Tears spilled from her eyes as she spoke. "Yer da's gone, Amos. Burned ta nothin' on that mound out there. There's no one left ta care fer us but you. Would ya send yer sister inta the wood, then? Would ya send me?"

Simeon wanted to run from the cottage. He looked first to Phebe, whose tears gathered in the groove of her scar and dripped onto the cloud of wool in her lap, then to Amos, whose hand was clenching in and out of a fist, causing his arm guard to move up and down.

"Five years, Ma." Amos's voice was low, his anger just restrained. "Five years 'til I come of age. Ya know how Da felt about me huntin' without him. Ya sat at this very table. Ya heard what 'e said."

Wynn sat down and continued her work. The spindle dropped low, twisting the length of wool into smooth yarn. "What choice do we have, Amos?"

Amos rose, sending the blade and branches clattering to the floor. "Ya weren't there, Ma! Ya don't know what it was like. Ya didn't see the gashes or feel 'is heart stop its beatin'!" His voice had risen to a strangled scream. His eyes shimmered with unshed tears. "Ya don't know. Ya don't know anything!"

Wynn stopped her rocking and gazed into the bright embers of the fire. Dark skin cracked away from bits of wood to reveal the orange glow beneath.

"Ya think yer da wasn't afraid o' the wood?" she said. She looked over her shoulder at Amos. "He did what 'e had ta do."

Amos kicked his sister's cot and sent it crashing against the wall. In three long strides he reached the door, and he turned to his mother before leaving. "I'm not afraid," he spat, and disappeared without another word.

Simeon could hardly bear the tension. This was not the cottage he'd grown to love as his own. This was not the family that had welcomed him into their midst, asking nothing in return. Abner had been their solid foundation, and without him, everything was reeling, tumbling. Simeon longed to leave, to run for the door, but he could not force his legs to move. He looked toward Phebe, who still sat methodically carding her wool. He watched her square her shoulders and take a deep breath. Then she stood from her work and asked, with as much cheer as she could muster, "Will ya stay fer some venison stew, Sim?"

He glanced at Wynn again, sure she took no notice of him now, then nodded to Phebe. He would stay, for a little while. He would press down his grief and horror and linger here in this dying house, not for Wynn, not for his dearest friend, not even for the man he had loved as a father. He would stay for Phebe, the scarred girl who sang like a nightingale and offered him stew while her world fell to ruin.

There's no knowing what wild inclination drove Amos to the river that day. At any other time he would have honored his father's wishes. He would have run for Linden Lake. But whether it was grief or rebellion or the seeking of oblivion that brought him, on that day Amos found himself seated on a bank of smooth, black stones, looking out on the dark expanse of the River Meander. All things seemed to end there, at the river. The other shore, however far it lay to the west, was obscured by mist and darkness. From this vantage point, the whole world was floored with rippling black and walled with shapeless shadow. And somehow that seemed fitting.

Why him? Amos thought. *Of all the men who set out on the Great Hunt, why did Da have to be counted among the dead? He was a warrior, strong and skilled, wise to the ways of the wolves. He shouldn't have died.*

Amos relived every detail of that final day with his father. Again and again he saw the bared fangs of the wolf. Again and again he saw the pool of blood on the forest floor. But his mind could no more make sense of the tragedy than his eyes could make out the opposite shore of the river.

Day after day, he sat by the river, staring absently into the void. The black dark of early morning faded to pale gray and darkened to pitch again. And still he sat, thinking. He thought about his father's story of the Great Cataclysm. He saw the story in a whole new light, now that his own world had been unmade, and nothing could ever restore it to its former beauty, its former innocence. He thought long on Evander and the sons of Burke. Visions of sun and stars had given them hope, and that hope had sustained his father in the face of immense opposition. Truly, it was wonderful to imagine that something better, something lovely and unblemished, lay just outside the skin of their world. Amos's earliest memories were bright with that possibility, and he had never questioned his father's words.

But Evander and his entire tribe were lost a thousand years ago. The sons of Burke were taken and defiled by the Shadow Lord. And Abner was dead. Had any of them ever set one foot firmly on the soil of a sparkling new world? Had any one of them broken through the Shadow? If Evander and Abner and the heroes of old had not found the strength to survive, to triumph, where did that leave him?

"Never thought I'd find ya here," Simeon said, some days after Amos had stormed from the cottage. "Ma said she saw ya by the river, and I told 'er she was mad."

Amos glanced briefly at Simeon, who was settling himself onto the black rocks.

"I never got ta tell ya," Simeon said, after a time. "I'm sorry, Amos." His voice broke. "I'm so sorry about yer da."

Empty words, Amos thought. They meant nothing, changed nothing. Abner was dead, and sorrow couldn't bring him back. Amos understood, though, that Simeon grieved Abner's death almost as deeply as he did. He managed a weak "Thanks."

"There's somethin' I've been meanin' ta tell ya." Simeon

fidgeted with the rocks beside his feet, lifted one as if to skip it across the water, then thought better of it and dropped it back to the ground. "I think . . . well, I might've had a warnin' . . . might've known . . ." His voice trailed off.

It was one of those moments when Amos longed for silence, when his friend's nervous questioning grated on him.

"What're ya talkin' about, Sim?"

"I had a dream, the night before the hunt."

"A dream? What do ya mean? A real dream, while ya slept?"

"Aye. I was sleepin', but it felt like I was awake."

Amos tried to make sense of this new revelation. He knew of Dreamers, knew that Penelope, Giver of Dreams always chose the fair-haired and fair-eyed, but until now he'd been sure that Simeon was an exception to the rule. Much as he loved his friend, nothing about Simeon, save his unusual coloring, suggested that he'd been specially chosen by the gods.

"You *are* a Dreamer, then?" Amos could scarcely conceal his shock.

"Aye. Seems so."

"But ya said ya had a warnin'. What did ya see in the dream?" A thought hit Amos with the force of a penetrating arrow. Perhaps Abner wasn't supposed to die after all. Hadrian's words hadn't been so clear. Lark might only have been tormenting the family she loathed. What if Simeon had known what was coming, had had the chance to stop it? "Did ya see Da? Did ya know 'e would die?"

Simeon retreated from the intensity of Amos's questions. "I didn't see Abner. I don't know what I saw."

"Ya said it was a warnin', Sim! Ya must've seen somethin'. Tell me!"

"I saw the wolf," Simeon answered, beads of sweat breaking out on his pale skin.

"*The wolf?* Ya saw the one that killed Da?"

"The eyes were the same . . . I don't know. It didn't do anything in the dream. I didn't know what it meant, Amos. I swear by all the gods."

Maybe Simeon really hadn't known. Maybe he wasn't responsible. But the idea that someone was to blame besides himself, that some force besides the relentless cruelty of the Shadow had been at work . . . it was too appealing for Amos to discard just yet.

"Why didn't ya tell me, Sim?! How could ya not say? We could've done somethin'!"

Simeon sat shaking his head, his face a picture of desolation, before whispering, "I'm sorry" once more and walking back into the village.

Amos rested his elbows on his knees and dropped his head into his hands. Almost, almost, he ran to catch Simeon. Almost, he begged forgiveness for his senseless cruelty and restored the bond he held with the person who knew him best in the world. Almost. But he didn't. He sat on the shore, unable to discover what power lurked in the deep places underneath his grief and rage, unaware that someone had been watching as he brooded by the river. Someone was hunting him even now.

$Sixteen$

pair of glittering green eyes surveyed the riverbank. They swiveled in a wide arc from left to right, waiting for the moment when Simeon disappeared into the magistrate's hall. Slowly, the bird spread its wings and flapped them once, twice, three times. Then it leapt from its perch high in the skeletal branches of the tree and began its descent. Broad wings stretched to an impossible span, the tips of the bird's feathers hardening, shifting, molding into fingers. Thin legs lengthened and thickened. Gray-brown feathers fused into a black leather coat. The fiery light of the creature's gaze held Amos in its grip until it stood on the bank, a man. Wild waves and curls of black hair hung around his face. His skin was fair, cheeks and chin covered with short, stubbly hair. And his eyes . . . his eyes were bright, the savage eyes of a wild animal.

Amos had seen nothing but the rocks at his feet. He had heard nothing but the haunting cry of an owl. Until someone spoke in a

113

deep, lilting voice.

"Can it be?" The man in the black coat stepped up beside him. "Are you ... Amos?"

"Aye," Amos replied. He looked the stranger over from head to foot, wondering at his odd style of dress, the peculiar sign branded into his belt (it didn't belong to any clan that Amos knew of), the strange make of his dagger. This man was certainly not from Emmerich.

"I've heard tell of you, even in my village," the man continued. "The boy who slew the Shadow Wolf." The man's voice was laced with wonder, awe.

"Aye," Amos answered, feeling not a hint of pride. "As how many others in Shiloh've done?" He turned to face the water.

"Not at seven, lad, and not as you did. Not with fire from their own mouths. They call you the true son of Hammond." The man sat down on the bank a few paces from Amos, his eyes fixed on the boy's profile.

"There've been others in the Fire Clan who could do the same. I'm no hero." Amos chucked a stone into the river and watched as circle upon circle rippled outward.

"Not so many as you might think. Not one in a hundred years has your gift, Amos." The man hesitated. "Could it be that Amos, Wielder of Fire, has yet to discover the full extent of his power?"

Amos looked back at the stranger. Who was this man? Where had he come from? And how did he claim to know so much about Amos's "gift?"

"Who are ya?" Amos asked, eyes narrowed in suspicion.

"Mordecai," he said, extending a hand to grasp Amos's forearm.

"Ya said you'd heard o' me in yer village. Where's that, I wonder? Do the tales tell the shape o' my nose and chin? How did ya know me from any other boy in Emmerich?"

"It was the guard," Mordecai said, pointing to the wide band of leather strapped around Amos's left arm. "They say it was strapped to your arm, already branded with the sign of the Fire Clan, when you came from your mother's belly." He laughed softly. "Is it true?"

Amos relaxed a little. "No. 'Course not. Besides, some o' the other boys wear 'em."

"True. But then, none of the other boys lost their da in the Great Hunt, did they?"

Amos flinched as if he'd been struck. It took him a moment to realize that the story of his father's death would have traveled back to dozens of villages on the lips of the hunters who'd seen the attack. A wave of nausea swept over him as he imagined the tale being told again and again to anxious listeners in homes and alehouses all over Shiloh.

"Isn't that why you're sitting by the river . . . alone?" Mordecai asked. And in his voice, Amos heard something like compassion, something like understanding. He looked down at his knees to hide the tears that came to his eyes. He didn't trust his voice, so he made no reply.

"What will you do now?" Mordecai asked. "Your family's looking to you, I imagine." He sighed. "Can't be easy for a boy of twelve to take on such a burden . . . to go back there, into the wood."

Amos's chest ached with the hard beating of his heart. He struggled to hold back the tears, to play the man.

"Your family's not much loved by the villagers, I've heard. There's no one here who might help you . . ."

Whether Mordecai's last statement was meant as a question, Amos could not tell, but his mind went immediately to Caedmon's mocking voice and Lark's cruel cackle. He did not think about Orin, or Jada, or Darby. He did not even consider that Simeon would be willing to brave anything for him, that that boy would endure any darkness by his side, even the deep dark of the Whispering Wood. No, Amos saw only hopelessness and desolation. All the world was a great iron door, clanging shut against him.

"I could help, you know." Mordecai lowered his voice. "I could teach you."

"Teach me what?" *Archery?* Amos wondered. *Or gardening, perhaps?* What could this man possibly teach him that would change anything?

"To conquer the fear."

The words were like a splash of cold water on his face. There had been a time when Amos had not known fear, had not understood its crippling power. Could it really be conquered? Could he regain the bold, easy confidence he once had?

"How?" he whispered.

Mordecai's green eyes flickered, and he smiled a broad smile. "With fire," he said.

"Fire?"

"Yes. You don't yet know how special you are, Amos. You have yet to use your gift to its fullest extent. But I can teach you. And then . . . then, you will fear nothing." Mordecai stood to go. "Meet me tomorrow, northeast of the village, on the border of the wood."

"The wood?" Amos asked. Surely, Mordecai wouldn't ask him to go there. Not so soon.

"You can go home and starve with your women, if you like."

Amos was stunned by his words. They flew in the face of everything he thought he knew about this stranger. Yet he couldn't deny the truth in them. What else was he to do? He raked a shaky hand through his hair and drew in a breath to give his consent. But when he opened his mouth to speak, Mordecai was gone. Amos sat alone on the bank of the River Meander. There was nothing to see but the rippling black of the water and the darkening gray of the sky, nothing to hear but the sloshing of the waves against the rocks and the hooting of a distant owl.

The next morning, Amos had crept from the cottage before the women woke, stealing through the dark toward the southern border of the wood. He had carried his father's lantern with him, but he marveled now that he had ever had any need of it. It sat, forgotten, on the floor of the wood, and a golden ball of fire hovered above Amos's palm. As he curled his fingers inward, the flames shrank, drawing in, fading, until he closed his hand and they disappeared altogether. Then, slowly, he opened his hand again, spreading each finger to its fullest span. As he did, the burning orb appeared and grew, tongues of fire stretching up and up.

"Good," Mordecai said, his once-green eyes reflecting the orange glow of the firelight.

After only a few hours with Mordecai, Amos had learned to call flame out of nothing. He needed no breath, expelled in the heat of an attack, to summon it. Whether it sprang from his mind, his muscles, or some unseen power of the gods, he could not tell. But it was obedient to his will, and the sense of power it gave him was exhilarating. From this day, lanterns and candles would seem mere children's toys, the tools of lesser men.

"Thirsty?" Mordecai asked from his seat on a fallen log. Amos dropped his hand to take a leather skin from Mordecai, and the ball of fire disappeared. Though he had hardly noticed the passing of time, the day had already ripened to a pale gray haze. His body was weary with the strain of the morning's instruction, and he was desperately thirsty.

Without thought, Amos lifted the skin to his lips and drank. The water was unlike anything he had ever tasted. It was so sweet that, at first, he thought it must be some sort of ale, some exotic offering from Mordecai's village. "What is this?" he asked, before drinking again, more deeply, from the skin.

"Miri's blood," Mordecai replied.

All the rich color of Amos's face, gathered from the morning's labor and the warmth of the flames, drained away. He knew the story only too well, knew where Ulff had spilled his daughter's blood.

"It's water?" he choked out. "From the river?"

"Yes," Mordecai said. "What of it?"

"I don't drink from the river!" Amos felt he'd been poisoned, tainted somehow.

"Why not? It's good water."

"Da forbade it! He said there's evil in the water."

Mordecai laughed as if Amos had made some joke. "Evil, eh? Every man in Shiloh is raised on Miri's blood. It's mother's milk to us."

"He said it makes ya forget," Amos pressed.

Mordecai let out a sharp breath and drew his dagger from its sheath. From another pouch on his belt, he took out a small stone that shone liquid-black. He drug metal over stone with quick, precise motions, sharpening the blade, and in the flickering light of the lantern that rested on the ground at Mordecai's feet, Amos caught a glimpse of the symbol on the hilt of the dagger. It matched the one on Mordecai's belt. There was a circle, incomplete, with five marks around it. Little flames, perhaps, or claws.

"Forget what, Amos?"

Amos was beginning to feel foolish, but he gave the answer his father would have given. "Who ya are. And what lies beyond the Shadow."

Mordecai smiled. "I don't think even you knew who you were before today, Amos." He continued the methodical sharpening of his dagger. "And it's only madmen who believe in some mysterious world beyond the Shadow."

Amos bristled. "My da was no madman!"

"Have you ever seen it, Amos, this 'sun' Evander spoke of? Have you seen bright lights in the sky, these so-called 'stars'? Have you ever spoken to a man who saw them?"

Amos shifted on his feet, wishing he had some other answer. "No," he admitted.

"Did Evander ever find what he was looking for? Or the sons of Burke?" Mordecai paused before dealing the final blow. "Was there anything but Shadow for your father?"

The muscles in Amos's jaw clenched.

"It's past midday, Amos. Take a look around you. What do you see?" The thick dark of the wood surrounded Amos on three sides. His eyes could discern only the nearest of the branches and shrubs that crowded together in the dusk. To the south, where the wood ended, the meadow was obscured by gray haze.

"I see darkness," he said at last. "Shadow."

"Of course you do. That's what is. Your eyes don't deceive you, Amos. You see Shadow because the Shadow is all that is real."

"But what about before the Shadow fell?" he argued, remembering his father's words about the Cataclysm. "Wasn't there a time when things were different, when men didn't live in darkness?"

Mordecai's voice was calm, his words sounding steadily over the ring of metal on stone. "There's no *before* the Shadow, Amos; no *beyond* the Shadow."

No *before* the Shadow . . . no *beyond* the Shadow. The phrases were heavy. Sharp as iron, hard as stone. They filled the stretching silence and Amos slumped to the ground, overcome by weariness.

The hairline fracture in the foundation of his life was broadening. He felt the shifting, the shaking of all he had once held sacred.

It seemed a great risk, now, to argue with Mordecai. This stranger had an air of such confidence, such certainty. But Amos ventured one more question.

"Have ya been ta the watchtowers, Mordecai? Or ta the other side o' the Black Mountains? How do ya know there's nothin' beyond the Shadow if ya live right in the heart of it?"

Mordecai's eyes flashed a brighter, fiercer green. "I've traveled far, boy," he said, as he rose to his feet, pocketed his stone, and sheathed his dagger. "I've lived longer and seen more. And I won't waste breath on a mad whelp, no matter what his gifts." He took two steps away from Amos before turning and speaking again.

"If you hold to this madness, you'll come to the same end as Abner." He paused, raised his brows, and said, "You're more than that, Amos. Don't waste your time, your power on some fool's hope. Let it die with your father."

Seventeen

$\mathcal{E}$cho grew into a fine horse, and Isolde spent many an hour braiding her shiny black mane. To Echo, she told everything that she could tell no one else. All that lay unspoken in her heart found a voice in the quiet of the little stable, where the chestnut mare stood twitching her ears and nickering softly. Whenever the atmosphere within the cottage became unbearable and the weather prevented her from summiting the hill, Isolde fled to Echo's side, leaning against her neck and feeling the animal's warm breath in her hand.

In the winter of Isolde's seventeenth year, not long before she was to come of age, the snows from the Pallid Peaks swept down on the village of Fleete. Hunters kept to their cottages, and lean times became starving times. Still, the sisters sat before the hearth and braided each other's hair, talking of the coming-of-age celebration, the gifts, the blessing.

"Do ya think they'll bring weapons?" Isolde asked, half teasing. Weapons were not traditional gifts for a girl coming of age, but she would prefer them to pots and blankets and shifts.

"No decent woman o' marriageable age would carry them," Rosalyn answered back, smirking.

"I'd be glad of anything, so long as it's not another wretched shift." Isolde yanked at the long gray gown, pulling it up into a wad above her knees.

The two sat listening to the wind tear through the village, screaming around the corners of every cottage and stable and shop. Isolde could sense that Rosalyn was troubled.

"The man I told you of, he's been hangin' around the cottage again. Yesterday, I nearly cried out when I saw 'is face in the window."

"The window?! So close?" Isolde whipped around to face her sister, and the half-finished braid slipped from Rosalyn's fingers. "Let's be rid of 'im, then! He'll flee ta the peaks, ta the arms o' the dragons themselves when I have done with 'im."

Rosalyn gave a sad smile and rose to peel the few potatoes that would serve as their evening meal. It was dangerous to be beautiful in Shiloh. Her dark, flashing eyes, full lips, and luxurious curling hair were more a curse than a blessing.

"I have ta marry some time, Isolde. It's been three years since I came of age." Her voice fell to a whisper. "Never thought I'd make it this long."

"It isn't graven in stone! You don't have ta marry!" Isolde wanted to shake her sister, to break her thoughts out of their familiar tracks.

"It's no more than our own mothers did. We can't all break with tradition, Isolde." She diced the now-peeled potato into little squares and scooped them into the kettle. "And I know what you're thinkin'. But ya can't protect me. There'll come a moment when you're not here, when you're not lookin'. And someone will come fer me."

"But what if you're carried away south o' the wood or inta the western villages? What then?!"

"Oh, you'll find me, daughter o' Valour." Rosalyn touched the sun charm that hung on her neck. The door swung open, and Sullivan stumbled in.

"It's no use. There's nothin' left ta kill, and I couldn't see it if there were. The valleys fer miles 'round are full o' snow and ice." He sat heavily in a chair in front of the hearth and said no more, while the girls busied themselves with boiling potatoes and keeping the fire fueled with dry logs from the dwindling stack in the stable.

The blizzard roared and howled through the streets of Fleete for days before Sullivan made up his mind to butcher the horse. By then, his stomach was tight with hunger.

"No! Not Echo, Da. Ya can't!" It had been some years since Isolde had taken the risk of defying her father. In seconds, she remembered why. The man moved with remarkable speed and agility when he wanted to, and before she could draw her dagger, Isolde's neck was twisted back at an awkward and painful angle. The lovely red hair at the back of her head was wadded in her father's clenched fist.

"It'll be you, Isolde, if not the mare."

There was no anger in his voice. Just the still, cold certainty of his resolve. After a moment, he released his grip.

"Now go and make some use o' yourself. Get some wood from the stable." He drew his knife from the sheath on his belt and pulled a whetting stone from the pocket that hung on his other hip. He would slit Echo's throat, hack her lovely coat to bits, and feast. He would do it without the smallest thought for the animal, for his daughter's feelings, for anything but the need of the moment.

Isolde threw a cloak over her shoulders and stepped into the cutting wind. She had just the briefest start, just the tiniest window of opportunity. And she took it. Echo was saddled in record speed, and the two companions pressed out into the white-dark.

To the north of Fleete were the Pallid Peaks. To the east and west, hill country. Isolde rode south, pushing Echo as hard as she dared through the blinding snow.

They traveled hour upon hour. Isolde's legs ached and burned with cold and weariness; her cheeks were chapped from the fierce wind. Echo's mane and lashes were coated in ice when they saw the faint lights of the first village to the south of Fleete. Girl and horse huddled against the wall of one little cottage, beneath the overhanging roof, and rested for a while out of the wind. But Isolde had made up her mind to take Echo beyond her father's reach. And when the blood had just begun to flow, hot and pricking, into her legs and feet, she mounted and rode on.

Next morning, the blizzard came to an abrupt end, and they soon passed through towns untouched by the storm. By midday, they had reached the village of Dunn on the northeast corner of the Whispering Wood. Isolde hoped that her father would never venture this far in search of an animal he would have butchered without a thought.

She left her lovely chestnut mare with a wizened old stable keeper, giving her mother's dagger in exchange for Echo's lodging and food. It was all she had to give, though far too valuable for what the aged man would expend on the horse's care. He wrapped some dried venison, a hunk of soft cheese, and a skin of water in a bit of rough cloth and handed it to Isolde with a little reassuring pat on her shoulder. She said goodbye to Echo then, rubbing her neck and stroking her nose.

"I'll come back, ya know. I'd stay, but I can't leave Rosalyn. Not now." Echo stamped and tossed her head, snorting.

"You'll be safe here." Isolde swallowed hard. "Goodbye, my friend."

The journey home took the better part of four days. It was only the mercy of the gods, or perhaps the thick-piled snow, that kept the Shadow Wolves away. But Isolde trembled to think what punishment awaited her.

When she stepped across the threshold, foot-sore, weary, and aching with hunger, Sullivan rose from his seat before the fire. He took his daughter's flame-red hair in his hand and drew his sharpened dagger from his belt.

"Da, NO!" Rosalyn grabbed his arm. Sullivan thrust his elbow into her face and knocked her to the ground. Isolde had no strength to wrestle free from his iron grip, but she cried out when he cut the shining hair from her head, gouging into the tender flesh on the back of her skull. He tossed the silken mass into the fire and stalked out. The reek of burnt hair filled the cottage.

Rosalyn clambered up to embrace her sister, and the two wept as the blood dripped down Isolde's neck. Rosalyn cleaned the wound and bandaged it. There was nothing else to be done. The ragged remnants of hair were too wild to be tamed into a braid.

As it happened, the next day was Isolde's coming of age. She should have been richly dressed, in a white shift embroidered with the sign of the Sun Clan. Her hair should have been braided and adorned with flowers. The villagers should have come throughout the day to flood the cottage with gifts. They should have returned in the evening to see Isolde receive the blessing. They should have gathered in the square, feasting and dancing into the close black hours of the night.

But the hard winter and the blizzard had left them all in want. There was nothing to trade for the white wool to make a coming-of-age gown, no one able or willing to offer a blessing. Two or three villagers tapped lightly at the door, left some small token, and hurried back to their cottages. But the ceremony and the feast were forgotten, impossible. Isolde was left to enter womanhood in silence, bearing the wounds of her father's brutality and the grief of her people's neglect. Far into the night she sat at the summit of the hill, staring into the immense, unknowable darkness, searching for flashes of dragon fire and dreaming of Valour's Glass.

&ighteen

hen Amos came through the door, he found his mother distraught. She paced back and forth between the windows and the hearth, wringing her hands and shaking her head. Her eyes were wild. "She's gone," Wynn said when she caught sight of Amos. "They came and ya weren't here, and she went out inta the night. She's gone." She had the look of a frightened, abandoned child. "Ya weren't here," she repeated. "They came back, and ya weren't here ta protect us."

"*Who* came, Ma? What happened?" Amos asked.

But Wynn could only shake her head and mutter, "Ya weren't here."

Amos glanced around the cottage and felt his heart skip a beat. There was no sign of Phebe. He spun around and raced back through the door.

He scanned the lane, the fence, the meadow, the garden, frantically seeking some sign of his sister, but his eyes told him nothing. His ears spoke more clearly, answering his questions with what they did not hear. The wind was still, the sheep silent. *Oh, no . . . no, no, no . . . not the cats. Is it the cats who've come and gone? Where is Phebe?!* He turned, running toward the sheepfold with more speed than his legs had ever known. And there was his sister, kneeling on the ground, her shift soaked in blood. *No!* his heart screamed. *Not her. Not Phebe, too!*

"Phebe!" he shouted, dropping to his knees beside her and grabbing her by the shoulders. In the torchlight, he could see her face, wet with tears and pale with exhaustion. Her head fell onto his shoulder, her body shaking with sobs.

"They came back, Amos." She gestured toward the fold, littered with the half-devoured remains of the sheep. The cats had wiped out their entire flock. On the ground beside Phebe was a little lamb, its face distorted by bloody gashes. The pitiful creature made a gargled, strangled cry, twitched, and was still. It was the lamb's blood that stained Phebe's shift and not her own. Amos sighed with relief.

"And Da wasn't here . . . he's not here," she continued. Behind them, the ruin of the mound hovered, ghostlike, on the edge of sight.

"What're we goin' ta do?" Phebe sat up and looked hard into her brother's face. Her eyes begged him for some flicker of hope.

Amos held his sister's eyes for a moment, aching for her. He lifted a hand to her cheek, brushing his thumb lightly over her scar. Phebe reacted automatically, jerking away from his hand and turning her face to the shadows. She took a shuddering breath before looking back at him.

"Please, Amos. What're we goin' ta do?"

Amos gripped the claw that hung around his neck. Once, it had been his trophy of battle. Now it mocked him. The boy who slew the Shadow Wolf was not strong enough to shoulder the burdens of this dark, new world. That Amos could not survive in a world where Abner was dead, a world where winter was closing in and his family was without meat, without wool, without protection. He would have to become someone else, someone stronger. He would have to be wildly powerful and utterly fearless.

"Don't fret, little bird," he said. "I'll take care o' ya."

He thought he heard a voice, a whispered plea from the burial mound. *There's still hope, Amos. Ya mustn't forget.* But Amos saw only one path before him, and Mordecai waited on its threshold. So, with determined fingers, Amos extinguished the shining flame of hope that had lit all his boyhood years. He yanked the cord from his neck and tossed it out into the brush. His choice was made.

Next morning, Mordecai was waiting for him. Nothing else was said about Amos's choice, about his father, about anything before or beyond the Shadow. All that was laid to rest, and Mordecai resumed his training.

He began that day by reviewing with Amos the skill required to focus his mind, his energy on calling up fire. At first, Amos had to breathe deeply, and wait long, his muscles tensed in anticipation. But as the days passed, Amos progressed. With hardly a thought, he could send the flames shooting up from his palms or sprouting out of his fingertips.

Late one evening, Mordecai took his instructions to a new level. "Can you see the shrub over there? The one just this side of the thicket?"

"Aye."

"I want you to focus all your energy on that shrub and set it alight. Have your bow and arrow at the ready."

"But I've never burned anything that way before," Amos protested. "I need ta have my hand free." He had forgotten about the arrow that killed the wolf on the last day of the hunt. It burst into flame in midair, though Amos's breath hadn't touched it. He had willed the arrow to burn, and it had obeyed.

"No, you don't. The power doesn't lie in your hand, Amos. Now burn it."

"Mordecai," Amos asked, "why don't *you* have power over fire? Ya know a great deal about it."

"Wielding fire is not my particular gift," he answered.

"Then what *is* yer gift?"

"Call it adaptability. Now . . . focus, Amos. Set fire to the shrub, and have your arrow ready."

Reluctantly, Amos dismissed Mordecai's cryptic reply and pulled an arrow from his quiver. With all the easy grace and skill of a master bowman, he fitted it to the string and gripped it lightly with three fingers. Then he lowered the bow and fixed his eyes on the shrub's dark leaves. They looked as if they'd been burned already. He took a deep breath and held it.

An image of the Shadow Wolf, dissolving in vapor and smoke, conquered by the light of one fiery arrow, came to Amos's mind. He remembered the fading glare of the cat's eyes as it succumbed to fire and drifted away. And then he saw his father's body, licked up by insatiable tongues of flame. That bright, hot force was master of the wolves and cats, stronger even than his father. And Amos was master of the flame.

He let out a controlled breath, and as he did, he saw a worm-like curl of orange on the tip of a black leaf. It spread, until the whole leaf was glowing, then another, and another. The bush was burning! Flames overtook it, and something scurried out into the open. It was a small brown rabbit, escaping the desolation of its cozy home. Suddenly, Amos understood. He knew what Mordecai was expecting him to do. He killed the poor creature without a moment's hesitation.

"Well done!" Mordecai said.

Amos gave him a half-smile, then grabbed the rabbit and threw it over his shoulder. *At least we'll eat well tonight*, he thought. He took no pride in such a kill, but that mattered little now. He would ignore the sinking sensation in his belly, for what other choice had he, really?

That night Simeon dreamed again. He stood in front of an immense bonfire, taller than the height of a man and very broad. He could hear the snapping of twigs and branches as they were eaten up by the flame. He could feel the heat of the blaze. It burned his eyes.

At first, there was only the bonfire and the dense, enveloping darkness that surrounded it. Then Simeon saw the black silhouette of a bird, wings spread wide, talons drawn in tight. Its eyes flashed green, burning hotter than the flames. He could feel the rush of hot wind on his face. The ashy fumes made him cough. But he could not look away. The bird's gaze held him captive.

Just when he thought he could bear it no more, the bird transformed. The level of its eyes remained steady while the form of a dark, tall man took shape. He towered over Simeon, shielding him from the heat and smoke. But there was no escape from the raging fire in his green eyes. When Simeon woke, panting and sweating, the image of those eyes stayed with him.

Nineteen

The dead rabbit was heaped on the floor, forgotten.

"She hasn't eaten anything." Phebe had whispered the words, glancing furtively at her mother, when Amos came home with his kill.

"Still?" Amos had asked.

"Not since . . ." Phebe's voice had fallen away. There was no need to speak of it again. When the cats had killed the flock, and Phebe had rushed out, Wynn had been hysterical. She'd wearied herself with muttering and pacing, then sat down in her rocking chair and taken up her spindle. When Amos left in the early morning hours to meet Mordecai by the wood, she was there, rocking steadily and gazing into the fire. When he returned in the deep dark of evening, he found his mother as he had left her.

"Ma, I've brought a rabbit," Amos said, walking over to his mother's chair and placing a hand on her shoulder. "Phebe can make a stew. It's yer favorite, isn't it?" He sat down on the hearth.

Wynn was growing steadily weaker, steadily thinner. The square bones of her jaw and brow stood out sharply in the fire light, leaving room for shadows to creep into her sunken cheeks and eyes. Her shift hung loose and limp over her shoulders. She was fading away.

"Everything's goin' ta be alright, Ma."

Her eyes flickered to her son's face. Amos waited for her to smooth his hair, to touch his cheek, to pinch his chin. But, as quickly as it had come, her gaze returned to the orange-gold light of the fire. She carried on with her spinning as her chair creaked out a weak pulse.

Amos sighed and looked around the cottage. His father's chair sat in its usual place by the fire, empty and haunting. Abner's quiver and bow were propped against the wall beside the door, and his cot had been neatly made, his extra tunic hanging from its usual hook. The other cots were neat as well, with gray blankets folded at the feet. The stone floor was swept, the woven rugs freshly beaten. The table had been wiped clean. Only the rabbit seemed out of place.

Phebe pushed past him to stir the broth that simmered in the kettle, and Amos moved to the wooden trunk against the back wall. That trunk held everything of any value they owned: his father's tools, the embroidered shift his mother had worn on the day she became a wife, the silver glass he'd found in the Whispering Wood, the smaller bows his father had carved for him through the years, and other odds and ends from his parents' past. All were packed neatly and put away: a box of memories bearing the sign of the Fire Clan.

"Just a little today, Ma, alright?" Phebe said. "Just a little broth, fer Amos's sake?" She held a wooden spoon to Wynn's mouth as she pleaded. But Wynn only rocked and stared, spinning all the while. So Phebe laid the spoon on the hearth, sat down in her father's chair, and sang. It was her last and greatest weapon against the despair that hung like a shroud over the cottage.

"Listen, can ya hear them?
Voices all around

Carried on the breezes
Rumblin' in the ground
Fallin' from the branches
Slidin' over stone
Turn ta find the whispers
Suddenly they're gone
Do the beasts o' Shadow
Plot against their prey?
Do the trees remember
Somethin' they must say?
Does the mother cry out
Fer her little daughter?
Do the shifters wait
The Seekin' Clan ta slaughter?
Listen, can ya hear them?
Voices hushed and fey
Linger not, oh trav'ler
'Til the close o' day"

The last note hung in the air after Phebe stopped singing. Amos stared at her, marveling at the light that shone from her skin. The little rag doll on her cot, its apron adorned with colored yarn, belied his sister's strength. After all she had endured, she burned with a radiance as bright as her brother's had once been.

When Wynn failed to react to the song, Phebe left Abner's chair and sat beside Amos. "How's Sim?" she asked.

"Don't know."

"What do ya mean ya don't know? Haven't ya been spendin' yer days with 'im, in the village?"

"No." Amos didn't want to talk about his last meeting with Simeon. And he didn't want to breathe a word about Mordecai, or his newfound power. Better that Phebe not know.

"What've ya been doin', then? Why haven't ya been here?"

"What I've been doin', I've been doin' fer you, fer both o' ya!" he snapped back.

"But Amos," she continued, "whatever you're doin', how can ya do it without Sim? He's like yer brother. He's family."

"I don't want ta talk about Sim." He would no more understand than Phebe would. Amos opened his mouth to speak again, but he was interrupted by the sound of a feeble cough. He and Phebe turned to Wynn. Could she have thinned and faded still more since he'd come home? Was it possible? She looked almost translucent.

Amos knew what was coming. He felt it in his bones. And he didn't want to watch it happen. He left the cottage, running out into the darkness, running hard, pushing himself until his lungs burned for air. He gritted his teeth and pressed on, faster, faster. On the bank of the River Meander, he fell to the ground and cried until exhaustion overcame him and sleep took him.

When Phebe woke the next morning, her mother was dead. Her vacant eyes stared into the ashen remains of the fire; her thin hands still grasped the drop-spindle. Phebe took one of the now-cold hands in both of hers, then collapsed to her knees, sobbing. Like a candle flame before a strong wind, her light wavered violently. It guttered, faltered, fighting for life until Phebe wiped her eyes, wrapped a blanket over her shoulders, and took the lantern from the table. She stepped out into the lane and headed north, toward Emmerich.

She was not yet ten. Her father and mother were dead. She could have wept long in the cottage, wallowing in the cursed misery of her condition. Instead, she bolted shut the door of her heart and willed her mind to take control. *We'll have to burn the body today*, she thought. *And I can't lift her. I'll need someone strong. A man.* Where

Amos had gone, she could not tell, and she knew of one house in the village where she was sure to find help. *I'll go to Darby*, she decided. *She'll know what to do.*

Darby did indeed know what to do, though at first she gave an anguished cry of grief and wept, drawing the dry-eyed Phebe into her arms.

"I fear for ya, little nightingale. 'Tis too much. 'Tis too much ta bear, I know. Yet ya mustn't give in ta despair like yer mother. They'll come fer ya, they will, sure as the endless night o' this wretched country, they'll come."

Darby quieted after a time and stood. The stones at the base of the loom were uncommonly still as the two stepped out into the road and made for the blacksmith's shop. Some of the villagers watched as they passed. Caedmon emerged from his usual seat in Payne's shop to see what new calamity had befallen. Lark peeked from behind the counter where she measured wicks. She kept her bitter words to herself, perhaps guessing what had happened.

Orin sent word to Jada and Simeon. They all hurried back to the cottage with Phebe and Darby, and without ceremony, without even a song, Wynn was given back to the light. Phebe stood rigid as the fire burned. Darby stayed close, the light of the flames reflecting strangely in her milk-white eyes. Orin and Jada watched without a word. Simeon gripped Phebe's hand as if he would never let go. There was no sign of Amos.

Phebe was the first to leave. As Wynn's bones blackened on top of the mound, the others followed her to the door.

"You'd be welcome ta stay with us, Phebe," Jada said. Darby echoed her invitation.

"No. Thank you. I'm alright," she replied.

"We could stay," Simeon offered, gripping her hand more tightly than ever.

But Phebe wanted to be left alone. It took some argument and many reassurances of her wellbeing to send Orin and Darby, Jada and Simeon on their way. But when, at length, their figures disappeared down the lane, she bolted the door, slipped off her boots, and untied her belt. She stretched her long legs under the gray blankets on her cot and stared up at the wooden beams of the ceiling, remembering Darby's words. It was too much grief, too much to be borne.

And the worst was still ahead. The night weavers were coming.

Twenty

"You didn't come to the wood this morning," Mordecai said and squatted down beside him.

Amos was damp, disheveled. His body ached from sleeping on the stony riverbank.

"I passed your cottage on the way to the river," Mordecai continued. "I saw the flames from the pyre. Your mother?"

He didn't know that Wynn had died in the night, but he'd known it would be soon. He'd sat on the bank for hours thinking, remembering, raging. He'd made hard choices for her. How could she have given up so easily?

"I could've taken care of 'er, ya know." Amos's voice rose as anger and wild despair bubbled up within him. "Why did she do it? What was she so afraid of?!" He needn't have asked. He knew. She feared what they had all feared from their first gasping breath. The Shadow.

"You're stronger than her, Amos. Different from her. With your power, you never need fear anything." Mordecai took a small cup from the leather pouch that hung on his belt, inside the folds of his long, black coat. He stood, walked to the edge of the river, and plunged the cup beneath the surface, filling it to the brim. He held it out to Amos. "Why not make an end of it now? Leave behind your father's delusions and your mother's weakness."

Amos stared at the cup and the inky liquid. "What do ya mean?"

"Miri's blood can be mother's milk to you, too. It has much to offer." Mordecai looked at the contents of the cup, tipping it momentarily towards him. "Let me give you a gift, Amos."

"What gift? Water?"

"Yes," Mordecai answered. "Drink deep, drink long. Leave the lake behind. Leave it all behind." Mordecai's eyes were bright as he spoke. "Forget the past. Forget the fear."

Through all the empty hours of the morning, Amos had pictured his father's face as he told stories by the fire. Amos had sworn to remember them. "I'll never forget, Da. *Never.*" The words rang in his ears, repeating themselves endlessly. "Never." "Never!" "NEVER!"

But the days of boyish adventures and fireside tales were gone. He had traded his glory for a bit of power. There was no going back. He reached out and took the cup from Mordecai's hand, savoring the sweet taste of the black water as it touched his lips. He leaned back and swallowed the rest, emptying the cup to the last drop. Then he knelt by the river and filled the cup again. Again he drank, and again he emptied the cup. Amos drank deeply. He drank until he felt nothing at all, until the searing ache in his chest had vanished and the tormented rushing of his thoughts had stilled.

After that day, Amos wasted no more time carrying water from the lake. Like the villagers, he bathed in the river, swam in the river, drank from the river. He imagined he had never felt better, never been stronger, never seen the world more clearly. He was wrong.

The days ran together, one day holding no particular distinction from the last. The stillness inside the cottage was almost unbearable to Phebe at first, for Amos never came; within the cold stone walls the bright warmth of home and family were mere memories. She woke one morning to find that she could no longer stand to see her parents' belongings lying empty and unused on cots and tables around the cottage.

She indulged herself one last time, inhaling the scents of father and mother, of spices and earth and smoke. Then she cleaned and folded the blankets and clothes with tender care and packed them away in the trunk, stroking the aged wood of the lid as she closed it.

But this labor hardly filled the long, quiet hours of one evening. Next day, she cleaned, scrubbing floors and windows until her back ached. She beat the rugs and mattresses. She mended the torn hem of her shift. She scoured the iron kettle and carded the last of the wool. And all this was but the toil of a single day. One day. Outside, winter was waning. The faintest breath of yellow brightened the branches of the nearest trees, and the grasses in the meadow across the lane were ripening to pale green. But inside the cottage, there was no time, no change, no relief from the oppressive, unending quiet.

Sometimes Phebe found herself lying on her cot, staring up at the wooden beams of the ceiling, until a newly lit tallow candle had dwindled to nothing. Worse still, she came to herself with a start one evening as she sat spinning wool and gazing into the fire. It was just what her mother had done when she had forfeited all hope, and Phebe knew, with terrifying certainty, that she mustn't allow herself to wander down that road.

She would truly have gone mad, that winter and early spring, were it not for Simeon. He came to visit often, and when he stepped over the threshold the cottage seemed reborn. Those were the brightest hours for Phebe. Her face lit the walls with golden radiance, and she thought, *If only Amos were here, we could have a grand time, all of us together.* It would feel, perhaps, something like it had felt before the Shadow had fallen so heavy on their lives. In the darkest, secret places of her heart, she knew that it could never be so. Already, she felt that Amos was lost to her, but she clung to the hope of his return. There was almost nothing else left to cling to.

Simeon plunged the tongs right into the heart of the embers and pulled out an axhead. At least, it *would* be an axhead when he was finished. He placed it on the face of the anvil, holding it firmly with the tongs in his left hand, and raised the hammer in his right. A resonating clang rang out with the first blow of the hammer, and the reddish skin that covered the axhead cracked and flaked onto the floor. Beneath, Simeon could see the golden yellow color of the heated iron. Over and over, he brought the hammer down with a clang, each blow bringing the lump of metal closer to its destiny.

It was Jada who had pressed him to accept the blacksmith's offer of an apprenticeship. She had seen his melancholy after Abner's death, had noticed Simeon's estrangement from Amos. Simeon knew that she grieved for the family, but he also sensed her relief. Skilled artisans could trade services for food. Many of them never even had cause to go into the wood.

When he was happy with the shape of the axhead, Simeon put out the fire in the forge, hung his leather apron on a hook, and walked to the stable. Orin's horses were there, munching on hay. Simeon had come to love Brand and Willa, the white stallion and the gray mare. He often went to the stable to visit them, stroking their necks and brushing them down before walking back through the village to the magistrate's hall.

That had been the plan for this night, but Simeon had been plagued all day by a nagging anxiety, a restlessness he couldn't quite define. The dream-image of the owl's eyes still haunted him, and he wondered if this dream might prove to be some kind of warning as well. Instead of walking home as usual, he turned off the main road, cutting between Lark's and Aspen's shops and winding his way through the scattered cottages of Emmerich. The night was warm, remarkably so for early spring. Once or twice he caught the ripe scent of dung. He passed the open doors of several cottages and heard the chattering of families around their supper tables. He tripped over the low hedge of someone's garden, and nearly collided with a woman holding a fussing child. *What was I thinking?* he wondered. *What am I doing? There's nothing to worry about.*

He was nearing the river, headed home, when he heard voices.

"I know ya took it, Ferlin. There's no one with stickier fingers in the whole village."

Simeon recognized that voice. It was Amos's, though it sounded somehow altered.

"I didn't steal yer bow!" Ferlin shouted back.

"I left it here on the bank last night. It didn't walk away, that's fer sure. Now hand it over!"

Finally, Simeon got a clear view of the speakers. Amos stood to his left, hands clenched in rage. Without his bow on his shoulder he looked like someone else entirely. *It's not just that, though*, Simeon thought. *He's changed. Something's wrong.*

Behind Amos stood a tall man in a long, sable coat. His face was hidden in the shadows. Across from the two was Ferlin, shifting his considerable weight from one foot to the other.

"I said I didn't steal yer bow! I wouldn't touch the cursed thing!"

"Cursed?" Amos asked, daring Ferlin to explain himself.

"Aye, *cursed*. I wouldn't touch anything belongin' to a madman who was taken by the Shadow."

Simeon expected Amos to attack. He would never stand to hear his dead father insulted. But Amos replied with total calm, and it chilled the blood in Simeon's veins.

"Yer a liar, Ferlin."

Ferlin lunged. Amos lifted his hand and thrust it forward. A ball of fire shot out from his palm. It flew toward Ferlin in an arcing stream, and his tunic went up in flames.

Simeon was frozen by the boy's screams, by the sound of the fire licking up the wool, and the smell of burnt flesh. He looked at Amos, who was already turning away. He looked at the man in the dark coat, whose features were now lit by the bright flames on Ferlin's tunic.

"You!" Simeon screamed, for the face of this man was the face of the man in his dream. And his eyes . . . those eyes. Beads of sweat appeared on Simeon's forehead. His pulse raced and his breath caught in his throat. For a moment, he held the man's gaze. Those burning green eyes challenged him, laughing, mocking. *What will you do now, Dreamer?* they asked. Then, as if Simeon had stepped into a waking nightmare, the man extended a long black tongue from his mouth. He flicked the forked end in the air, drew it back behind his teeth, and smiled. *He's mine now, boy. There's nothing you can do to stop it.*

Only Simeon had seen. Only Simeon knew. His mind raced even as his muscles refused to act. Who was this man? What had happened to Amos? Had the gods gifted him with another warning only to see him fail?

At last, Simeon moved. He could do nothing for the friend that walked away into the shadows, but he could do something for Ferlin. He ran to the boy, throwing all his weight into Ferlin's back and knocking him into the river. The water hissed and steamed as the flames were quenched.

Simeon made several futile attempts to drag Ferlin onto the shore. He cringed each time he touched the bubbling, blistered skin, each time Ferlin cried out in agony. Fortunately, the villagers nearest the river overheard the commotion. Men and women came running, and Ferlin was loaded onto a cot and carried home. Lark came undone when she saw her son. Simeon felt sick. Shaken and trembling, he slipped away from the crowd and ran to find Phebe.

Twenty-One

The light of the fire had dwindled, and the cottage was swathed, within and without, in shadow. Phebe sat in her mother's chair, a rising sense of panic in her breast, sifting through Simeon's words. *How could it have come to this?* This was the stuff of legend, of history; surely her family had not come to *this* end. Surely this was not her story. "But how can ya be sure, Sim?" she asked. "Amos would never . . ."

Simeon added logs to the fire and used the iron poker to shove them into place. "I never thought 'e could do what I saw 'im do ta Ferlin."

"What're we ta do? We can't sit idly by and let the Shadow take 'im." Tears welled in her eyes and spilled onto her shift, staining the gray fabric with dark blotches. "We've got ta find 'im."

Simeon reached for Phebe's hand. As he did, the cottage door swung open and crashed against the wall. Amos stormed into the cabin, looking eerily unlike himself, and behind him, guarding the threshold, was Mordecai.

"Amos!" Phebe and Simeon shouted together and sprang to

their feet. He took no notice of them, pushing past the old wooden table and throwing open the lid of the trunk that sat against the back wall. Inside, neatly folded and wrapped, were Abner's tunic and quiver, Wynn's shift and spindle, even the blankets from the cots where the two had slept. He rummaged through the contents of the trunk, roughly handling the treasured memories of his past, and called out to Mordecai.

"How much?"

"All of it." His green eyes flashed a warning to Simeon.

There was a dull clanking of iron and groaning of wood as Amos closed the lid of the trunk. He lifted one end by an iron handle and dragged it toward the door.

"What're ya doin', Amos?" Phebe demanded.

He didn't even glance in her direction. He only dragged the trunk across the stone floor and heaved it out into the lane in front of the cottage. Mordecai had preceded him. He stood smiling by the fence where the first tiny buds of jasmine were creeping from the vines.

Simeon and Phebe followed them into the lane. They stood confused and terrified, unable to stop, or even quite believe, the scene that unfolded before them.

"The other things as well," Mordecai was saying, his eyes moving over Amos's clothing and weapons. "You've no need of them now."

Amos laid his bow and quiver on top of the trunk. He drew out his dagger, removed his leather belt, and heaped them on the pile. Last of all, and with just an instant's hesitation, he unstrapped the leather guard from his arm. There was a pause: a deep, still, silence when all the world held its breath.

Then Mordecai whispered, "Go ahead." And without a word from Amos, or even the faintest flutter of motion, the trunk burst into flames.

"No!" Phebe screamed.

Simeon grabbed her arm, pulled her toward him, and held her tightly. She pushed and fought, determined to run to the trunk and beat out the flames with her own hands if need be.

"Amos," she cried, "how could you?"

He looked back at her then, his expression holding something like pain, something like remorse, something like love. For a second, he looked like the Amos who had killed the Shadow Cat to save her. Then his eyes clouded over, and he followed Mordecai down the lane and faded into the darkness.

"May the light shine upon you, brother," she whispered through her tears.

"What's happened to 'im, Orin? I don't understand."

Simeon paced the floor. Orin's cottage, situated just behind his workshop on the eastern edge of the village, looked much like Phebe's cottage. There was a wooden table and benches, a cot, and a chair by the fire. If the ironwork on the walls and door was rather more ornate, it was no surprise, for Orin was a master blacksmith. The tongs and poker that stood by the fire boasted handles of delicate wrought iron worked into the sign of the Clan of the Builder.

Orin's clan, Simeon knew, had dispersed after the sons of Burke were taken by Ulff. The watchtowers had been abandoned, and families had spread, integrating themselves into other clans in villages all over Shiloh. The unfamiliar clan sign stuck out, drawing the eye away from the symbols of the Fire Clan that seemed to brand every other part of Emmerich. Simeon had noticed, during one of his visits to Orin's cottage, a small blanket embroidered with the sign of the Clan of the Builder, folded on the trunk in the corner. He wondered at it, for it was far too small to be of any use to Orin. It looked like a child's blanket.

"And what o' the man? I've never seen him in Emmerich before." Simeon stopped his pacing to watch Orin, who sat at the table studying the grain of the wood. He had taken off his leather apron and hung it on the wall with his thick leather gloves protruding from the pocket.

"You're sure it was the same man ya saw in the dream?" he asked.

"Aye." Simeon sat down on the hearth. "I could never mistake those eyes."

"And you've not seen Amos behave in such a way before, not even once?"

"No!" He remembered their foolish attempt to take Hadrian's lantern. But that had been different. It was nothing like the display of cruelty and indifference he had just beheld.

Orin released his breath slowly and straightened in his seat.

"Sim, I fear ta say it aloud, fear what it bodes fer the days ta come, but I believe you've seen a shifter."

Simeon stared at Orin. He had heard of the shifters. Everyone had. They were Ulff's most cunning servants, his most elite warriors. But no one in Emmerich, Simeon least of all, had ever considered the possibility of a shifter moving among them. Shifters were part of history and legend; they seemed no more of a threat than the spawn of Sirius, closeted in the remotest reaches of the Pallid Peaks. Shifters here, in Emmerich, now? He could not take it in.

"A shifter?" he asked. "Do ya mean the same kind as took the Lost Clan?"

Orin nodded, his face grave. "Aye, the very same. According ta legend, the shifters waited in the Black Mountains, disguised as trees. Evander's men were surrounded, beset, before ever they knew they were hunted. If any survived, I don't know how."

"But I saw an owl and . . . a snake. Can a shifter change 'imself into a tree?"

"Anything, Sim. They can take any form, so long as it's alive."

"But . . ." Simeon groped for words. "Why Amos? Why now?"

Orin swung his legs over the bench and took his seat by the fire. He studied Simeon's face.

"Have ya ever heard anyone say that Amos or any of 'is family was 'marked' by the Shadow?"

Simeon remembered Lark's and Hadrian's words with perfect clarity. He'd heard others make similar statements all his life. He'd seen some people avoid Abner's family as if they carried the blue ague.

"Aye," he answered. "The villagers mostly."

"Have ya ever considered that they might be right?"

"No!" Simeon threw back the words. "They just don't understand. They don't believe Abner's stories. That's why they're afraid."

Orin rested his elbows on his knees and looked down at his hands. "Simeon," he said, before looking back at the boy, "did ya know that Amos was born one thousand years, ta the day, after Evander? There are some few of us in Shiloh who still mark the days, who remember. Amos and Evander were both born on Midsummer's Day, a thousand years apart. I believe that Amos is the true son of Evander."

The words didn't penetrate. They swarmed in a mass around Simeon's head. "I thought 'e was a son of Hammond, because of 'is gift with fire. Evander's not even o' the same clan."

"Clans don't matter so much as ya might think." With his thumb and forefinger, Orin pinched the iron symbol that hung around his neck. "Amos has a stronger bond with Evander than with Hammond, whatever sign 'e wears on 'is guard. And as Evander was marked, so, I believe, is Amos."

"But why? What has Amos ever done ta bring down the wrath o' the Shadow?"

"It's not so much what 'e's *done*. It's who 'e is and what 'e believes." Orin leaned back in his chair, hesitant to move into sacred ground. "Abner was a threat, Sim. Amos is a far greater threat. He's known far and wide, revered by many. Men would follow 'im as they followed Evander. And Ulff knows it. He'd send an army o' shifters if 'e had to."

Tears pooled in Simeon's eyes. "Is Amos goin' ta die as well?"

Orin looked into the fire. "I can't say, Sim. But ya don't have ta die ta be removed as a threat ta the natural order o' this world." He glanced at the little blanket on the trunk. "There are other ways. Most merely lose hope."

The fire crackled and hissed in the hearth. Little tongues of flame licked the logs and lapped at the air as the men sat silent. Finally, Simeon spoke, his voice and his face pleading with Orin.

"What can we do?"

"I wish I knew. But if ya dream again, ya must tell me at once." Orin rose and took a small jar from its shelf. "Fer Lark," he said, handing the jar to Simeon. "It'll help with 'er son's burns."

Simeon nodded, heading for the door. He turned before leaving, struck by a sudden thought. "Orin," he asked, "how do ya know so much about Evander, about Amos? Don't ya think they're mad like everyone else in the village does?"

Orin's eyes lit. His skin flared with a brief burst of light, and he winked at Simeon. "One day, Sim," he said. "One day I'll tell ya all ya wish ta know."

When Amos reached the Meander, Mordecai beckoned him onward. "Come," he said. This time, he made no attempt to hide as he shifted into the form of a great owl and flew across the dark expanse of the water.

Amos first knelt down to drink. The events of that night had picked at the scabs of old wounds. He didn't want to remember Phebe's words or her screams. He didn't want to remember the anguished look on Simeon's face. So he drank again and again.

He looked down at himself, at his tunic, his leather trousers and boots. He looked like any other boy in Shiloh, stripped of everything that hinted of his former identity. Those things had been no more than leather and wood and string. Now they were nothing at all. Just ashes consumed by the power he carried with him, the power he carried within him.

He removed his tunic. He lifted his hand, the tips of his fingers growing hotter and brighter, and burned the sign of the Wolf into his chest: a circle, incomplete, surrounded by five pointed claws.

He jumped into the water.

Beneath him, through undulating weeds and darksome currents, he could make out a pale luminescence. He dove deeper to get a closer look, and a wan face emerged from the riverbed, its eyes glowing a livid blue-green.

"Welcome, Amos, Wielder of Fire."

A hand rose out of the weeds, looking much like a lank weed itself, and moved toward Amos's face. It stretched across his eyes, grabbing him at his temples. First he saw nothing, then there was a flash of fire, and then the hand was gone. The pale face looking back at him was not the face of a single creature as he had thought, but rather a writhing, twisting mass of worms that only resembled a face. The Nogworms. Amos had never seen them, but they felt right at home with him. They felt at home *in* him, in nearly every person in Shiloh. They were the parasites that filled the waters of the river. They were the decaying remains of the beautiful creatures that lived in the crystalline currents before the world was unmade. They were the dulling, numbing, warping, forgetting power that had settled into every corner of Amos's body. The mass of Nogworms moved in unison, drawing the blue-green lips into a feral smile.

Amos swam the last stretch of river, emerged on the opposite shore where Mordecai watched from his perch high in the branches, and disappeared from Emmerich.

Twenty-Two

ight hundred years and more have passed," Darby began, "since the first was taken. In those days, Burke had not yet been born, and no Clan o' the Builder had raised the Hall of Echoes or the bridges over the River Meander. In those days, the wolves roamed in packs, and there were as yet no Hunter's Paths through the Whisperin' Wood. Those were times of great hunger, for most feared ta enter the wood at all, and families survived on what little could be grown or killed near the villages." Darby pushed her chair back from the table, raised unseeing eyes to the rafters, and took a deep breath.

"In a village some ways west o' the wood, there lived a man named Rider and his wife Mariah. Like you, child, Mariah was a singer. There was light and magic in 'er voice, and ta the people o' the village, she was a marvel. Her daughter, Imogen, was much like 'er; she sang with a voice as high and clear as a bird, and she shone with a fierce light long after the other children o' the village had faded." Here Darby stopped, her hands fidgeting in her lap. "'Tis a dark story, Phebe. Why must ya hear it at all?"

Phebe didn't answer right away. She and Darby sat at a table in the back room of Darby's cottage. The room was spare, just a cot in the corner and the two chairs at opposing sides of the table where they had eaten. She pushed back her empty plate and mug and stared at her wrists. They stuck awkwardly out of the sleeves of her shift.

"I don't know why. I only know that I must hear it, Darby. Please tell me. What happened ta the girl?"

Reluctantly, Darby carried on. "The story goes that one day, Imogen's father ventured inta the wood in search o' game. The winter had stretched long, and the family was lean and hungry. So Rider took 'is brother and 'is nephew and braved the wood, and on the very first night o' their hunt, the wolves surrounded 'em. Rider's brother survived, but the others were taken. Lost and devoured. When the brother returned, wounded sorely by the claws o' the beasts, he brought the awful news ta Mariah and Imogen. He stumbled through the door o' their cottage and said, 'Rider's dead, taken by wolves.' Mariah cried out and Imogen with 'er. And then the man spat out one more bitter thought. 'We'll all go likewise, for no man can escape the jaws o' the Shadow.'"

"They say it happened in an instant, in the blinkin' of an eye. Imogen's light faltered and then disappeared altogether. She stood frozen, dull as iron, but around 'er, across the floors and down the walls, somethin' moved. It was as if the walls and floors grew a thousand legs and gathered in toward the girl. They say the Weavers moved up 'er legs, 'er shift, 'er face, 'er hair. They spirited her away, cloaked in webs o' Shadow. She vanished before 'er mother's eyes."

"The Hall o' Shadows," Phebe said. "That's where the night weavers took her, isn't it? Ta the crystal teardrops. Is she there still?"

"The tales say as much. They say the Hall o' Shadows is the path ta the door o' Shadow Castle."

"What happened ta Mariah?"

Darby shook her head as though she spoke against her will. "She searched the wood, the Black Mountains, everywhere, until she found 'er daughter. There's no knowin' how she survived."

"Why didn't she bring 'er back?"

"She tried, it seems. The poor woman cracked under the weight of 'er grief. When she came back from 'er journey, she was wild, ravin' about bein' too late. The story and the songs were pieced together from fragments, really."

"She said she was too late? Is there more ta the story?"

"Ta the song. I've heard the village children singin' about the Hall o' Shadows far, far away. But there's a verse they don't sing, a verse they don't know. My mother sang it ta me when I was a girl." She closed her eyes, remembering, and sang.

"Turn, turn away from the gatherin' darkness
Erebus will still the cries and bind the hands
Time slips away, and the days are fleetin'
Come and take yer children ta yer arms again"

Phebe shivered. "But, Darby, everyone in Shiloh fades. Ya never see a grown man or woman who shines still like a new babe."

Hardly ever," Darby said, "but there are some, you among them."

"How can ya tell?"

"Some things I see that my eyes never told me. There are other ways o' seein', child."

"But why don't the night weavers come fer everyone whose light fades away?"

"Ahh, there's a difference between givin' away yer light and havin' it stolen away. Imogen's uncle stole the child's hope as sure as 'e stole 'er light. 'Twas he who snuffed out the girl's flame."

Phebe considered a moment. "Was 'e sent into exile then?" she asked.

"The four eternal laws had not yet been written, my girl. The tale of Imogen's takin' spread such fear that MacDowell, Father o' the Fire Clan at the time, called the leaders o' the other clans together. They drafted the laws and sent messengers all over the land. The stonemasons had their work cut out fer 'em, engravin' the laws on a stone in every village."

It was enough for one day. Phebe had heard all she needed to hear. "My thanks ta ya, Darby. Truly." She grasped the weaver's hand and made for the door to the front room. In all their years of friendship, Darby had never invited Phebe into this back room, this inner sanctuary. As she turned to go, she noticed for the first time a piece of embroidery displayed on the wall above the door. At first glance, it looked to be no more than the sign of the Fire Clan, but on closer inspection, dozens of tiny figures appeared. Men clothed in tunics of bright crimson and blue danced with women in deep purple and green shifts. Children, carrying flowers and branches heavy with golden leaves, wove their way through the other dancers. They, too, were dressed in rich colors: red clay and flaming orange. All these gathered, in three great tongues of flame, from the outer edges of the circle to the inner core where red and gold threads mimicked the edanna from the mosaic in Market Circle.

"Oh," Phebe gasped, and Darby understood.

"'Twas my comin'-of-age gift," she explained. "My Ma must've guessed I'd have no need of a white dress ta be wed in." She laughed a little to herself.

"Won't ya stay fer a cup o' cider?" Darby said. "Cora brought it only this mornin'. Payne just finished a new batch."

"It's kind o' ya, but I best be goin'," Phebe answered. She went out into the familiar front room. Bolts of cloth still covered the shelves, and the table where customers bought and sold sat in its usual place. The coveted basket of colored yarn still beckoned from the back wall, and the vertical loom, tall as a man, waited in the front corner for Darby to take up her weaving.

"Wait!" Darby called out, jumping from her seat and hurrying into the front room. "I nearly forgot." She snatched up a large sack and handed it to Phebe. "Ta pass the time," she said.

Phebe pulled open the knotted cord at the top of the sack and peered down at its contents. Raw wool.

"It's not been carded yet, mind ya," Darby said. "But once it's spun, ya can trade me fer cloth ta make a new shift."

She wondered how Darby could have known. The woman couldn't see her wrists protruding from her sleeves.

"Ya grow as if ya spent all yer days feastin, child," Darby said with a smile. "I hear the change in yer voice, the change in yer movements. And besides, every young girl needs a new shift now and again."

Phebe didn't know how to thank her. She tightened the cord at the top of the sack and slung it over her shoulder.

"Be off with ya now. It's gettin' late." Darby sat at her loom, her hands moving in graceful rhythm over the threads.

Phebe scooped up her lantern. She would make just one more stop before returning home.

Under the Shadow, beneath the stifling weight of the darkness, year had faded into year. In the village of Emmerich, the cottages and shops remained much as they had been when Phebe was a small girl. But the terrible blue ague, that fever so feared by the people of Shiloh, had come with a vengeance a few summers after Amos's disappearance, and hardly a family had reached the first frost unscathed.

The ague always came on a wind from the south, infecting the people with an unseen fire. Men and women groaned and burned with fever; then, in a sudden turn, the fires went out, and their bodies turned cold and blue. Elah, the apothecary's husband was the first to go. Then Lark, the chandler, and one of Payne's sons; Caedmon lost two daughters.

Phebe never fell ill. While Jada oversaw the burning of the dead and the tending of those without able-bodied nurses, Phebe cared for Simeon. She hovered over his cot, bathing the sweat from his face, as he mumbled and shouted, nearly senseless with the raging fever. He spoke often of Abner and of Amos during those weary nights, and it brought fresh grief to Phebe's heart. Her father was lost to her forever, and Amos?

She had stopped looking for him after the first year or so. When the door of the cottage swung open, she no longer held her breath. When a flash of fire appeared in the distance, she no longer imagined that it was Amos coming home. She didn't forget. She couldn't forget. But hope was a merciless companion, and she buried it.

Amos did not come back to her for many lonely years. What came to Phebe instead were snatches of stories and whispered rumors of one who opened a path for the night weavers. Men who sat drinking and cursing in Payne's alehouse could not speak their name without dropping their voices and sending furtive glances out into the street where the children played. Travelers spoke of a spreading despair that moved faster and struck harder than the blue ague. For, if Amos, Wielder of Fire, could fall prey to the Shadow, what hope could there be for any of them?

The apothecary's shop was crowded with the scents of dried herbs, of strange flowers, of fire and smoke. Just inside the door was a long table, covered with fresh and dried leaves and roots, stems and buds. A mortar and pestle sat at one side, crusted with powdery green residue. Hanging in bundles from innumerable hooks in the ceiling beams were morning glory, flowering tobacco, night phlox, belladonna, and mandrake. The walls were lined with wooden shelves, each heavy with the weight of a dozen clay pots, piles of wooden pipes, and a smattering of glass vials.

"What brings ya, Phebe?" Aspen shuffled in through a side door, carrying an armload of firewood. She was bent with the toil of nearly ninety winters, and her hair was white as Darby's finest wool. Her dark eyes had always flashed with life until her husband's death. Elah had kept the stables at the southern corner of the village, and he had been her steady companion through many weary years. His death had been a heavy blow, and Aspen was tired. Without Elah, even small tasks drained her, and she wasted no breath on pleasantries or idle chatter.

"I've a fresh mandrake root prepared if it's sleep yer needin'. The bark'll help ya through the long nights."

"It's kind o' ya, but I've come fer . . ." Phebe lowered her head and turned the left side of her face toward the wall.

"I see," Aspen said, rising from the hearth and seating herself at the long table. "You've come about the scar. Is that it?"

"Aye," Phebe answered. "I thought, perhaps, ya might have somethin' that might make it fade, even just a little."

"Yer da came, when it first happened, ya know. It grieved me ta tell 'im so, but there's naught I can do ta heal the marks o' the wolves and the cats. I've no medicine ta cure so deep an ill. Were ya scarred from a fall, or even the point of a dagger, the night phlox would wipe away all trace. But, as it is . . ." With effort, Aspen stood and circled the table. She stretched a gnarled hand to brush the silky hair back from Phebe's shoulder. The girl turned her face away, but Aspen placed a hand on her cheek and turned her back.

"Ya always were a lovely girl," Aspen whispered. She spoke the truth, for Phebe's fair skin and flowing hair, the fine set of her nose and brows, the coal-black spark of her eyes were indeed beautiful. "No scar could outshine so much beauty."

Phebe flashed her a look of such cold disbelief that Aspen dropped her hand and returned to her chair. This girl was too deeply marked for an old woman's words to leave any impression.

"Won't ya take some mandrake bark, just in case?"

"No," Phebe said.

"I'm sorry, Phebe," Aspen said, and meant it.

"I best be goin'." Phebe hurried out into the street, shouldering the heavy sack of wool and raising the lantern to light her way. As she passed, she felt the cold presence of the stone, lying just outside the circle of light cast by her lantern. That silent sentinel, for more than eight hundred years, had spoken alike the doom of the guilty and the innocent. Phebe imagined tendrils of black mist stretching out from the stone, grasping the hem of her shift, weaving dark fingers into every thread until she was clothed in darkness and rooted to black earth. Its power had taken hold, and it would never let go. Its words would haunt her, weighing more heavily with every struggling step homeward.

For any who steals a man's goods, payment in kind.
For any who steals a man's name, payment in flesh.
For any who steals a man's life, payment in blood.
For any who steals a man's light, payment in exile.

Twenty-Three

Sullivan's travels carried him farther and farther into the hill country, and in his absence Rosalyn came once more under a watchful gaze. The man could not be called a suitor or an admirer. He was more akin to a predator. At times he came very near the cottage, his eyes searching the interior for any sign of her. But more often, he paced along the lane that led to the cottage, growing increasingly agitated as the hours passed. Isolde sat in the empty stable, watching him with her keen, quick eyes, the anger simmering deep in her.

"I won't let 'im take ya," she told her sister one morning. The sisters sat across the table from each other, chopping herbs and wild onions.

"If not him, it'll be someone else," Rosalyn said. "It's the way o' the clansmen. Ya know that."

Isolde slammed the blade of her cutting knife into the table. "It doesn't have ta be that way! Ya don't have ta lie down and take whatever they give, whether it's a boot in yer ribs or a child in yer belly! Ya can run! Ya can fight!"

"Not I, Isolde," Rosalyn said, shaking her head and wiping her tears with the back of her wrist. "It's you must go, you must fight, fer those of us who can't."

Isolde fled. As dear as Rosalyn was to her, she couldn't understand this resignation, this despairing acceptance of fate. A long line of days unbroken by joy or hope or change lay before Rosalyn. It was a future too unbearable for Isolde to even consider.

She ran down the hillside, snatching at her long shift and pulling it away from her boots. Through the dim light of mid-morning, she raced to the cherry trees in the valley. She dropped to the ground beneath their spreading branches and looked up at the dark leaves and the thickening darkness beyond. She breathed, in and out, in and out, quieting her racing pulse. She listened to the rustling of leaves and the distant roar of the wind in the mountains. She let the moments slip away.

If Da were dead, she thought, *I could leave this place*. Sullivan could not keep her locked in the cottage forever. He had neither the power nor the desire. Her father would have rejoiced if someone carried *her* away to be his wife. There would be one less mouth to feed, one less useless mouth at that. What was it, then, that kept her chained to this stagnant, changeless place? *Rosalyn*. Apart from a cryptic prophecy about her fate and a chestnut mare that might still be waiting for her in Dunn, Isolde had nothing, nothing but her sister. What if she were to take Rosalyn and run? What if they took up Valour's quest together? The risk was great, the road fraught with dangers. Their beauty would kindle the lust of cruel men; the warm blood coursing through their veins would rouse the hunger of the beasts; the darkness would hinder their every step.

To linger in Fleete, though, was to die a slow death, giving way to the comfortable despair of their people. She had to move. She had to overcome the gravity of doubt, of hesitation, the gravity that held all that remnant of the Lost Clan to their solitary hill.

She stood and hurried up the path toward the village, running when the climb wasn't too steep, pushing herself until her lungs burned and her legs were weak beneath her. She ran to the cottage and flung open the door, her eyes searching for her sister.

"Rosalyn!" she shouted.

The iron kettle hung on its hook above the fire, its contents boiling over and hissing and steaming in the coals below. The blankets of Rosalyn's cot were disheveled, and the floor was smeared with mud. But no one was home. A matter of moments, the separation of one argument, had changed everything. Rosalyn had been taken.

"Rosalyn!" she cried.

Isolde slumped down onto the cot, despairing. Her hand came to rest on something, and she flicked it away without thought. It landed on the stone floor with a little "ting" that made her look down. It was Rosalyn's necklace, the leather cord and the charm with the sign of the sun.

She didn't wait for Sullivan's return. She tied the cord around her neck and took what hunting gear was left in the cottage; an old saddlebag, a water skin, a bow and quiver, and a coarse gray blanket. She took the Red Map, carefully concealed beneath the straw mattress on her cot.

On the threshold, Isolde turned back for a last look at her home. On the edge of the village, she turned again. But her gaze could not penetrate the gloom that enshrouded the summit of the hill. So she set her face to the unknown. She wrenched free of the cords that had kept her so long bound and stepped out on the road. She would find Valour's Glass, find what remained of the Lost Clan, find the fabled sun, and return to find Rosalyn.

Twenty-Four

ive years after Amos's disappearance, in late spring when Payne finished brewing the year's first batch of huckleberry ale, Simeon came of age.

In Shiloh, births were not much celebrated. There were no weddings, and funerals were dark, savage affairs. But when a young man or woman came of age at seventeen, the whole village joined in the celebration. It didn't matter if he or she was particularly liked or accepted by the community. People were slow to buck tradition, and even slower to pass up a chance for feasting and dancing.

Coming of age meant that a boy could take on his father's work, and a girl could take a husband and have children. It was the single greatest transition of a person's life, and as such it was accompanied by several time-honored traditions. A young man always received a special weapon or tool from his father. Often, he would also receive a quiver, belt, or guard with the mark of his clan. A young woman received a white shift or apron embroidered by her mother.

Throughout the day of the celebration, people would come and go, bringing gifts to the young man or woman. They would drink and talk and return to their work at their leisure. Then, in the evening, the village magistrate would come at the head of a great procession. Every villager watched as the father offered a blessing to his son or the mother offered a blessing to her daughter. Many in the procession carried firewood, which they piled and lit to make a bonfire. Others brought food, benches, and tables. And there, in their makeshift banquet hall around the fire, they feasted and danced late into the night.

For all his childhood fears, Simeon's coming-of-age celebration was a great success. The villagers were generous, bringing blankets, candles, dried herbs, tools, and earthenware mugs and bowls. All these he set aside to furnish his future home. Phebe brought him a tunic she had sewn herself. He put it on at once, and praised her embroidery work on the hem and neckline.

In the evening, against tradition, his mother spoke a blessing over him, and both she and Orin presented him with gifts. Hers was a very old bow, carved with leaping flames that sparkled with inset edanna. This was a great heirloom of their clan, and where she had kept it all these years, Simeon could not tell. Orin's gift was a hammer and anvil. He had made a four days' journey to the west of the river to buy it, and Simeon was deeply moved. The celebration that followed was wild and joyful. There was roast venison and sweet bread, cheese and ale, and the drums and the panpipes and the flutes played loud and long.

The passing of five years had changed Simeon. The frail, frightened boy of twelve had taken on the look of a fierce and able man. The villagers argued among themselves, that year, about what exactly had wrought such a change in Simeon. Some said it was his appearance, and the normal physical changes a boy experiences as he grows into a man. Though his hair and eyes were fair as ever, his skin had darkened a shade or two, toasting in the constant heat and light of the blacksmith's furnace. His arms, once unable to conquer the weight of a yew bow, had thickened and strengthened.

His chest was broad, and his jaw, much like Orin's, was covered in yellow-brown stubble.

Others argued that it was Simeon's confidence that had changed him so, and they made a strong case. For one thing, he had excelled at the craft of blacksmithing. Under Orin's careful instruction, Simeon had progressed rapidly. The iron seemed to bend to his will and not merely to the heat of the forge or the pounding of the hammer. Men traveled from neighboring villages with commissions for Simeon. At seventeen, he could breathe life into dead iron, making it sprout from the base of a candlestick into the delicate branches and cascading leaves of a willow tree.

Simeon had also gained skill with the bow. Abner, of course, had taught him to shoot, but it was Orin who taught him to hunt. Whenever their work permitted, Orin would mount Brand, the white stallion, and Simeon would take Willa, the gray mare. They would travel sometimes west, over the river, and sometimes south of the village. Once or twice, they worked their way back along the Hunter's Path that Abner and Amos had followed so many years ago. There, to his great surprise, Simeon made his first kill, a large bull elk. He had smiled to himself sadly as they journeyed home that night, remembering Amos's ambitions for the Great Hunt.

Yet another group in Emmerich argued that it was Orin who had brought about Simeon's transformation, and there was considerable truth in this as well. No master craftsman could have treated his apprentice with more patience and respect. No friend could have invested more time and care or given more freely of his resources. No father could have shown more love to his son.

But while Simeon had benefited from all these changes in appearance and circumstance and company, it was Amos's absence that had done him the most good. Truly, he grieved his friend's loss, felt it to his core. But Amos had always cast too great a shadow. Amos had filled up the room, filled up the village, with power and destiny and confidence. As a boy, Simeon could hardly help seeing himself in contrast to his friend. Their looks, their abilities, their histories had been so different that Simeon had only ever imagined standing beside Amos or following along behind him. Simeon had been like a sapling struggling to soak in the meager light that filtered down through the dense branches of a mighty tree. With Amos's disappearance, the mighty tree was felled. And Simeon had room to grow.

Not long after the celebration, Orin took Simeon for a drink at the end of a grueling day's work. Inside Payne's shop were two other patrons: Caedmon, in his usual seat near the brewer, and another man drinking quietly at a table in the corner. Orin requested two mugs of beer and sat with Simeon on the opposite side of the room.

"What's on yer mind, Sim?" Orin asked. The days following the coming-of-age feast had seen a change in the young man.

By this time, Simeon felt fully at ease with Orin, but this conversation was difficult to begin. "It's my ma," he said at last. "She asked ta talk with me a few days ago."

"Thinks I'm workin' ya too hard, eh?" Orin chuckled as Payne brought two mugs, brimming with foam, and set them on the table.

Simeon gave a half-hearted smile and took a drink. "It's just . . . well, I always thought my father had died o' the ague, or been killed on a hunt. I always thought Jada had borne me. She never said . . . until the other night, that is . . . she never spoke o' my birth, never told me."

Orin gave him time, waiting in silence.

"Ma said she found me by the river, that I came ta her as a gift from the gods." He drank again from his mug. "She said I should've been half drowned, but I wasn't. I was laid up on the bank o' the river, just waitin'. I can't understand it, Orin. I thought it was a misery havin' no father, but now I've no mother either. No history, no clan." He looked up. "I'm no one at all."

Orin's dark eyes clouded. That look held grief and confusion and something else Simeon could not identify. There was a scuffling as two men came into the shop to refill their jugs, and the sound drew Orin out of his reverie.

"I'm sorry, Sim. I didn't know," he said. "The ague did strike the village around the time ya were born. I left Emmerich that year, and when I returned, too much had changed fer me ta question anything. Suppose I always imagined you'd been orphaned by the fever, that Jada had taken ya in."

"Ya knew, then? That Jada wasn't my ma?"

"I knew only that she'd never married, Sim, and I don't believe any man would lay a hand on 'er, not with her bein' magistrate." Orin leaned in and lowered his voice. "But what ya say about bein' no one, about havin' no history, no clan . . . it isn't so. Not knowin' yer history isn't the same as not havin' one. And the dreams," here he lowered his voice further, "they're a sign o' bein' specially chosen by the gods. It's likely, Sim, that you're *more* than ya thought, not *less*."

"'e's the one I told ya of, Jeremiah." Caedmon's booming voice broke into their quiet conversation. He had had more than his usual seven or eight mugs. He was unsteady on his stool, waving a hand in Simeon's direction and glaring bleary-eyed at Orin. To Caedmon, Abner's and Wynn's deaths, along with Amos's disappearance, had been no more than perfect justice. For a time, he had settled down, confident that Emmerich was safe, and the 'clan o' the madman' had been forever silenced. But the loss of two daughters had renewed the fires of his rage and bitterness, and he spent more and more time with Payne, neglecting his work, his wife, and his remaining daughters.

"'e's the one that followed 'im around, day after day, like 'e was 'ammond 'imself, or one o' the gods." Then Caedmon spoke to

Simeon directly. "What do ya think of Amos now, Simeon? What do ya make of all 'is fool stories?" He laughed and choked, teetering dangerously on the edge of the stool.

"You've had enough, Caedmon. Why not go on home and lie down, eh?" Payne took the empty mug from the man's hand and tucked it beneath the counter.

"You'd 'ave given yer right arm fer 'im, wouldn't ya?" Caedmon continued. "You'd 'ave died fer a murderin' servant o' the Shadow Lord. Friend o' the shifters and gatekeeper fer the night weavers! Better 'e 'ad died with 'is da in the wood!"

"Enough!" Orin jumped to his feet, knocking his chair to the floor with a crash. "Ya spout off rumor and gossip as if you'd seen it with yer own eyes!"

"Ah," Caedmon replied, rising from the stool and stumbling forward. "I've not seen it, maybe, but 'e 'as." He waved a shaking hand in the direction of the man in the corner.

Orin knew the man. They were brothers of the same clan. Jeremiah was a stonemason who worked as a journeyman, traveling from village to village as he was needed. He came and went from Emmerich every few years, and Orin had never known him to be dishonest. The extent of Jeremiah's travels and his association with people of many villages and clans made him, in fact, a very credible source of information about Amos. But it served no one, Simeon least of all, to know more of the doings of his friend.

"What Caedmon says is true," Jeremiah said, looking from Orin to Simeon. "But I meant no harm ta you or the boy."

"No 'arm?!" Caedmon roared. He was poised for another screaming assault on Simeon when, suddenly, his face flushed red, his eyes rolled back in his head, and he tumbled forward, upsetting a table as he fell. The lantern that had rested on the table fell to the stones and shattered, the oil inside splattering onto the woven rugs that littered the floor. Flames spread across the floor of the shop, the fire licking at the legs of chairs and tables, hungry for anything that could be consumed. While Orin hauled Caedmon over the threshold and out into the street, Payne rushed to the back with Simeon on his heels. Jeremiah joined them as they snatched up casks and jugs and rags. Payne led them to a huge water barrel just behind the shop. They filled everything they had with water and raced back to douse the spreading fire.

"Orin!" Simeon shouted, tossing him a handful of wet rags. They beat at the burning mats, the chairs and tables that had caught fire, holding the flames at bay while Payne and Jeremiah brought water again and again. Just when the last sparks had been quenched, and the men dropped the rags and casks to catch their breath, there was a cry from the street. It was Caedmon.

Orin was first out the door. Some small spark of fire must have caught hold of Caedmon as he was dragged from the shop. It had taken time to catch, for the air was thick and damp. But, as Caedmon lay in a drunken stupor and the others fought to rescue Payne's shop, the spark had worked its way into the fibers of Caedmon's tunic. The pain of the burning had wakened him.

Orin wasted no time. Without a thought, he tore the sweat-soaked tunic from his own back and beat out the flame on Caedmon's sleeve. When the man was out of danger, Orin sat on the street. He wiped the sweat from his forehead, then stiffened, realizing what he had done.

The others stared out the doorway, fixated on a mark at the base of Orin's neck. It was a tattoo no larger than the palm of a man's hand: a small circle surrounded by sixteen pointing rays. None of the men had ever seen it before, but they knew the legends well enough. This was the sign the sons of Burke had taken before they fell into the hands of the Shadow Lord. This was the sign of the Star Clan.

Twenty-Five

'T'was my young wife who believed, far more than I," Orin began. He and Simeon had returned to his cottage, escaping the questioning stares of Payne and Jeremiah. Caedmon had seen nothing. "Not every man and woman in the Clan o' the Builder had taken the sign o' the star when the watchtowers fell. But there were some, some who believed the word o' their fathers and brothers and husbands, though they'd never seen the lights with their own eyes. And when the sons o' Burke returned from the dark halls o' the Shadow Lord . . . when the stargazers returned, rather, and the clan was dispersed, some came ta settle in Emmerich, livin' off their skills with stone and iron. My father's fathers've been blacksmiths here fer generations. And I'm the last o' my clan in the village. Last o' the Star Clan, at least, now Lila's gone."

"She was yer wife?"

"Aye." He smiled. "I met 'er on the first night o' the Great Hunt many years ago. Around 'er neck, she wore the sign o' the Clan o' the Builder, but 'er eyes told me there was more to 'er than that. She saw more, hoped more. We danced that night . . ."

"Was it the ague that took 'er?"

"No. 'Twas the river. She drowned some few days before the birth of our first child."

Simeon grieved for the man. He had no comfort to offer, nothing that could take away the ache. At the same time, he felt a stirring of anger in his chest.

"Why did ya never say? Why do ya hide the mark o' yer true clan? It would've been such a comfort ta Abner, ta know that there were others."

Orin offered no defense, no excuse. "Like I said, Sim, it was Lila who was the true believer. I always doubted, even as a child, when my father told me the story o' the stars, even when I took the mark o' the clan. It seemed too much ta hope. And when I lost my wife and child . . ." He paused and sighed. "I lost the courage ta hope. I'm sorry ta disappoint ya. I've been a coward."

They looked at one another for a long moment. Orin could see Simeon's struggle. He felt he had betrayed the boy's trust. He wished now that he could go back and stand beside Abner. He wished that he had risked exposure, rejection, that he had stood for something, anything in the years since Lila died. But he could find no words to explain these feelings to Simeon, and the boy left without so much as a backward glance.

Isolde was near death when she escaped from the lair of the dragon. She had gotten it into her head that Valour's Glass might be there in the Pallid Peaks. All these long years, it might have lain just outside her reach. The dragons were known for hiding things in their caverns. Old things, secret things.

Two nights she had waited outside the cave, searching the air and the snow-blanketed cliffs for signs of blue fire. She had seen none. She made the ascent on the third evening, cursing her cloak and shift all the way. Her feet slipped on the ice, her fingers burned with cold, but she would not give up. She reached the dragon's lair and stepped inside.

The cave bored straight back into the mountain, and it reeked of ash and rot. Inside, the faint glimmer of her own skin was Isolde's only light. She could see bones strewn about, and here and there claws and teeth, but nothing more. She was wondering how many such caves were tucked away in the Pallid Peaks, wondering how long it would take her to search them all, when the cavern was illuminated by blue flame. The Shadow Dragon had come home. Its ragged black wings filled the mouth of the cave. Its scales clanked; the mountain trembled as it rushed in. It roared, spewing pale fire. Isolde shrank against the wall.

This was a foe too terrible for her to defeat. Of that she was certain. And yet, the midwife who spoke the prophecy had been no less certain that Isolde's story would spread far and wide, that it would endure for ages to come. If the dragon devoured her here, no one would ever know what became of her. She had a destiny to fulfill, and even this monster could not stop her.

The moment the realization struck her, her skin flared with new fire, and the dragon retreated. It screamed in rage and settled its bulk at the mouth of the cave, black wings stretching to block out all light from outside. Smoke and steam curled from its nostrils. It watched with unblinking eyes, and waited.

She ate the last of her food on the fifth day, sipped the last of her water on the eighth. On the tenth day she risked everything and made a wild rush for the dragon. She ran with an arrow at the string, willing herself forward. When the dragon opened its mouth and the deadly blue fire poured out, Isolde took aim and shot. The arrow passed through the flames and carried a spark deep into the dragon's eye. The beast reared back, Isolde scrambled beneath it, and its sable claws only grazed her shoulder as she tumbled onto the mountainside.

The raging and stamping of the dragon brought the snows thundering down. They buried Isolde, and she waited until the sounds of beating wings and rushing wind faded. Under cover of blackest night, she dug her way out of her icy tomb and fled from the Pallid Peaks.

Echo was waiting for her in the village of Dunn, and tears pricked Isolde's eyes when she was reunited with her friend. The wizened old stable keeper slipped her mother's dagger back into her hand and patted her arm as she left.

There was hardly a corner of Shiloh Isolde did not see during the subsequent years, and Echo proved the steadiest and gentlest companion. She used the Red Map to guide her along the countless branches of the River Meander. In every village, she inquired about Evander and the Lost Clan, about Valour and the glass. But none of the tales told the fate of her people or the whereabouts of Valour's gift. She grew weary and frustrated. She questioned the prophecy, questioned her choices. But the days of hard riding, the nights of cold rain, the hunting and the hunger and the flaming arrows loosed on the enemy all served to transform a passionate, impetuous girl into a warrior.

For a time, she lived with a widow and her children in a village called Hanley, filling somewhat of the gap left by a dead husband and father. In exchange for fresh meat, they gave her shelter and a stiff sort of kindness. Better still, the widow outfitted her with clothes more suited to riding and hunting. She tailored her husband's leather trousers and vest, cutting out large panels to use as arm guards, and shortened the sleeves of his tunic.

When Isolde left the widow's home, she was a curiosity. No woman in Shiloh, not even in story or song, wore leather trousers, a long gray tunic, a leather vest bound with cords, a belt with a dagger, and guards on both forearms. Isolde cared nothing for that. She smiled to herself as she rode through the grasslands with her flame-red hair flapping behind her.

Twenty-Six

It was market day. The hush that had fallen over the village in the wake of the blue ague was years forgotten, and the streets and shops crawled with activity. Travelers from neighboring villages and families who lived in the hills outside Emmerich had gathered with the locals to buy and sell, to commission work, to have furniture and tools repaired, and to claim their share of the latest gossip. Market Circle was cluttered with carts and stalls, alive with the shouts of buyers and sellers, haggling over prices. Men boasted to one another or stumbled out of Payne's brewery with ale sloshed on their tunics. Women chattered unceasingly, made offers in the doorways of shops, and scolded the children that scurried through every open space, criss-crossing the alleys between cottages. Horses were tied to posts outside the stables, dogs sniffed and scrounged for scraps and discarded bones. Sheep were herded, by twos and threes, to be sold or traded in the market, and the air was filled with the varied scents of roasting meat, herbs, leather, smoke, sweat, and animal droppings.

Phebe passed the stone and moved toward the heart of the

village, wishing she could avoid the cramped, crowded streets. A basket of golden potatoes, ripe red tomatoes, and sweet peppers hung over her arm. She hoped to sell them for enough to buy a bit of white cloth and some colored yarn. Maybe then she wouldn't make such a pitiable figure at her coming-of-age celebration. She had only a few weeks to prepare, and the thought of the approaching day filled her with dread. There was no one to offer a blessing, and the only family heirloom that remained was a silver glass that had been unharmed, undarkened even, when Amos destroyed the old wooden trunk. Lovely as it was, it held no special meaning for Phebe. It sat on the mantle above the hearth.

With effort, Phebe shrugged off the melancholy thoughts and wound her way through the crowd. Outside the stables, a group of children chanted familiar words in sing-song voices.

"Far, far away
In the crystal teardrops
Hangin' from the branches o' the silent trees
Gone, gone away
Ta the Hall o' Shadows
Peerin' through the mist with eyes that cannot see

Shine, shine away
Keep the lights a'burnin'
Never let the embers o' the flame go out
Run, run away
For the Shadow Weavers
Come ta take a trophy ta their Master's house"

Phebe's legs turned to stone beneath her. She felt cold, dreadfully cold. She remembered her father's horror as she sang those words in her little girl's voice. She recalled the words of the forgotten verse, the words Darby had sung years before.

"Turn, turn away from the gatherin' darkness
Erebus will still the cries and bind the hands
Time slips away, and the days are fleetin'."

Someone whistled, drawing her back to the present, and she looked up to see Simeon standing outside Orin's shop. He wore his leather apron and gloves. His face was drenched with sweat, his cheek smeared with soot. He smiled and winked at her, and she warmed, returning his smile and waving with her free hand. He'd be far too busy to talk with her now, for several men were lined up outside the shop holding tools that needed mending. So she fought through the cramped street, making her slow way toward Market Circle.

She glanced into the chandler's shop as she passed. Ferlin stood where his mother had once stood, behind a low counter. He was taking an order from a woman with a filthy child on her hip. Her other children scurried about the shop, snatching up tallow candles to jab one another, then replacing them in untidy piles and making a general mess. Phebe tried not to think of the slabs of scarred flesh concealed by Ferlin's tunic, so she focused instead on the heavy scent of dried herbs wafting from Aspen's shop and walked on.

"There's a choice bit o' meat, and no mistakin'."

Phebe turned to see who spoke and *to whom* he spoke and came face to face with a broad, heavily-muscled young man. His hair hung lank about his bearded face, and he stank of sweat and stale beer. Beside him another man stood. He was smaller, with pointed features, and it was he who spoke next.

"That one's marked, Garmon." His lip curled as his eyes traced her scar. "Ya don't want 'er."

His argument fell on deaf ears. The larger man surveyed her from head to foot, taking in the flowing dark hair that hung loose to hide her face, the long, graceful arms and legs, the narrow waist wrapped round with a leather belt, and every curve of the shift as it fell over her body. Phebe shrank from his gaze and searched frantically for some break in the wall of people before her.

"She'll do alright, marked or no. I like the look o' this one." He took a step toward Phebe. "Get the ropes, Finch."

"Ya sure she's come of age, Garmon? Ya don't want trouble with the magistrate."

"Ah, we'll have no trouble there, Finch. Emmerich's got a woman fer magistrate. I'd like ta see 'er stop me." He advanced two more steps and took Phebe's arm with a thick, meaty hand.

"No," she whispered, her voice catching in her throat. "Please, leave me alone. Please. Ya don't want me."

Garmon pulled her to him, taking a few strands of her hair in one hand. "Ya mustn't speak so humbly. I *do* want ya." He leaned in to whisper in her ear. "And if ya come quiet, I won't hurt ya."

There was an instant, just one instant before she screamed when she thought about going quietly with Garmon back to his village. In that instant, she saw her life before her, an unchanging nightmare of drudgery and despair. And how different was that from the life she lived already? Then, she pictured Simeon's grin, remembered the strength of his hands and the great depths of his kindness, and the spell was broken. She screamed his name once, twice before Garmon clenched a hand over her mouth, twisted her in front of him, and pushed her off the main street.

As they moved farther and farther from the center of Emmerich, the lights grew fewer, the shadows longer. They were not ten paces from the last stone cottage, the northernmost point of light in the village. Beyond was vaporous darkness, and Phebe was convinced that once they plunged into that abyss, no one would ever find her. She heard footfalls behind them. It must be Finch, she thought, *carrying the ropes that'll bind me to this foul man forever.* But no. The next sounds were the twang of a bowstring and the sharp whistling of an arrow's flight. Garmon groaned, loosened his iron grip, and collapsed.

So great was her relief that Phebe nearly fainted when she turned and saw Simeon rushing toward her.

"Are ya hurt?" he asked, gripping her elbows to support her.

"Simeon," she breathed, leaning all her weight against him.

"Phebe, please. Did 'e hurt ya? Are ya alright?"

"Aye, Sim. I'm alright. I'm alright now."

Simeon scooped her up into his arms and made for the river, slipping into the magistrate's hall from the back and avoiding Market Circle. Gently, he placed Phebe on his own cot, bringing a chair from the next room so that he might sit beside her.

"It won't be much longer now, Phebe."

She was quiet for a while. Then, she swung long legs over the side of the cot and sat up to face him. "'Til I come of age, ya mean?"

"Aye," Simeon replied, searching her face. "And 'til ya have a protector."

"It seems I already have one." She smiled and laid her hand on Simeon's.

He took her hand in both of his, cursing the clammy sweat that broke out on his palms. "What I mean ta say is, it won't be much longer 'til we can be married. If you'll have me, that is." And he saw how Phebe reacted to those words, saw the flushing of her cheeks, the racing of her pulse, the flashing warmth of her eyes. Wild with hope, he rushed on ahead. "I can earn a good livin'. We can have a cottage in the village. That way you'd always be close ta me. You'd be safe."

Phebe was lost in the pale blue of his eyes. Since Amos had gone, Simeon had seen to her every need. In eight years of solitude, she had not once chopped wood for her fire, had not once gone without meat or drink. The cottage never fell into ill repair. If Simeon could not patch the roof and mend the hinges on the doors, he had brought Orin to do so. And what was more, what was infinitely more, were the hours of quiet joy spent by the fireplace. Phebe could picture Simeon sitting in her father's chair on countless nights through the years. In the beginning, the large wooden chair had dwarfed him, but he would sit with her, telling tales of his mistakes and misadventures at the forge. Later, he would prop long legs on the hearthstones and tell her of his travels with Orin. Through his eyes, she had seen the villages of western and southern Shiloh, and she had rejoiced with him over the success of his first kill. In the end, when he filled Abner's chair and seemed quite at home there, he spoke of the challenges of his trade and of his dreams for the future. Phebe knew, sure as the endless night of that dark country, that she would have died like her mother were it not for Simeon. She loved him. With every fiber of body and soul she loved him. But she would never set foot under his roof and call herself his wife.

"Simeon," she began, with a slight shaking of her head that warned him of what was to come. He gripped her hand more tightly. "There's no better man in Shiloh. None. A man like you doesn't want *me* fer a wife. Not *me*, Sim. Ya want a woman who's not been marked. Ya deserve that much, at least." She turned her face away from him and tried to pull her hand free. He wouldn't allow it. Instead, he gripped her wrists and drew her up with him as he stood.

"Little nightingale. Phebe . . . this is the face I've always loved. Were one strand o' yer hair altered, I'd know it, and grieve fer it." He brushed her hair away from her face and let his fingers fall lightly to her waist.

She didn't know what to say. She wondered if Simeon could hear her heart pounding. "No one's called me nightingale in ages."

"Ya don't sing like ya used ta. But that'll be different. It *can* be different. Everything can."

"That's just it, Sim!" she said, jerking away and putting several paces between them. "It's not only my face that's marked! It's my whole family, my whole life. Don't ya see?! If ya married me, then *you'd* be marked as well. You'd bring *my* doom down on *your* head. I couldn't bear it."

"No! That's over. It's done. Ya don't have ta share in their fate."

184

"Don't I? What proof have ya? And what has my family ever brought ya but misery? What have we ever given that wasn't snatched away ten-fold?"

He could see in her eyes that the door was shut against him. There was a finality in her words that filled him with dread. What desolation did she believe waited for her? And how could he ever make her see that he would risk any darkness to free her, to protect her, to hold her?

"I should go," she said, turning to leave. With a hand on the doorpost, she looked back over her shoulder. "Thank you, Sim." The words felt so small. What was she thanking him for, after all? For eight years of companionship and care, for preventing her abduction, for his offer of marriage, his love? The iron shroud that was her constant adorning felt heavier than ever before. Her vegetables, her plans, her coming of age were all forgotten, and the dim silence of her cottage felt like the very arms of death itself, opening wide to receive her when she returned.

Twenty-Seven

O
rin shook his head in wonder. "It's a marvel, Simeon. I've never seen anything like it." It was not a lie, not even an exaggeration, and it had nothing to do with the pride Orin took in the young man who'd become like a son to him. The lantern was nothing short of marvelous.

"Do ya think she'll like it?"

The older man just smiled and chuckled. He patted Simeon on the shoulder and walked out of the shop.

Simeon stood a while, gazing at his masterpiece. He'd been working steadily for over a year, at times fearing that it could not possibly be finished before the celebration. But here it was: complete, beautiful, perfect.

"I'll know soon enough," he said aloud. Then, indulging in the briefest of smiles, he wrapped the gift in a cloth and carried it home.

That night Simeon dreamed again.

In the dream he walked eastward, away from the village, and he held Phebe's lantern in his hand. He glanced down as he passed the stone and plunged into the darkness that surrounded the lighted village. A sense of panic rose within him, for without intending to, he was taking the same path that he and Amos had followed on the night when they tried to steal Hadrian's lantern. Why was he taking that path? It was madness! Yet his feet continued to betray him. He was being drawn toward something. *To* what, he did not know. *By* what, he could not imagine.

There was a flash in the field up ahead, just the briefest flickering, as if someone had lit a candle and then snuffed it out in the same breath. To his left, another light appeared. It rose out of the tall grasses, then disappeared as quickly as it had come. Out of the corner of his eye, he caught another flash, this time to his right. He stopped walking to watch. They were everywhere! All around him, the air grew thick with dozens and dozens of tiny flames. They came together, assembling in front of him, organizing themselves into one body of light.

The apparition had six wings. The highest set was pointed upward, high above the creature's head. The rest were long and pointed, almost feathery, and all were a brilliant white. Arms and legs took shape, and a gown of luminous silver. Then a face appeared. It was not the face of a child, not the face of a woman. It was altogether different. The blazing light cooled enough for Simeon to look into the creature's eyes. He was not afraid.

"Simeon," she said, and her voice burned up the air between them. "Dreamer, the time draws near."

In this dream, Simeon could find no voice. He could not question, could not answer. He stood silent and transfixed by the smoldering energy of the fiery creature.

"The Shadow hangs heavy over Shiloh," she continued, "and deep darkness waits at the threshold. Your threshold, Simeon. But the Children of the Morning are not forgotten. The Bright have preserved you for this day."

No words formed on Simeon's lips, but his mind rebelled at the thought that he should be chosen by the gods. Amos had been the chosen one.

"You see yourself through the eyes of the Shadow, Simeon. Do not be fooled. I am one of the Nelya, the Fire Children. And it is to you that I am sent. It was not by chance that Jada found you in the Meander, not by chance that Penelope blessed you with the gift of dreaming."

The edges of the Nelya were giving way. Little flecks of light drifted out in every direction until first her wings, then her legs, then her arms disappeared. Her silvery gown broke apart into in- numerable fragments of light.

"Others will follow. Step out of the Shadow, Simeon."

His mind raced with questions, but he found no voice, no time, to ask them. Her face was no more than a few points of flame that spread and settled down in the grasses. The night was once again utterly dark, and Simeon woke to find that Phebe's lantern was lit.

Her dread grew with each passing day. She wished that some- thing might happen to delay the coming-of-age celebration. Any fate, even death, seemed kinder than what lay ahead.

Ma, at least, should've been here, she thought. Nothing could have stopped her father's death. Of that, she was certain. And as for Amos, she could only think that he had been driven to madness by his grief. At least he still lived, somewhere; at least he had not faded to nothing.

A spark of rage long buried rose up in Phebe as she lay on her cot in the stretching twilight hours. Wynn had simply given up. A little voice echoed on the stone walls of the cottage, and it whispered to Phebe that her mother had found no reason to live, no reason to fight. Her children had not been enough. Her daughter had not been enough. In those, the darkest moments, Phebe felt the walls of the cottage closing in around her, pressing against the edges of the cot. The great wooden beams of the ceiling descended until they hovered just a fingerbreadth from her face. The air was close and hot, the weight suffocating, unendurable. Surely death would be sweeter, kinder than this, whether it truly brought her back to the light or only delivered her into oblivion.

With what strength remained to her, Phebe clung to memories of the way her mother had smiled when she called her little bird, of their travels to the village, their work in the garden, the pleasant hours of sewing and spinning together. There was just the faintest shimmer about her skin and eyes, just a thread of hope remaining.

There was a rap at the door. Phebe rose from the chair by the fire, wondering if one of the villagers had mistaken the date of the celebration and come a day early. Outside were Darby and a young girl from the village, one of Payne's little daughters. The girl stepped quickly inside the door and scooted against the wall, while Darby took Phebe's hand, crossed the threshold, and deposited a basket on the table. It was covered with a gray cloth.

"Is everything alright, Darby? I've plenty o' food and plenty o' wool fer a while yet. Ya needn't have troubled yerself ta come all this way." She was unaccustomed to having guests in the cottage, apart from Simeon. She felt nervous and awkward at the presence of even so dear a friend as the weaver.

With a sparkle in her unseeing eyes, Darby pulled the covering from the basket. "It's not ta bring food or wool that I've come, child." She lifted a bundle of white wool and ran her fingers over the cloth, feeling for something. "I know it's breakin' custom, but

I've brought yer gift a day early." She pinched a corner of the fabric between her thumb and forefinger and unrolled the bundle.

Phebe gasped. Darby stood there, in her barren, gray cottage, holding the most beautifully and brightly embroidered coming-of-age gown she had ever seen. The white wool, so precious and rare, looked like palest candle flame, and the threads of yarn that bordered neck and sleeve and waist and hem dazzled the eye with every imaginable color. Bright green leaves and vines, bursting with jasmine in the softest of yellows wound their way around the neck-line and down both sleeves. Every flower was woven as if in full bloom, and each had a rich golden center. At the wrists, the sleeves were loose, embroidered with nightshade that flowered in indigo and purple. The sign of the Fire Clan stood out in flaming red at the center of the waistline, and branches laced their way around the gown to form a kind of belt. On some of the branches, birds were perching. The hem was embroidered with night phlox. Their feath-ery leaves were worked in vibrant green, and their delicate flowers shone in blood-red and flame-orange.

"Oh, Darby," Phebe whispered. It was all she could manage. She had dreamed of such a gown since the moment she had first set foot in the weaver's shop and seen the basket, overflowing with skeins of colored yarn. What this gift must have cost, what time it had taken to weave, she could not fathom.

"We couldn't have ya in gray on the day o' the celebration, now could we?" Darby beamed at her, folding the dress in half and drap-ing it over Phebe's outstretched arms. "We'll be goin' on. Have ya everything ya need fer tomorrow? Enough ale? Candles? Wood fer the fire? You'll need plenty o' light. Most o' the villagers haven't been out this way in many a year, ya know."

"Aye, Darby. I know."

"Alright then." She clutched Phebe's hand and drew her in to kiss her cheek. "Ya ready ta go, Willow? I'll tell ya a story and you'll forget all about the dark road." The two made a slow start down the lane, the girl holding a lantern in her free hand and Darby already spinning a tale.

As the weight of a man holds him down to the earth by some unseen force, so the weight of darkness over Phebe's cottage drew all things to itself. Isolde was caught in that sweeping current.

She checked the map as she rode into town, confirming the name with Willow and Darby as they hurried home. Emmerich. *How strange*, she thought. *Didn't the stories say that Emmerich was the home of Amos, Wielder of Fire?* She shivered.

Isolde listened for the sound of horses, and soon found the stable where Brand and Willa were kept. She tied up her mare, lay down in the straw, and fell asleep.

Twenty-Eight

The day of the celebration dawned foggy, and dim and gray as ever. Phebe got out of bed, braided her hair, slipped on the beautiful white shift, and lingered for a moment, admiring the embroidery work and running her hands over the twisting threads. This was a day for rejoicing. Not one day of her life before or after would be so celebrated, so honored. Yet she felt no joy. The woven vines around the hem of the gown might as well have stretched to the ground and rooted her to the soil, so great was the weight on her mind and heart.

She straightened the cottage in preparation for visitors, sweeping the stone floor for the dozenth time, refolding and restacking the blankets on her cot. On the table, she set out every mug she owned. There were five, and they would be washed again and again today. Every guest expected to toast her health with a mug of beer or ale, and Payne had been kind enough to give her a barrel of each as his family's coming-of-age gift. She sat down by the fire and fidgeted, wishing the time away. She wrapped strands of black hair around her fingers and tugged at them, like her brother had done when she was a girl. Then, hardly knowing why, she walked out the door and across the lane to gather a few sprigs of the night-blooming jasmine that covered the fence by the meadow.

The air was pungently sweet, saturated with the rich fragrance of the blooms. Phebe took a moment to arrange the flowers in the braid that wrapped her head like a crown. She remembered how her mother had woven them into her hair when she was young, how Wynn had loved the sweet scent of the flowering vine. She remembered the first night of the Great Hunt, when her father had carried her on his shoulders and Simeon had spun her in a wild dance that whipped the blooms from her hair.

The tears rose in her eyes, but she refused to let them fall. *I mustn't think of all that*, she thought, *else I'll never survive this day*. Instead, she steered her thoughts to more practical matters, reviewing again the list of preparations to be made. That was when she remembered. Firewood. Simeon had not come in several days, and it was he who had always chopped wood for the fire. The few logs that remained in a stack on the hearth would not be enough to last the day. She could only hope that he had left some store of firewood beneath one of the trees in the glade. She grabbed the small torch that hung in its iron brace beside the doorway and made for the chopping block.

A chill wind blew from the north, drawing the mist in its wake. Phebe had not gone ten paces before the light of her torch was all but lost in a sea of gray. The torchlight could not penetrate that thick fog. Once, it would not have mattered so much, for she herself would have cast a light across the path. Now she shone only faintly, with the memory of glory.

She stumbled past the garden and the old sheepfold, into the stretch of woods that bordered Linden Lake. A stiff wind began to blow, and the fog lifted. In the weak mid-morning light, she could see the chopping block, and nearby, a sizeable store of firewood. She sighed her relief, and took one step into the glade before stopping again. The familiar landscape felt distinctly unfamiliar. Something was wrong with the trees. Fog still clung to their branches, weaving them together in webs of hazy light. *Webs.*

Phebe stifled a scream. In the breath before she turned and fled toward the cottage, she noticed something moving on the trees. Did the bark itself crawl, or did something move beneath it? She didn't wait to find out. Not until the door of the cottage closed behind her and she fell against it, panting, did she let herself wonder. Could it be? Had they come for her at last?

Phebe jumped when she heard the knock. She opened the door, just a crack, and found Simeon standing on the threshold with a bundle in his hands. She flung open the door and threw her arms around his neck, clinging to him desperately. He smelled of fire and wood and clean earth. He was solid and good, and she relaxed into the strength of his arms and chest.

"It's just me, little bird. What's frightened ya so?"

He never got an answer. Before she could reply, Orin's voice sounded from the lane.

"I see you've beaten me ta the door, Sim." He gave the young man a sly smile. "And I wanted my gift ta be the first." He turned his smile on Phebe, then, and presented her with a new kettle.

Close behind him were a handful of villagers, carrying candles, baskets, and woven rugs. Many were eager to offer their best wishes, and all were eager for a mug of beer. Simeon was shuffled to the corner of the cottage, where he leaned against the window, watching her.

He thought about the first time he saw her. She was four years old then, just a slip of a girl, just the sister of his friend. And then she had sung, a haunting song about a nightingale. Her voice had been like a beacon, like a rip in the fabric of darkness. From the moment she'd opened her mouth she had captured him. He thought about her singing at her father's funeral pyre. He remembered the choking sound in her voice as she willed her way through line after line of the lament. He thought about the countless evenings he'd spent with her in this cottage. He would bring meat or bread or some trinket from the village. She would cook for him or sing for him or sit with him in easy silence before the fire. She would listen and encourage him as he told of his progress at the forge or his success in the latest hunt.

Looking at her now, his heart was so full of love for her and so broken for her. He saw her loneliness and pain, even as she forced a smile, greeting villager after villager. He knew she hadn't wanted to face this day, but she'd done it all the same. There was strength in her that she knew nothing of. But Simeon knew. He had always known.

The day was drawing to a close when he was alone with Phebe again. Soon, the procession would arrive. The celebration would begin. He had so little time.

"What've ya got there, Sim?" she asked, falling into the chair beside him.

"Do ya remember the night I told ya I was goin' ta be a blacksmith?"

"Aye." Phebe laughed at the memory. "Ya thought you'd never amount ta anything, that you'd be stokin' fires fer the rest o' yer days."

"Ya asked me then if I'd make ya somethin', when I learned how."

"I was naught but a silly girl, Sim. Ya owe me nothin'. 'Tis I who am in yer debt. A thousand times over."

Simeon brushed the statement aside and continued. "There's somethin' I've wanted ta make fer ya . . . well, always. Took years ta learn how." He was hesitating, a mixture of anticipation and embarrassment. He wanted the moment to be perfect. At last, he pulled the cloth from the bundle in his hands and dropped it to the floor, revealing an exquisite lantern.

Here were no glass panes bordered by crude iron bands. No, this lantern was made entirely of tiny vines of wrought iron that twisted and curled in a hundred directions. Little iron leaves adorned the vines here and there, and on one side of the lantern, nesting among the leaves, was a small bird. Phebe knew without asking that it was a nightingale.

He picked up the lantern then, opening a hinged door on one side, and blew into it. From nowhere, a dozen small lights appeared, circling each other like bees around a hive. The lantern's warm light filled the cottage.

"What are they?" Phebe whispered.

Simeon never got to explain. Again the two were interrupted, this time by a knock at the door. It broke the spell. Their moment was gone.

Phebe and Simeon went to the door together and found Jada standing on the stoop. Behind her, some hundred people waited with torches and lanterns and baskets of food. Several men were already preparing the bonfire and setting up tables and benches.

Phebe found comfort in the familiar faces that dotted the crowd. These were people for whom her scarred face held no surprise, no horror. Darby was there, and Aspen. Payne and Cora were there, with their children gathered around them. Orin stood at the front of the group, and Caedmon hovered near the back, scowling. Many other faces she knew, but could not name, and there was one face in particular that caught her eye. It belonged to a young woman not many years older than her. Her hair flamed red in the torchlight, and her eyes were as blue as Simeon's.

It was understood that Phebe would walk out of the house and stand with Jada while the people circled around to hear her blessing. Without anyone to offer a blessing, however, she was uncertain of what to do. She glanced back at Simeon, who was carefully placing the lantern on the mantle. He knew that Jada planned to offer a blessing for Phebe, so he smiled, motioning her out to the waiting assembly. She squared her shoulders and went, Simeon closing the door behind them and standing in the shadows to the side of the group.

There was a hush, and Jada began.

"Phebe, daughter of Abner and Wynn, we have come ta celebrate yer comin' of age. From this day, you are a woman of Emmerich, free ta take a husband and bear children. Since yer mother is not here ta offer a blessing . . ."

"I'll offer one instead."

The voice came from the darkness beyond the crowd of villagers. Every eye turned to see two shapes moving closer, silhouetted against the firelight. One appeared to be in motion. Its edges were indistinct. Only its green-gold eyes never wavered. The other walked with long strides and a familiar confidence. And though he had changed markedly, several people in the crowd recognized him. Simeon was the first, and he rushed to block his path.

"Stay away from 'er," Simeon said.

"Amos?" Phebe stared at her brother over the top of Simeon's shoulder, then pushed past him to get a better look. The man before her stood taller, with a broad chest and muscular arms and legs. He wore no arm guard, carried no bow or quiver. But his red-brown hair was still boyish and untamed.

"Did ya think I'd forgotten ya, sister?"

A dam of pent-up emotion gave way in Phebe's heart. She wanted to touch her brother, to be sure he was real. She wanted to scream at him, or slap him in the face. She wanted to embrace him. She wanted to weep. But everyone was watching her, waiting. What should she do?

"What blessing do ya offer, brother?"

Amos gave a half-smile and raised a glass vial full of black liquid. "The blessing of forgetting."

A low murmur ran through the assembly, for the villagers thought it a strange blessing. They all drank the black water from the River Meander. They always had. Still, they feared the worst from Amos and his companion. Maybe some darker power was at work in the water he offered.

He held the vial to his lips, took a sip, and offered it to his sister. "Drink, Phebe."

She stood motionless, taking in the bizarre and unreal scene before her. The light from the torches did not flicker. The air was still. No one breathed. Phebe looked into her brother's face, struggling to piece together the mystery of his disappearance and his dramatic change. Until now, she'd never seen him drink from the river, but she remembered clearly enough her father's warnings.

She looked at Simeon, who shook his head, his eyes urging her not to drink. He was burning with an intensity she had never seen.

"No," she said at last. "It's not a blessing ta forget, Amos." She wished she could sound more convincing. There were so many painful memories, so many black days.

He sneered and flung the water from the vial at Phebe. Before the inky liquid reached the precious white fabric, Simeon exploded into action. He pulled a dagger from his side and held it to Amos's neck, catching him off-guard. But Amos merely looked at the arm that held the dagger to his throat. A bit of skin reddened and bubbled up. Simeon screamed and dropped the knife, but he stood his ground.

Orin moved in, and other men of the village stirred.

Then Phebe spoke, and everyone stilled.

"Remember the first time ya shot a rabbit, Amos? You were so proud, but I cried the rest o' the night because I wanted ya ta bring it back ta life."

Amos stared back at her, unmoved. There was no life at all in his eyes. "Ya must remember the cat, Amos. I'd have died were it not fer you. Ya wore the claw 'round yer neck fer ages."

Still nothing.

"Remember how Da used ta tell us stories by the fire?" Her voice broke. "He'd come through the door and greet his 'dear ones'.

Then he'd sit in 'is chair, oilin' 'is bow, and tell us tale after tale."

There was a flicker of recognition. Amos clenched his jaw. "Why are ya doin' this?" he asked, warning.

"Remember how many times Ma had ta mend yer shirts when ya were little? Ya kept hangin' 'em from the trees and usin' 'em as targets."

Out from the deep well of Amos's pain poured a river of hurt and hate.

"Ya want me ta remember *Ma? You?* Of all the people in Shiloh —"

Phebe stopped. She'd been moving toward Amos almost imperceptibly. "What do ya mean?" she asked. But she already knew. He was raising the same question, making the same accusation she had been making in the silence of her heart for years. Only a thread of hope remained. It was so very, very fragile.

"Does it really bring ya comfort ta remember a worthless dog who didn't even love ya?"

Everyone heard his words. Everyone saw it happen. From every direction, the ground began to crawl. Or something under the ground was crawling. In the deepening dark, it was hard to know, but it was utterly silent, utterly terrifying. It looked as if the earth and the grass and the stones had sprouted legs, and all of them were rushing toward Phebe. The dreadful rippling movement reached her feet, crawled up her legs. The embroidery on her shift danced, and the white wool was alive with motion. Up and up it worked its way, distorting her face and finally reaching the crown of jasmine on top of her head. Thread upon thread of darkness was woven around her. Her gown, now stained with the deadly black water, was disappearing behind strands of gray-black web. It happened so quickly. Simeon had only time to scream her name before her light was snuffed out and the night weavers took her.

Twenty-Nine

Simeon's was not the only voice that rang out in the night. There were other screams as well. But while Simeon reached out to grasp the emptiness where Phebe had been, the villagers pulled away. They were grieved, horrified. The void left by the night weavers, that black hole hanging before them, had a gravity of its own. They feared they would be sucked into its grasp, and their fear aroused their rage.

Everyone had heard his words. Everyone had seen it happen. And the law was clear. After a breath of perfect silence, Caedmon's voice filled the air.

"Let's take 'im, lads," he said, and spat on the ground.

Women snatched up their children, holding them tightly in their arms, and the men moved as one to take Amos to the stone, where his judgment would be meted out. The first villagers to reach him hesitated, fearing his awful power, but he didn't fight. His eyes were fixed on the void where Phebe had been. They wrapped his wrists in a leather cord, led him through the darkness to the edge of the village, and placed him directly in front of the stone. Jada stood facing them all.

"Amos," she said, "you have broken the greatest o' the eternal laws o' Shiloh. You've stolen yer sister's light . . ." Her voice faltered, and she looked down at the ground. When she raised her head she looked at Amos with fiery eyes and spoke with unquestioned authority. "You are hereby sentenced ta exile, now and forever, from all the villages o' Shiloh. Messages declarin' yer fate will be sent ta the farthest reaches o' the land. Any man who attempts ta aid ya will fall under a sentence o' death. There is no safe place fer ya. We consign ya ta the darkness. Be gone." The people murmured their approval, and the air was tight with tension, with waiting.

He could have burned the village to the ground, could have killed every last person assembled at the stone. Instead, Amos looked at Jada, then scanned the faces in the crowd until he found Simeon, whose light was surging erratically. He locked eyes with his former friend. There was something in that look, some unspoken message. Only Simeon and Mordecai, perched on a nearby branch, read it clearly.

Caedmon and a handful of other men stepped forward, expecting that Amos would have to be physically forced from their presence. They were wrong. Without a word, he walked away.

When the crowd at the stone had thinned, Simeon cut a path to Orin. He grabbed the man by the arm and directed him past the forge and into the cottage.

"I need yer help," Simeon whispered.

"Anything."

"I need ta take Brand and Willa."

"Ya mean ta go after 'er, then?"

"Aye."

"I'll go with ya."

"Orin, wait. I'm goin' after Amos as well."

"Amos?! It'll do ya no good, Sim. I don't even know if 'e can be killed. Look what 'e's done ta ya already!" The heat blister on Simeon's arm was still bright.

"I don't plan ta kill 'im." Simeon struggled to explain. He knew only that he must go after him, that Amos was the path to Phebe.

"But 'e can't be trusted!" Orin's voice had risen almost to a shout when he heard a scuffling outside the workshop. He looked at the young man next to him, suddenly aware of the greatest danger of Simeon's plan. It wasn't Amos. "They'll kill ya, Sim," he whispered.

The latch on the door rattled, and there was a soft knock. Orin's hand went to the hilt of his dagger, and he stepped softly behind the door. An unfamiliar voice spoke through the wooden planks. A woman's voice.

"Please, I must speak with ya." Orin sent a warning glance to Simeon before opening the door a crack. A striking woman slipped inside. She was outfitted for battle, with a dagger hanging from her belt. She carried her bow and quiver with easy grace. And she was very bright, blazing with purpose and determination.

"I hope you'll forgive my intrudin'. I followed the procession. I saw what happened ta yer girl."

Simeon and Orin were too stunned by her strange dress and her sudden appearance to comprehend what she said. It was as if she had materialized in the air outside the door.

"Isolde," she said, reaching out to grasp each of the men by the arm. "I mean ta go with ya."

Simeon found his voice. "Go with us? Where?"

"Over the mountains, ta find yer girl."

Simeon looked to Orin, but the older man only blinked at him.

"I've spent years in search o' somethin' ta lead me out o' this cursed darkness. Too many years. I'm tired o' waitin' and wanderin'." She looked from one man to the other. "And if ya take my advice, I think we should follow the Wielder o' Fire. Seems the most likely person ta lead us ta the Hall o' Shadows, doesn't he?"

Hope rose in Simeon's heart. "Ya have a horse?" he asked her.

"Aye," she said, and smiled.

They looked at Orin, their eyes asking what he would do. For a moment, he stroked the stubble on his chin. Then he turned to Simeon. "Saddle Brand and Willa," he said. "I'll get the supplies. We leave within the hour."

While Simeon and Isolde crept to the stable, Orin gathered blankets, weapons, water skins, torches, and food. He tossed everything into a sack and tiptoed to the back of the cottage. He scanned the alley, looking left and right before stepping out.

"Simeon, is that you?" Darby shuffled along the lane, her fingertips brushing against the walls of the cottage. Orin knew she'd heard him. He had to stop.

"No, Darby, it's Orin." He reached out to take her hand, and she leaned in, whispering.

"Tell him ta hurry, Orin. 'Time slips away and the days are fleetin'.' Tell him ta bring 'er back before it's too late."

Orin saw the pained expression on her face. He squeezed her hand and rushed to the stable, where Simeon had Brand and Willa saddled and ready. They mounted and set off, with Isolde and Echo following behind.

Except for the forgotten benches and baskets of food that littered the ground outside, the cottage looked much the same. The last remains of the bonfire crackled, sending fragments of light dancing over the stones of the cottage wall. While Orin and Isolde kept their seats, Simeon dismounted and stood in the lane. He had hoped to see a scar in the ground, a hole, a burn, anything to mark the place where Phebe had been taken. There was nothing.

Inside the cottage, the blankets were still folded on her cot. The table was piled with gifts. The embers of the fire in the hearth still glowed. But the room was barren without her light, silent without her voice. All the life in that place had been sucked out. It was a dried husk, the leavings of the night weavers. He took the lantern down from the mantel, trying not to think how Phebe's face had shone when she saw it. The only thing left on the mantel was the silver glass. He tucked it into his belt, took a long look at the cottage, and closed the door behind him.

"Let's go, then." Simeon mounted Willa and turned her face to the east.

As the horses broke into a run, their hooves pounding the soil of the grasslands, Orin thundered, "We go now inta the very heart o' darkness. May the light shine upon us all!"

Thirty

East of the village, a vast stretch of grasslands rose to the looming bulk of the Black Mountains. They crouched on the horizon like wolves stalking their prey. Even in the thickest darkness of the night, people could feel the presence of those mountains. But not a man in Emmerich could tell how long it would take to reach them. Not a man of them had made that fearsome journey. Not even Amos.

Further north, beyond the River Meander, the Whispering Wood stretched close to the base of the mountains, and Amos had traveled there often. But this was a piece of land he had never crossed. Any other man would have been terrified, walking through unknown territory into exile, with no food, no weapons, no light. But this was not Amos's first exile.

When he left Emmerich the first time, he had traveled as he pleased, where he pleased, by day or night. There was no one who could stand in his way. What he'd needed, he'd taken, though Amos remembered little of food or drink during those years. He remembered little of anything, for that matter, except the power that coursed through his veins and the ever-shifting presence at his side.

Mordecai's absence was more unsettling than his presence. The shifter was cunning. Amos had seen him take the form of an owl, a wolf, a black-horned Daegan, even a nightshade. Though there'd been no sign of him since the stone, Amos knew he could not be far.

Any other man would have been terrified, but fear was not the thing Amos felt most keenly. In fact, he didn't know what he felt. Only one thing was clear. He had to find Phebe. He had to undo what he had done. So, carrying a flame in the palm of his hand, he made his way east into the heart of the Shadow.

Black night rushed past him, and wind whispered through a sea of dry grasses. Over the heavy breathing of the horses and the relentless pounding of their hooves, Simeon could hear the jostling of saddle packs and the hushed voice of Isolde, coaxing Echo onward. Beyond the radiance of the riders themselves, casting a soft glow over the horses and over the land before them, Simeon could see nothing. At times, during that first long night of hard riding, he wondered if he had stumbled into some fearful dream. Perhaps he wished it to be so. But he felt too keenly the growing ache in his legs as they gripped Willa's saddle. And he felt too deeply the widening chasm in his heart. Phebe was gone; this was no dream.

Without thought, Simeon quickened his pace, and Orin and Isolde followed suit. Hour after hour they pressed on, sensing the slow approach of the Black Mountains. What secrets, what terrors did they hold? He could not imagine. To think that Phebe already knew, that she'd gone into the darkness ahead of him. He rode on, pushing Willa to the limits of her strength and endurance, until at last the vague promise of dawn crept through the blanket of Shadow, and Orin called for a halt.

"Have mercy on my mare, Sim," Orin said, as he dismounted and gave Brand a drink from his water skin. "The dark's easin' up a bit. We'll rest a few hours before movin' on."

"Aye." It took great effort for Simeon to climb down from Willa and give up his pursuit, even for a few hours' rest. Running his horse to the point of collapse, though, would do nothing to save his Phebe. He took a cloth from beneath his saddle and wiped the sweat from Willa's neck. "That's a good girl," he said, and he patted the side of her face and gave her a drink. Isolde did the same with Echo. The brown mare nuzzled her neck and nickered.

"You've a good mount there," Simeon said.

"Aye," Isolde replied. "I've known no friend but her these many years, no steadier companion. And most o' this dark country we've crossed together. She's fearless, this one." At that, Echo tossed her head and snorted before stepping away to munch on the dry grass.

Isolde unrolled a thick blanket and spread it on the ground. She ate a little cake of dried berries from her pack. Then, with the ease gained from many years' lonely travel, she rolled onto her side, rested her head on her pack, and fell asleep.

Orin slept as well. Simeon only dozed, drifting in and out of a shallow sleep and finally waking with every muscle tensed and sore. He groaned and sat up. By then, it was midday and time to be moving.

They found him as night closed in. He sat on the ground with legs crossed and back hunched. His head hung down on his chest, and his hand rested on his knee. Little sparks of flame erupted from his open palm in fitful bursts, and he made no move to rise or speak when the horses approached and the riders jumped from their saddles.

"Amos." Simeon was first to step forward. He crouched down, and Amos lifted cold eyes to meet his.

"You've come then," he said, without affection, without pleasure.

"Aye, we've come."

Amos raised his head to survey the others. "Have ya any water?" Orin grabbed the water skin from Brand's side and carried it to Amos, who lifted it to his lips, drank, and fell into a fit of coughing and spitting.

"Ugh! By the gods, what is that filth?" he choked.

"Water," Orin replied, "from a spring outside the village."

"You've nothin' else?!" Amos was doubled over, grasping his gut.

"No. And if ya mean ta live, ya must drink it. You're weak already from thirst. Just take it slow."

Amos raised the skin to his lips and drank again until he cried out and tossed the skin to the ground. He pushed himself, slowly, to a stand, the last of the spring water dripping down his chin and onto his tunic.

"Ya mean ta kill me, is that it, Sim?" A wicked smile broke out on his face, and he looked pointedly at the blister on Simeon's arm. "Challenge me now, even in this state, and I fear you'll fare no better than before."

"Challenge ya?" Simeon asked. "We've come in search o' ya! I saw yer face at the stone, Amos. Ya mean ta go after her. I know it. And you'll need help."

"Help?" Amos said. "*You* came ta help *me*? *You* plan ta march inta the Black Mountains and take on the Shadow with yer bow and arrow, eh? If there's anythin' I recall about *you*, it's that ya couldn't hit the broadside of a wall from three paces."

Simeon had strung an arrow before Amos finished speaking. With surprising speed and grace, he drew it back along his jaw and let it fly. It whizzed by Amos's face, touching his hair as it passed, and landed somewhere out of sight.

"So you've improved." Amos looked at Orin and Isolde, standing silent and holding the reins of their horses. Then he turned back to Simeon. "But ya don't know what lurks in the darkness, what waits fer ya. Ya can't survive it, and ya can't help me."

Amos's face darkened, and Simeon wondered how much he knew, what horrors he had seen and done. He wondered if Amos meant to die in this pursuit, wondered why he pursued at all. Then he was assaulted by the memory of Phebe in her coming-of-age gown. She was gone, and it was Amos who had taken her. A flood of savage rage overtook him, and Simeon lunged at Amos, grabbing him by the throat.

"You! You took 'er from me! If it hadn't been fer you, Phebe would still . . ." His voice failed him, even as he felt the growing heat beneath his palm and loosened his hold. Simeon took a step back, took a moment to breathe. "It doesn't matter what waits fer me. I *must* go. I *must* find 'er."

"It's yer life, Sim," Amos said. "Whatever comes, it won't be on my head."

"You've enough lives on yer head already! What's one more, Amos?!" Simeon's eyes were burning a path through the night. This was a challenge indeed, but Amos didn't take it up.

"There's a river runs through the Black Mountains, the River Lost it's called. If we follow it north, it should lead us ta the Hall o' Shadows."

Amos read the question in Simeon's eyes. "I know nothin' more than that."

"You'd follow 'im, then?" Isolde asked, looking at Simeon.

"Aye, Sim." Orin said. "Who's ta say this boy can be trusted? Who's ta say it's not a trap?"

"It's almost certainly a trap, old man," Amos spat back. "If ya don't trust me —"

His words were interrupted by a long, wailing howl. It echoed in the darkness beyond their small circle of light. It was joined by another voice, and another. The horses stamped the ground, anxious to go. The Shadow Wolves were on the hunt.

"We can't stay here, regardless," Isolde said. She turned to Amos. "You ride with me. My horse carries the lightest load."

They rode hard all through the night. The following day, the mountains filled their vision. Behind them was the spreading emptiness of the grasslands; above and beside them, there was only black. They plunged in.

Thirty-One

Isolde's Red Map came to an end where the Black Mountains began, and there were no tales that told what made the mountains black. In some secluded corner of his mind, nearly every man had answered the question, had filled the empty space, with whatever reality seemed most fearful to him. Some imagined that the mountains were covered in dust and ash, or jagged rocks. Others saw the mountainsides black with the thick fur of the wolves or clothed in a net of impenetrable Shadow. The travelers discovered that the mountains were covered in dense, black forest. The branches of the trees were woven together so tightly that they appeared, from a distance, to be one solid mass of darkness. But they were not impenetrable.

A few shafts of hazy light fought through the canopy above as the riders picked their way through the forest. Damp mosses covered the ground, deadening the sound of the horses' hooves, and black rocks jutted between black trunks dusted with dim green lichen. There was no telling the height of the trees. Amos could see the dark pillars climb up to the height of five or six men, perhaps, but beyond there was only mist. The sight recalled a memory of the Hall of Echoes, with its stone pillars reaching into the endless dark of the sky. With the memory came a nameless pain, then a dull aching in his head and a twisting in his gut. He pushed the thought aside to focus on the woman who rode in front of him, her red hair hanging down her back.

"Not so bad, is it?" she asked, over her shoulder.

She was right. The Black Forest made for much easier traveling than the Whispering Wood, where the undergrowth grew impossibly thick, blocking a man's path and sheltering his enemies.

Amos only grunted in reply.

At the end of the first day, they found the River Lost. While the main channel of the River Meander flowed west from the Black Mountains and gradually arced toward the south, this branch of the river broke off within the mountain range, emptying far down in the southern moors. The water flowed swiftly over dark stones, cutting a black path through black forest. The horses bent to drink, and Amos lapped at the water. The others drank from their skins, rested, ate. Then, for some hours yet, they traveled into the inky night, listening for the sound of rushing water at their side.

When they finally made camp, none of them slept much. They kept Phebe's lantern lit, but made no fire. And above them, from the invisible heights of the branches, came the lonely hooting of owls, the fluttering and brushing of wings. Once or twice, they heard the screech and hiss of a cat. When morning broke, and they set out, it was not only Amos who knew they were being followed.

On the second day, the trees drifted from their tight ranks, and the riders moved more quickly. It was easy traveling, except when the path was blocked by dry creek beds that snaked off from the river. Some of these were deep, their steep sides choked with stones and the leaves and fallen branches of uncounted years. At times, they had to lead the horses far from the water to find safe places to cross. They would dismount and guide the animals down into the dry beds, searching for safe footing, then coax them up again onto the forest floor before returning to the river. That was when it happened, when the first assault came rushing in.

Orin had crossed first, leading Brand down into the bottom of a dry creek bed, maneuvering around roots and piles of rocks. Brand had followed, gingerly resting his hooves on the ground to test its strength before stepping forward. He made it out of the gulley and stood stamping on the other side. But Willa was more stubborn. She tossed her head, eyes wide, nostrils flared, refusing to step down into the ditch. Simeon coaxed and tugged at her reins. He stroked her neck and spoke softly into her ear. It was no use. She would not move. Isolde stepped forward, curious about Willa's behavior and eager to try her hand at leading the horse. Then three things happened at once. Isolde's hand came to rest on the gray mare's back, Amos jumped from the edge of the bank into the creek bed, and Simeon shouted.

"Amos, wait!"

Two wolves were moving down the length of the gulley. Their heads were low to the ground. Their eyes flickered with yellow-orange light. Their fangs were bared. The horses screamed and drew back, while Simeon grabbed his bow. He had an arrow strung and in the air before the first wolf reached Amos. But the arrow only passed through the beast and stuck fast in the ground.

Amos's fingers exploded with fire as the wolf bore down on him, knocking him from his feet. Its claws were just slicing into his shoulder, when Amos's hands burned into the heart of the beast and it dissolved in wisps of smoke.

The second wolf was close on its heels, but Orin and Isolde stood helpless on the banks. They had no fire, and it was only fire that conquered the wolves. Orin finally jumped down behind the animal, in hopes of cutting off its escape, and Simeon pulled another arrow from his quiver and sent it flying. Amos, lying on his back, saw what he must do. The moment the arrow passed above him, the instant before the second wolf was upon him, he focused all his energy on it. The arrow burst into flame and hit the wolf between the eyes. The beast halted in mid-leap and drifted away into nothing. The Black Forest was silent again.

Amos was bleeding. He leaned against the side of the ditch, pressing hot fingers to his shoulder, melting the torn pieces of flesh and bonding them back together. Simeon turned away, unable to watch the gruesome display. Instead, he stroked the soft dappled gray of Willa's neck and patted her nose to quiet her. The others said nothing. When the animals had calmed, they led them across the dry bed and back to the river.

They traveled late into the night. When they made camp, building up a large fire and lighting torches to guard them, they were quiet, each unwilling to voice the thoughts and fears that rose to his mind.

Of the four who sat around the campfire that night, though, Isolde's mind was the least burdened. For her, there was some comfort, some higher purpose in this quest. No matter how dark the road became, it still seemed to Isolde that it was the right road. If she died in the passage of the Black Mountains or in the uncharted lands beyond, still she would die as she must die, following in Valour's footsteps. She laid aside her water skin and her bundle of food and began to sing a homely, happy little campfire song she had learned on her travels.

Shiloh

Come in out o' darkness
Rest ya here a while
Watch the flames go dancin'
And the embers smile

Hear the golden fingers
Play their little song
If ya know the melody
Then sing along

Sing,
'Hiss, hiss, crackle, crackle
Lean in close
Thaw yer fingers and yer frozen toes'
Sing,
'Hiss, hiss, crackle, crackle
Wood burns bright
Through the mist and shadow
o' the fallin' night'

Orin had heard the song before. He tapped out a rhythm as she sang. Meanwhile, Amos watched the others: the older man he hardly knew, the beautiful stranger, and Simeon. He sat with his blue eyes fixed on the ground, his calloused hands tenderly holding an iron lantern.

Amos was reminded of him as a little boy, pale and thin, refusing to leave his friend to face Hadrian's wrath alone. Simeon had never been the strongest or the fastest, but a current of stubborn determination ran through his veins. Once he'd set his mind to do something, he'd see it through. No matter the cost. Once he'd set his heart on someone, he'd fight for him. He'd fight for her. To the end.

Amos was reminded, too, of how he and Simeon had made plans to escape the Shadow when they were boys. It had seemed so easy then, as if they could march right up to the Shadow Lord and command him to be gone. There was a sweet sadness to the memory, and with it came a wrenching pain that began in his head and belly and radiated out to his fingertips and toes. The Nogworms. He moaned, gripping his gut and doubling over against Isolde.

"Water!" she called out to Simeon. "I think 'e needs water!" He tossed her a skin, but Amos refused it, swearing it was poison, that it only intensified his pain.

"Take these then." Isolde handed him a wad of nightshade leaves. "Fer yer shoulder."

Amos stuffed the wad inside his cheek.

"I keep it with me always," Isolde continued, moving her tunic aside to reveal jagged scars on her right shoulder.

"Wolf?" Amos asked.

"Dragon," she said, and saw his surprise. "Don't tell me that Amos, the boy who slew the Shadow Wolf with fire from 'is mouth, has never seen a dragon!"

He looked away.

"I grew up with the tale of Amos, Wielder of Fire. My sister . . ." Isolde dropped off, reaching to touch the braid that wrapped her forehead.

"You've not told us yer story, Isolde," Orin said.

"Another time, perhaps." She tossed a branch onto the fire. "I'll take first watch," she offered and said no more.

The next day, the landscape changed drastically. The light overhead remained thin and weak, the tops of the trees indistinguishable. The water rushed along beside them, often dropping in foamy, white cascades. But now, the land on the other side of the river rose higher and higher, and, instead of forest, they looked over at sheer rock cliffs. To the left of the River Lost, where they traveled, the change in the landscape was even more remarkable. Here and there, among the innumerable black trunks, were trees as white as Brand's snowy mane. They were startlingly bright. And their color was not the most marvelous thing about them. Their roots seemed to be all above the ground, twisting and interweaving across the forest floor, encircling the trunks of the surrounding trees.

The company led the horses along the edge of the river, knowing the animals would struggle to find their footing in the maze of roots. But Brand and Willa and Echo grew restless as they traveled. At midday, when the pallid light of the forest had reached its peak, they were attacked again.

Amos saw them first: five sets of eyes glaring down from the ridge on the opposite side of the river.

"Sim!" he shouted, pointing up at the wolves.

This was a much more serious attack than they had yet faced. They had their torches, yes, but there was nowhere to run for safety. The roots of the white trees kept the horses from moving with any speed, and only the river stood between predators and prey. To his right, a bow twanged. Isolde sent a flaming arrow right into the heart of the pack, and with a rushing of wind the first beast was gone. Simeon and Orin joined in, leasing a volley of fiery arrows on their attackers.

But Amos, surely the most dangerous of the group, hesitated. One of the wolves was watching him, its green-gold eyes fixed on his face. The predator had marked its prey. All of a sudden, Amos was keenly aware of the mark of the Wolf branded into his chest. While the others emptied their quivers, he watched the pack grow. More and more eyes appeared over the edge of the cliff, and then the pack divided, some skidding down the rocky descent to the river and others moving forward along the ridge.

Brand reared up, pawing at the air. Willa screamed. There was no more time to consider. They had no choice.

"Go!" Orin shouted. He slapped the animals' backs and sent them running into the wood. "All o' ya. Now!" He turned and ran after the horses, dropping his torch as he fled.

Amos was first to go, then Simeon. Isolde shouted at Echo to go on ahead. But the horse waited for her. When at last she turned and ran, the brown mare followed . . . followed but would not over-take her. Echo was guarding Isolde from the rear.

Without any plan, without any clear sense of direction, they ran, zigzagging through the trees. They could hear the panting of the wolves and the rumbling growls that filled the forest as the ani-mals closed in. They pushed themselves harder, leaping over stones, nearly tripping on the myriad white roots that snaked across their path.

A dozen wolves, perhaps more, were gaining on them. These monsters never tired. They moved in like fog, surrounding their prey. And the flashing green of the leader's eyes sent trickles of cold sweat down Amos's back.

A terrible scream cut through the trees behind them. Ahead, to the right, Orin roared in rage and pain. In the instant before the wolves reached Amos, his foot caught on a large white root, raised a few inches off the ground. He lurched forward, knowing his end had come. But his knee, instead of landing on the floor of the forest, bumped into another root that appeared from nowhere. His arms, held in front of him to break his fall, caught hold of yet another root. The tree was helping him. Its white roots had risen to form a sort of ladder. He scrambled into the branches, out of reach of the wolves, and hoisted Simeon up behind him.

They turned to look for the others and saw Isolde rushing back to defend Echo. One wolf had descended on the horse, and another bore down on Isolde. Simeon took his bow from his shoulder and snatched up the last of his arrows. He locked eyes with Amos, and the arrow burst into flame before it ever left the string. Simeon's shot was fierce and true. It whistled through both wolves, dissolving them into vapor, and landed on the forest floor half a pace behind Echo.

"Isolde, the tree!" Amos called to her, but she hovered over the wounded horse. "It's you they want!" She tore herself away and scurried into the branches of the nearest tree.

"Boys!" Orin shouted from another of the white trees. Blood dripped from his left leg, staining the bright bark as it fell. At the base of the three trees the wolves circled, snapping. "What now?"

Amos followed the movements of the green-eyed wolf as it pulled away from the group.

As if in answer, dozens of white roots rose up and snaked around the paws, the tails, the backs of the wolves, dragging them into the ground.

There were muffled yelps, as black soil closed over them, and then . . . silence.

"Take comfort, Children of the Morning," said a voice. It came from somewhere between the two branches where Simeon and Amos were perched. They searched the tree for the source of the voice. Deep grooves ran up and down the white bark, sometimes curling in perfect circles. And there were smaller grooves that cut across the others. One of these opened when the voice spoke again.

"The Shadow cannot touch you while you rest in my shade," it said. The two men realized at once that the horizontal slash in the bark was the tree's mouth. The grooves above were eyes — beautiful eyes, sparkling with life. And the curling circles resembled hair that wrapped around the creature's face.

"I am Sylva." The slightest movement in the lines of bark drew her face into a smile, and the bark around her face swirled. "I am older than the Shadow. It holds no terror for me."

Recognition dawned on Simeon's face. "Grosvenor! Are *you* the tree from the songs and tales? The tree o' the White Bow?"

"No. Another of my kin gave the White Bow to Grosvenor. For you, there is help of a different kind."

"Can ya lead us ta the Hall o' Shadows?" Simeon asked. Phebe was never far from his thoughts, and with every hour that passed, he felt a greater urgency to find her.

"No. But Ezra waits for you at the parting of the rivers. He has much to tell, much to give."

"Ezra?"

"Yes," Sylva answered. "Ram and the Bright have not forgotten you." The travelers did not understand her words, but the sight of a White Tree come to life out of legend and song had lifted their hearts.

"There's hope, then?" Simeon asked.

"Always," she said. "But you must hurry. Time slips away. The days are fleeting."

The roots that had dispatched their enemies rose in gentle steps to their feet, and Simeon and Amos stepped down onto the forest floor.

Isolde hurried to Echo's side. Orin was slower in coming. When his feet touched the ground, he tore a strip of cloth from his tunic and wrapped it around the wound in his leg.

"You'll need your horses." The roots of the trees spoke to each other in some unknown language, root touching root, one after another, and pulling aside to form a path. As soon as the way was cleared, Brand and Willa trotted up, tossing their manes and stamping. They nosed Echo and whinnied as Isolde helped the brown mare to her feet.

Simeon greeted Willa and took the lantern that hung from the saddle. He lifted it, opened one side, and blew softly, illuminating a circle of darkening forest. He turned to Sylva as the travelers set out toward the river.

"Thank you." Simeon said. "May the light shine upon you."

She brightened at the phrase, her bark flowing around her face. "And you," she replied.

Thirty-Two

The images flashed before him: black shapes silhouetted against flames. There was a cottage with fire leaping out of the windows, illuminating the slate tiles on the roof. There was a tiny ember, a pinprick of fire that brought the hay to life and pulled the stable down around the screaming horses. There were the clansmen who had heard of his coming and organized an attack. They were consumed in a great inferno, a wall of fire that Amos cast before him as he came.

There was a boy who had run to defend his father, who had cried out and slumped to the ground as line upon line of darkness was wrapped around him. And then he was gone. Amos had destroyed the boy as surely as if he'd sent an arrow through his heart or burned the flesh from his bones. In the wake of that encounter, the old fear had returned, and the fire in his veins had cooled. But he had not understood. Mordecai had offered him the path of power. Amos had nothing to fear. Nothing. What, then, was the trembling inside him?

Echo was badly wounded, with long, bloody gashes across the back of her right thigh. Isolde would not ride her. She led her limping along and spoke quietly into her ear. Orin, too, could do little more than limp, though Brand could bear him easily when the terrain allowed. One of the wolves had bitten deep into his left thigh, and his face was pale and drawn.

Their food stores were dwindling, their water supply nearly exhausted. While Amos and the horses drank from the river, the others would not touch it, for it sprang from the same source as the River Meander. As night fell again on the mountains, they camped by the River Lost.

"Think there's anything worth eatin' in this forest?" Isolde asked.

"I've seen rabbits, snakes, some small birds, but no deer or elk." Orin's voice was soft and strained.

"I grow weary o' this venison," she said, tossing a little piece of the dried meat into the fire and rising to sling her bow over her shoulder. She returned to the camp after a short time, carrying a large gray rabbit by the ears.

"Well, men o' Shiloh, great warriors and skilled artisans that ya are, do ya think ya might do the cookin' tonight?" She laughed and tossed the rabbit to Simeon, who took his dagger from his belt and started to skin it.

Isolde knelt down to pat Echo's flank, lifting the awkward bandage to survey her wounds. "Don't suppose we've got any mandrake root?" she said, to no one in particular.

Simeon tossed her a bundle from the pouch on his belt. "Here," he said. "We treated Orin's leg while you were gone."

"What's that?" Isolde asked, noticing how the firelight flashed on a shiny object protruding from Simeon's pouch.

"'Twas Phebe's," he said, without taking it out.

All at once, Isolde knew. This was it. It had been here all this time. The realization struck her with the force of a hundred arrows. Valour's Glass. "May I see it?"

Simeon took it carefully from the pouch and passed it to Isolde. She examined the inscription. "Until the day breaks, and the Shadows flee away," she read aloud, and laughed at the absurd turn of events. "This belonged ta Valour! It was a gift from the gods. I've dreamed o' findin' this glass fer as long as I can remember. I've searched the whole o' Shiloh fer it! How did it come ta Phebe?"

"A gift from the gods?" Simeon asked. The tale of Valour's Glass was well known to the remnant of the Lost Clan, but not to the rest of Shiloh. "I know nothin' of how it came ta Phebe. She didn't know the value o' the thing."

"I found it," Amos said.

"Drawn to it, I suppose," Isolde said. "Like a true son of Evander."

A memory flashed into Amos's mind: his father, seated before the hearth in their little cottage, taking pride in the insults of the villagers. "Mad as Evander, eh?" he had said. The memory felt like a dagger in his belly.

"'Twas chance. I saw a light off the Hunter's Path, and I took it. That's all."

"And yet ya find yourself here, journeyin' over the Black Mountains, just as Evander did." Isolde's eyes held a challenge, but Amos said nothing.

There was silence for a time. Isolde found it difficult to look away from Valour's Glass. The logs on the fire cracked and split and the juices from the roasting rabbit fell hissing into the embers.

Then Orin spoke up. "What gives *you* claim ta the glass, Isolde?"

"It belongs ta my people, my clan."

"Yer people?" Amos asked. "Evander's clan?"

"Not all the Lost Clan was lost." She hesitated, hating to admit the truth. "Some remained."

Only a few days earlier, this revelation would have stunned the men, but not here, after all they had seen.

"Take up the glass then, daughter o' Valour, and tell us what ya see," Amos returned her challenge. When she failed to act, Amos laughed. "You're afraid."

Isolde snatched the glass and stretched it to its fullest length. She took a deep breath, glared at Amos, then lifted the glass to her eye and peered through. Almost as quickly as she'd taken it up, she dropped it to her lap and tucked it into her belt.

"I see nothin'," she said. "Only dark forest . . . and trees." Her heart felt like stone within her, but she would never admit that to the others.

Amos snorted and reclined on his side, propping himself on his elbow. "What did ya expect ta see? The sun, perhaps? Or stars? A world *beyond* the Shadow?" He gave a bitter laugh. "I've traveled all over this black land, and you can be sure there's nothin' beyond the Shadow, nothin' more than Shadow. Only a madman goes in search o' what isn't there!"

"Yer da believed there was more." Simeon's voice came soft and clear from the edge of the firelight, and his eyes searched Amos's face. When Amos refused to meet his gaze, he stood and left, his pale hair and worn gray tunic disappearing into the darkness of the forest.

Simeon returned to the campfire long after the others had fallen asleep. He fell down onto his blanket, and slept, and dreamed. He stood in a long avenue, lined with towering trees. Their branches stretched high, and on each hung a little glass orb, like a drop of water suspended in air. Mist swirled within them, and eyes stared out of them: the eyes of little children and men and women. Phebe's voice called to him. *"Simeon! Simeon!"* But he could not see her. He ran up and down the lane of trees, searching the faces behind the glass. He followed the sound of her voice, searching frantically and crying her name. At last, he saw her, eyes fixed before her, dark hair swirling with the mist. "Phebe!" he cried. He reached out to touch the glass, to touch her, and she vanished. "Phebe!"

He woke to find Isolde crouching over him, her hand on his shoulder. "I thought ya might be a Dreamer," she whispered. She offered him what was left in her water skin and sat down beside him. "Chosen o' the gods, they say. Blessed."

"Dreams are no blessing. They show what I cannot change, what I cannot bear ta see!"

"Ya saw 'er?"

"Aye."

Isolde took a cloth and bathed the sweat from his forehead. "She was lovely. I saw 'er that night in the white gown so richly embroidered. She must've been much loved."

Simeon's face was stricken. He placed a hand on the lantern that rested by his blanket. Phebe's lantern.

"Sylva said there was hope, Simeon. There must be some purpose fer the dreams."

"What about Maeve's dreams, Isolde?" Simeon turned to her and searched her face. "Was there purpose in those? Or was it some cruel trick o' the gods ta lure Evander and all yer clan, or *nearly* all yer clan, ta their deaths? Have we been drawn inta the same trap? Do we go to our deaths even now?"

"Ezra will know what ta do. It can't be long now."

"No, Isolde, it can't. She'll be out o' reach, beyond hope . . ."

Isolde could not bring herself to say more. She watched him there, his pale eyes fixed on the lantern as if it were Phebe herself, until sleep took her.

Thirty-Three

They argued the next morning, as they ate the cold remnants of the roasted rabbit and stashed their blankets under the horses' saddles. "I say we find the source o' the river first," Amos insisted. "We know nothin' about this Ezra."

"We can't refuse the aid o' the gods!" Isolde argued. "Orin is badly injured, and Echo . . ." She flicked her hand toward the two. Orin was leaning against a tree while the others packed up. He was pale. The bandages had not fully staunched the bleeding in his leg. Echo was drinking from the river. The bandage over the gashes on her thigh was caked with dark blood, and she stumbled as she backed away from the riverbank. "Besides," Isolde said, tying an empty water skin to Willa's saddle, "we need water."

Simeon wanted to side with Amos, to argue against any delay. But when he looked at Orin, he knew the man's life was in danger. He was in desperate need of help, miraculous help. Simeon wondered suddenly if he would have to choose between Orin's life and Phebe's. It was a decision he couldn't possibly make . . . not now, at least. So he put off his choice.

"Either way, we follow the river."

Their journey grew more difficult as they traveled north. They were climbing ever higher into the mountains now, and the river fell away until it snaked along a deep gorge far below. They saw no more wolves and no more white trees, and they rode largely in silence. Something about that country made them reluctant to speak. Except for the distant noise of rushing water, the swishing of the horses' tails, and the groaning of leather, it was oppressively still.

They began to notice great piles of stones scattered here and there on either side of the river. At first, the tumbled stones seemed a part of the changing terrain. But it soon became clear that these were ruins. There were remnants of towers and walls cut through with crumbling archways. On some of the arches, the travelers could make out the sign of the Clan of the Builder. The watchtowers. And as they struggled on, Simeon thought on the fate of the sons of Burke and wondered how closely those servants of the Shadow still kept watch on the abandoned towers.

"Abner never told me what power Ulff gave ta the stargazers." Simeon whispered to Amos as they led Brand and Willa up a steep rise.

Amos was slow to answer. "He changed 'em . . . their eyes, their bodies."

"Aye, but why do men fear them so?"

"I've never seen the stargazers, but the Shadow Lord's curse was fittin'. He took those who sought ta draw out the secrets o' the stars and doomed them ta draw out somethin' else instead."

"What?"

"The secrets of men."

Simeon shuddered and was silent. They plodded along the river, until Orin fell from Brand's saddle and lay in a heap on the ground.

Simeon rushed to his side and placed an arm under the older man's shoulder. Orin's eyes were closed, his mouth tight and drawn.

"Orin! Orin, can ya speak?" Simeon watched as Orin tried to swallow. The loss of blood, the lack of water — he would not last long in this state.

"Sim," Orin managed, opening his eyes a little. "Forgive me. I've failed ya yet again." He tried to swallow.

Simeon lowered him to the ground and touched the bandage on his leg. He looked to Isolde.

"If Orin can stay in the saddle, will ya take him ta Ezra? Brand can carry ya both, and we'll follow behind with Echo."

She nodded and gave a longing look back at her mare.

"She'll only slow ya down. Don't worry, Isolde. She'll be alright." Amos and Simeon hoisted Orin on top of Brand and secured him to the saddle as best they could. Orin leaned against the horse's snow-white mane and looked at Simeon.

"I don't want ta leave ya here, my boy. This place . . ." His eyes closed. Simeon grasped his hand and fought to control his rising emotion as Isolde mounted the white stallion and rode ahead, fading into the mist and shadow of the mountains.

The silence around them was thickening. The air was heavy with . . . something. Expectation, perhaps, or foreboding. Their presence among the ancient watchtowers had not gone unnoticed.

In the darkest hour of the night, he came. His skin was deathly white, and the pale wings that rose above his shoulders made him look much taller than a normal man. The white feathers of his wings darkened as they descended, ending in a luminous blue. White straps studded with silver-blue stones hung over each shoulder, intersecting in the middle of his chest and wrapping into a belt. From the belt, white cloth draped to his knees. He was beautiful.

Amos had been sleeping when the creature arrived. Simeon was on watch, if such it could be called. The blackness around him was so complete, he had to rely on his ears to tell him when danger might be approaching from somewhere outside the small circle of light cast by Phebe's lantern. The two had camped in a ruin, under the shelter of an arch marked with the sign of the Star Clan. The sign reminded Simeon of Orin. It had given him comfort. He'd rested against the arch and looked up into the unbroken darkness, surprised to see a light moving from the east, falling in an arc. He had grabbed Amos's leg, shaking him from slumber, and the two had leapt to their feet, braced against an assault.

But the racing light had slowed, great wings beating the air and bringing the enemy to a gentle landing. They had taken in its pale skin, its smooth head, its eyes. And they were caught in the snare, spellbound. Eyes that were first white and opaque darkened to a black as lightless as the night around them. Simeon and Amos saw innumerable bright points moving inside those black globes. The tiny lights circling each other in Phebe's lantern were only a whisper of the depth and beauty of what they now beheld.

The stargazer took a step forward, spreading immense wings over and around his victims. Simeon hardly noticed when the fear within him emerged as cold sweat and clammy skin. But when his body withered, shrinking to the size of a small child, he began to sense that something was wrong. Instead of images of twinkling stars, he saw in the creature's eyes a picture of Hadrian hovering over him. The wicked man filled the sky, and Simeon shrank still more. He was so powerless. What was happening to him? And where was Amos? Surely Amos could save them. He glanced toward his friend, hoping to find him poised for battle. He did not.

From Amos, the stargazer drew out legions of wicked secrets. There were too many. They emerged as parasites, squirming and wriggling from every pore of his skin until they covered Amos's body, head to foot. They had long feasted on the decaying remains of his tortured mind, his wounded heart. Now they feasted on his flesh, and he screamed in agony. The sound chilled Simeon's blood. If he had had any faith in his own ability, Simeon would have fought to free his friend. But he had none. He was a trembling child again, paralyzed by fear, utterly helpless. He looked back into the stargazer's eyes to find an image of Phebe suspended high in a tree, far out of reach, crying for help. But he could do nothing. He was sure of it. He dropped to his knees, his heart hammering out his terror. He heard Amos scream again, and Simeon knew the stargazer was finishing his task. He cowered, covering his head with his hands, and waited for the end.

Then came a sound of consuming fire, burning through the forest with unspeakable speed and strength. He felt a rush of hot wind, heard the flapping of fiery wings. The roar of fire and wind rose to a fever pitch. Then all was still. Warm light broke into the clouded corners of his mind, and he saw the Neyla. Her face blazed with light; her voice echoed around him. *You see yourself through the eyes of the Shadow, Simeon. Do not be fooled. The Bright have preserved you for this day.*

In the midst of the battle, while Amos writhed on the ground beside him, Simeon willed himself to stand. He dropped his arms from his head, opened his eyes, and looked down at his body. It was no longer the body of a frightened boy. It belonged to a man. From his belt, he drew a dagger forged with his own hands. And he plunged it into the breast of the stargazer with a fierce cry.

The blade pierced the deathly white skin and stained it red. The creature threw back its head and screamed at the overhanging Shadow. It fell backward onto the rocky floor of the ruin. By the time it hit the ground, it was nothing more than a man, with dark skin and hair, and the sign of the Star Clan tattooed on his chest. One of the sons of Burke had gone back to the light at last.

Simeon knelt beside Amos. The loathsome parasites were thinning out, but very slowly, and Amos's eyes met Simeon's with a look of such despair, such shame. In that moment, Simeon was so overcome with pity that he forgave his friend for everything.

When the last of the parasites had disappeared beneath the surface of his skin, Amos surveyed the damage. His arms, legs, and chest were a solid mass of tiny wounds, and little flecks of blood oozed from the deeper ones. He raised a hand to his face and touched his cheek with a grimace. The skin was rutted and bleeding. His head fell back against the stony ground, and he looked up at Simeon with an odd smile.

"Sim, the warrior," he said.

They set out early the next morning, with Simeon leading the horses and Amos riding Willa. They descended a steep slope that brought them back to the banks of the river. This time Amos didn't touch the water, though the horses drank their fill.

As the day warmed to gray, they struggled to keep the river in sight. It dropped below them again, cutting a deep gash in the forest. Now the mountain slopes crashed into the water at a perilous angle, and men and horses were forced to climb rise after rise. Each was higher than the last, some jutting from the ground to immense heights, reaching up until their peaks were obscured by mist and Shadow.

The journey was a torment for Amos, but not because of his parching thirst and his stinging skin. He was haunted by the memory of a night long ago, when he had watched from the shadows as a man was lifted to a pile of stones and given back to the light. He had seen the fire move across the man's tunic, his boots, his hair. He had watched the golden-tongued monster devour the body until flames poured out of the darkening skull. He had felt the fear as never before.

Above him, the branches had creaked. Behind him, a cat had

hissed. On that night, he had known that the world was overrun with evil things, driven forward by the malice of the Shadow Lord. And he had known that he was among them, a pawn in the hand of darkness.

He would do anything, now, to have his father's guard on his arm, to feel his quiver hanging over his shoulder, to grip his old bow. He looked down at the ruin of his body. What had he become? What had he done to himself? To Phebe? To Simeon? To so many nameless innocents? And how could it ever be undone?

Thirty-Four

s the light of that day waned, they came to the end of their northward journey along the river. Here was the diverging of Meander and Lost. Ahead, a narrow stone bridge crossed a deep rift in the mountains, a rift cut by the Meander as it made its journey west. To their right, the Lost broke from its brother and cut its way south toward the moors.

Simeon led the horses across the bridge, hopeful that the crumbling rocks would hold the weight of both horses and men. Beneath him, only mist was visible, though he could hear the hollow echo of rocks tumbling into the water at the base of the canyon. Beyond the bridge, an overgrown path wound into the forest, leading them to an archway in an ancient stone wall. Vines wound over its surface, forcing their way through the cracks in the stones, and the roots of a time-worn tree curled down from the top of the wall. Simeon led the horses under the archway, walking into the ruins of what was once a great castle or fortress. This first room was open to the sky, and differed very little from the forest outside. But farther in, Simeon could see a room with a stone roof. Inside, a fire crackled.

"You are welcome here, Warriors of Light." The sound of the voice was followed closely by the man himself. He was radiant, ageless, and he smiled as he took Simeon's hand in both of his.

"Call me Ezra. I'm so glad you've come." His eyes took in everything, from the weariness in Simeon's face to the wounds on Echo's thigh. And he looked long at Amos. "Please," he said, "come in and rest. There's water in the basin, bread on the table by the fire. Isolde can take the horses."

"Simeon!" Isolde rushed from the interior of the ruin and wrapped him in a hasty embrace. "What's happened?" she asked, when she caught sight of Amos.

"An attack. Will ya help me?" Together, they eased Amos from Willa's saddle and helped him to a cot in a side room. Isolde leaned over Amos, searching for some place to rest her hand, to reassure him, to comfort him. But there seemed nothing she could do that would not cause him more pain. She laid a hand on Simeon's shoulder instead.

"Orin's sleepin' in another room. I'll go and tend the horses."

In that place, among the sundry corridors with their fading engravings, there was a quiet, a peace. Though the rooms were lit with the usual fires and lanterns and candles, there was an otherworldly brightness in them. Outside, the wind howled through the gaps in the mountains. Wolves and worse stalked their prey. And the Shadow covered all. Inside, the travelers found refuge.

Amos's skin, bathed many times in water from a deep well, was nearly healed at the end of one day. When another had passed, Orin's color had returned, though he was still very weak and walked with effort. By the end of the third day, when Echo's leg was sound and their supplies had been replenished, Simeon was growing restless. He was gathering their few belongings and making whispered plans with the others when Ezra approached him. The extraordinary man had hardly spoken since their arrival, choosing instead to focus all his efforts on healing the wounded. So Simeon was surprised when he asked them to stay.

"You've been most kind, Ezra, but we have ta get movin'."

"Where?" Ezra asked, as though he knew nothing of their quest.

"The Hall o' Shadows. Have ya forgotten?"

With maddening calm, he asked, "What will you do when you reach the hall?"

"I hoped you'd tell me that, Ezra!"

The others came at the sound of Simeon's voice, and Ezra beamed at each of them in turn. "Time is short, Simeon, and I would not keep you from your love. Tomorrow you leave, with gifts to help you on your journey. But first, a story."

"A story?" Simeon asked. "Now?"

"Your journey has been dark and weighted with Shadow, but surely you could not so soon forget the power of story."

Amos pulled up a chair, remembering with great pain and regret his father's fireside stories. Isolde took a seat on the hearth, her heart aching for one of Rosalyn's tales. Orin sat on the floor and stretched his wounded leg. Simeon was left standing, gaping at his friends. And it was not until Ezra began to speak that he sank into a chair and allowed himself to drift on the current of Ezra's words.

In the beginning, there was Ram. He was alone and apart from everything, and he was great and joyful and immensely strong and good. To begin, he created the sun, round and red and gold, and he loved its brightness and its warmth. But the sun shone down on an empty world, and Ram was grieved. He looked at the void and longed to fill it with color and life.

So Ram created other creators to help him fill the emptiness. Three sons and three daughters burst into being from the soil of Ram's thought. Leander, Rurik, and Vali were fierce, daring, brave. Petra, Callista, and Riannon were strong, beautiful, wildly free. These sons and daughters of Ram, like their father, were not bound by flesh. They could see into one another and discern one another's minds. And whenever one of the immortals (for so they came to be called) saw in another immortal an image that matched something in his own mind, that image came to life.

Leander and Riannon shared many visions of wild creatures, and it was not long before the world was filled with soaring birds and creeping beasts. Vali and Petra shaped the mountains, great windswept peaks tipped with snow, and Riannon and Callista formed the flowers, soft purple heather and delicate wild roses.

In this way, Shiloh was filled with life, and the immortals, at times, even created other immortals to share in their work. At the birth of Linden, trees spread over the land, gathering into forests and hedging the meadows, their great branches stretching toward the sky. Some of the trees were touched by Ram, and they took on a spark of the life of the immortals. At Maya's birth, rivers cut through earth and stone, laughing and rollicking their way across the land. Ram was so delighted that he filled the waters with nymphs, shimmering creatures whose eyes sparkled in the light of the sun.

But Rurik, as yet, had taken no part in creation. He went to his brothers, Leander and Vali, searching their minds for some vision that matched his own. It was not to be found. He went to his sisters, but neither Petra nor Callista shared any thought with him. Rurik was angry at this, for his brothers and sisters shared in their father's work and their father's glory, but he did not. He wished, in fact, that he might create alone, bringing into existence the thoughts of his own mind as only Ram could. It was not until Rurik went to Riannon that he discovered some trace of himself, for Riannon was the wildest of Ram's children and she, too, longed to be free of the immortals' one restraint. In her heart, as in her brother's, a dark sliver of rebellion resided. Riannon was neither cruel nor wicked, but, like the wind, she could not be contained, and she *hardly knew what she did when she stood face to face with her brother and brought into being the Shadow.*

The speaker's voice mingled with the crackling of the fire on the hearth, weaving from nothing a vast world of beauty and terror.

There was a hush in the Mount of the Immortals when the Shadow came, and all creation held its breath as what began as a point of darkness between Rurik and Riannon spread black fingers over the whole of Shiloh. Leander raged as every beast fled in fear from the Shadow. Vali turned his face from the darkened peaks of the mountains. Petra screamed as the Shadow blanketed the surface of the waters, and Callista wept when darkness drained the color from every leaf and wildflower. But it was Ram whose grief was greatest. The Shadow made a mockery of the sun, his first creation, and it made a mockery of all the glorious creative work of his children. Still, when they turned to their father and cried out with one voice for him to destroy the darkness, Ram did not. Rurik and Riannon were the work of his own hands, the vision of his own mind, and he would no more destroy their creation than he would destroy them.

Instead, he spoke, and the Shadow that had spread to the edges of the horizon stood still. In the east rose Aurora, hand outstretched to hold back the darkness. She blazed with orange and golden light. In the west, Vespera rose up, hedging in the night with brilliant reds and purples. Ram spoke again, and the immortals gasped as countless points of light broke through the night above them. Vega was illuminating the darkness with a thousand silver stars. Her sister, Selene, soon followed, appearing low on the horizon, shining round and pale against the black sky.

So the darkness was contained, held in check by sunrise and sunset, and moon and stars kept the night from ever reigning supreme in Shiloh. Then Ram returned to the Mount of the Immortals, and his children followed, but Rurik lingered in the Shadow. He felt no sorrow for what he had done. Rather, he felt a sense of wicked delight, for he believed he had created something more powerful than any force in Shiloh. And that made Rurik, in his own mind, the greatest of all the immortals.

Ezra's words rushed over them like wind, like water. They breathed them in, lapped them up, yearning to hear and to know, at last, the truth that had hovered, all their lives, just outside their reach.

It did not take long for Rurik to convince Riannon to partner with him again in creation, for though she harbored some regret, still she felt more of a kinship with Rurik than with any of the other immortals. One night, far from the Mount, Rurik and Riannon gave life to two daughters and a son. Infinite freedom and dark ambition gave birth to Fury, Savage, and Miri. Riannon never questioned her decision until the Shadow Wolves came.

While Ram and the Bright Immortals reveled in the beauty of their work (stained though it was by the Shadow), Rurik reveled in the power of his. He wore the darkness like a cloak, as a sign of his strength. And like his father, Savage loved nothing better than to dwell always in darkness. The two shared many visions of dark things, but their greatest collaboration spawned the Shadow Wolves: not one beast, or even a few, but a host of wicked wolves who moved silently through the night, stalking their victims and devouring them with darkness. They filled the forests of Shiloh, using the Shadow to prey on the innocent.

One evening, Riannon hovered on the edge of a meadow not far from the castle where she and Rurik now dwelt. As she watched Vespera rise up and usher in the night, a doe crept into the open with her young fawn. Riannon watched them with a sort of motherly tenderness. Her children had never been babes, had never been helpless, but they were born from her heart and mind, and she was fond of them and fiercely protective. Riannon's thoughts were interrupted by a low, calculating growl and a sudden rustle of leaves. She watched as doe and fawn fled in fear from the Shadow Wolf, as the monster overtook them and tore them limb from limb. It was more than Riannon could bear, for it was she and Leander who first shared the vision of soft eyes and red-brown fur, of delicate legs and twitching ears. No creator, no mother could endure the sight of such vicious cruelty. She raced home, full of horror over the part she had played in Rurik's dark work and fearing his next move. Only Miri could be found near the castle, so Riannon snatched her daughter into her arms and made for the Mount of the Immortals.

Riannon was wild and swift indeed, and she would have been long safe in the Hall of the Immortals had not Fury seen her rushing from their home. Fury felt betrayed for her father's sake and her own. In her haste, Riannon had rescued her youngest daughter but spared no time to seek out her eldest. Fury raced to her father in a rage and told him of Riannon's betrayal.

Cloaked in darkness, and moving with enormous speed and stealth, he tracked mother and daughter to the river. Riannon was moving lightly over the water, hardly rippling its surface, but Miri had pulled away from her and hung back. Something about the water frightened Miri, filling her mind with dark visions. Her hesitation was Rurik's invitation. He leapt from the riverbank, throwing the full force of his strength against Miri and forcing her beneath the surface of the water. She thrashed and struggled, and the fight was bitter, but the outcome was inescapable. Not even an immortal can overpower her creator.

A shudder ran through the river, and Miri was no more. She dissolved in a haze of black that spread through every ripple, raced along every current, leached its poison into every drop of water. The water nymphs could not escape. Their sparkling eyes dulled to pale blue and livid green, and their bodies fell into decay.

Riannon, once wild as the wind, was still as stone. Anguish and sorrow and rage and regret swept over her with such force that she could neither move nor speak. She hovered over the water, watching the river darken to the shade of her daughter's blood, until Rurik bound her in such chains as only the immortals know and carried her back to his castle.

Ezra paused in his telling, and the room was still until Isolde broke the silence with a thought and a question.

"I've never heard the story of Riannon so told, Ezra. Why?"

"Too much has been lost, too much forgotten. You will understand soon enough, Isolde." He let out a slow breath and began again.

So began the War of the Immortals, for the murder of Miri and the capture of Riannon were crimes too unspeakable to be ignored. Yet the battles of the Bright and Dark Immortals (as they came to be called), and all that was risked and lost, and the great and terrible deeds that were done live, in their entirety, only in the minds of the immortals. Little is known, for Ram thought the accounts too grievous to be recorded. In the end, the Bright Immortals were victorious, but not before the birth of another generation of immortals and the creation of man. This is how it happened . . .

The immortals did not primarily battle with weapons of war. Rather, they fought with the greatest power they possessed: the power to create. They believed that creating other immortals to oppose the work of the enemy was the surest road to victory. The Bright brought forth Olwen and Shula, Penelope and Colm, Ezra and Oriole and Cyrus. These all were born into a world at war, and, for a time, they knew nothing else. Nothing of the wonder of Shiloh in its infancy, when the dew was still wet on the grass, and not a petal of a single flower was darkened by the Shadow.

Rurik took a new name. He became Ulff (the Wolf), ruler of the Dark Immortals. He and his children also battled creatively, though they always gave life to dark and horrible imaginings. Morrison and Erebus, Tacitus and Hadrian, Cecilia and Leto never knew the rule of Ram or any world apart from the Shadow, but it suited their nature, and they served the Shadow Lord without question. Meanwhile, Riannon languished in the bowels of the prison that was once her home. Sorrow and regret were her only companions as, outside in the wide world, the immortals sought to destroy each other.

For the listeners, the immortals suddenly came to life. They had heard of Linden and Olwen, of Morrison and Erebus. But until this night, the immortals had never had faces. Penelope, Giver of Dreams, took on form and shape and purpose. She was born out of need, to heal a broken world. And she was only one of many.

"Ezra?" Isolde was first to find a voice. "You're the Ezra o' the story? An immortal? A god?" She meant no insult. It merely came as a shock to discover that she had spoken and eaten with one who had watched the passing of thousands of years of history.

"Indeed, Isolde," he replied.

"And Hadrian," Amos added. He and Simeon had exchanged glances as soon as the name was mentioned.

"It was he who led the shifters into battle against Evander and his men," Ezra explained.

The Nelya were born during the War of the Immortals, springing from the minds of Vega and Shula. Music too, and story were created to battle the deep, empty silence that Tacitus brought into Shiloh. Ulff created the shifters with the help of Cecilia, and these became one of his very favorite creations. He used them to murder Colm and Cyrus, disguising his servants as Bright Immortals and luring the two into a trap. That was a very dark moment in the war, and it was the moment when Ram stepped in.

To contain the destruction, Ram had to limit the power of the immortals. No longer could they create gods or monsters, nothing bright and strong enough to dwell in the Mount of the Immortals, nothing wicked enough to blanket the world in eternal darkness or sorrow. The immortals could create nothing that would last forever.

So flowers budded and bloomed and shriveled and died, and others rose up to take their place. So the animals fed on one another and were eaten in their turn. So summer turned to winter and dawn to darkest night. And the mighty immortals were humbled. Now nothing they made could either draw Shiloh closer to its former glory or draw it down into death at last.

For a time, the fighting ceased. A great silence settled over the land. The Bright and Dark Immortals were suspended at opposing ends of a strange and fleeting peace. They waited, and the world was still.

Then Ram began again. He had been dreaming of a new creation, something still resembling himself, but altogether different from the immortals. This creature would be limited, bound by flesh and blood and bone. It would bear the mark of Ram, but neither Ram nor any of the immortals would hold power over it. "It will be altogether free," Ram thought, and in his heart he felt a pang for his lovely Riannon. So, one shining morning as Aurora welcomed the sun into the Mount of the Immortals, Ram made Man. And because he wished for Man to multiply, and because his sons and daughters always created in partnership with one another, he made Woman. Ram called them Children of the Morning. He clothed them with fragments of his own glory, and they shone bright, brighter even than the sun.

Ram was indeed so pleased with his work that he held a great feast and invited all the immortals to come and bestow gifts upon the Children of the Morning. He invited not only the Bright Immortals, but the Dark as well, being firmly set in his wish that Man and Woman should be utterly free to do as they chose, and this confounded his sons and daughters. Their war with Ulff and his children had not yet been won, and they feared their brother would send his armies against the Mount.

But their fear proved unfounded, for Ulff regarded his invitation to the feast with suspicion. Thinking that Ram had laid him a trap, Ulff remained in his castle during the whole of the celebration. In the end, only Leto, the youngest of the Dark, traveled to the Mount of the Immortals and quietly observed from an unseen corner.

Man and Woman stood together before the Seat of Ram, robed in green and blue and bright silver. Leander and Vali were the first to step forward. They blessed Man with boldness and courage. Next, Petra and Callista endowed Woman with strength and beauty. And there were many more gifts: gifts of craft, of dreaming and magic (Olwen blessed Man and Woman with power. Their hands, their voices, even their thoughts could shape the world around them). There was no greater moment in the history of Man, and if the moment had lasted, if Man and Woman had lingered in that glory, the history of Shiloh might have been very different.

If only Leto had not been there, watching from the shadows as the Bright claimed this new race for their own. Leto was mistress of all things hidden and forgotten. Her eyes were dull, and she was careless, but her power was immense. As the Bright Immortals grudgingly drew aside and Ram waited in silence, Leto walked slowly up to Man and Woman, lifted her hand, and swept it in an arc before the faces of the Children of the Morning.

"What you know, you will not long remember
Your names, your bright glory will fade.
You'll surrender your gifts to the Shadow
And forget by whose hand you were made."'

"No!" Isolde cried out. For Orin and Simeon and Amos, the feeling was much the same. As the story unfolded, their anticipation had turned to dread. They knew to what end the tale must come, and their anguish was as great as if Man had been cursed only yesterday.

"We felt as you do, Isolde," Ezra said. "We pleaded with Ram. But he would not break the curse any more than he would annihilate Leto."

"Why not?" Simeon asked.

Ezra shook his head as he answered. "Only Ram could say. I know he was grieved, though, as grieved as Ulff was delighted when he heard of Leto's 'gift.'"

It was not many days before everything changed. Man and Woman, like the last generation of the immortals, had only ever known a

Shiloh that hung in the balance between day and night, between sun and shadow. When Aurora rose at dawn and welcomed the sun, Man and Woman were fearless and bold, powerful and beautiful, and their radiance outshone the sun. But as Vespera ushered in the close of the day and darkness settled over Shiloh, they forgot their boldness, forgot that morning would indeed come again. They were afraid, and their glory was dimmed. They forgot their creator, their gifts, their allies. Even Selene, the shining moon, and Vega, who lit the darkness with ten thousand stars, could not convince Ram's last creation of any world filled with light and color. And every night was the same, until Ulff came.

The Shadow Lord left his dark castle, crossed the River Meander, now black with his daughter's blood, and prowled through the night in search of Man and Woman. When he found them huddled beneath the branches of a willow tree, trembling with fear, he disguised himself, exchanging his cloak of darkness for a robe of brilliant white. He smiled as he spoke.

"Children of the Morning," he said, calling them by their true names, "why do you cower in the dark?"

"We are alone and afraid," Man replied. "We cannot rest, cannot move from this place, or the darkness will devour us."

"In my kingdom," Ulff said, "there is no one who fears the night."

Man and Woman were awed by his glory, and they longed to be free from their fear.

"Ram has abandoned you," Ulff continued. "There is nothing for you here."

Man and Woman watched as the Shadow pulled away from the glaring light of his countenance, the leaves of the willow tree standing out in relief, vivid green against the black night beyond. They thought nothing of the soft glow emanating from their own skin.

The Shadow Lord extended a shining hand. "Come," he said. His eyes flickered with malice. "Come with me."

Blinded and deceived, forgetting everything that mattered, the Children of the Morning followed their new lord into the very heart of darkness. *And when the great iron gates of his castle closed behind them, Riannon's screams rang through the air. She vanished out of the world forever, leaving her chains on the floor of the dungeon.*

Isolde raged against the blindness, the stupidity of the Children of the Morning. How could Man and Woman be so easily, so thoroughly deceived? How could they have chosen the darkness?

Again, Ram stepped in, and what the people of Shiloh would later call the Great Cataclysm was nothing more or less than the victory of the Bright in the War of the Immortals. Man and Woman had chosen the darkness. Their decision could not be undone, but Ulff's kingdom could be contained. So Ram and his children, full of righteous fury over the death of Riannon and the capture of the Children of the Morning, did battle against the Shadow. They broke up the very foundations of Shiloh to set a boundary around Ulff and his kingdom.

Petra tore away at the ground, thrusting up the Pallid Peaks and the Black Mountains to the north and west of Shadow Castle. Maya, still grieving the death of the water nymphs, changed the courses of the rivers and broke open the fountains of the deep to form a great sea to the east of the castle. Linden called the trees to his aid, setting them in ranks to guard the darkness. Leander and Vali came in like the tide, driving the Shadow Wolves before them. And Ram, flanked by the gods of morning and evening, of star and sun, closed in on the Shadow, forcing it to its knees in one small corner of Shiloh. There Ulff and his children would be imprisoned forever, while light and glory and beauty reigned supreme and unchallenged in the wide world.

Still, Ulff had his captives, and his revenge. He took Leto into his every confidence, for it was she whose curse had delivered the Children of the Morning into his hands, and it was she who touched the rivers with a careless finger and infused every drop of black water with the awful power of her curse.

"Only the rivers?" Amos asked, remembering with regret his father's warning.

"Yes," Ezra replied. "Ram would not allow her to poison all the waters, even in the Shadow Realm. In fact, the water from the lakes and springs is healing water. It is a counter to Leto's curse." Here he smiled. "That is Maya's gift to the Children of the Morning." He returned his gaze to the firelight and finished the story.

Man and Woman had made their choice, and instead of waking from *a nightmare, they woke into one. And the worst of it, the greatest tragedy of all was that the Children of the Morning had forgotten the dawn. They woke in a world of Shadow, a world drained of color and beauty, and they did not weep.*

But Ram would not leave them without hope. He sent Shula, the Flaming One to give the gift of fire. "May the light shine upon you," she said, and she placed a flaming torch in Man's hand and vanished. Then Ram brought to life one last immortal. Omega rose up from the Mount itself, as strong and solid as the rocks from which she had sprung, and prophesied an end to Man's captivity.

"The Children of the Morning will dwell in darkness," she said, "only until the day breaks and the Shadows flee away."

"Valour's Glass!" Isolde said. "'Twas a gift from Omega."

"Yes," Ezra replied. He would have said more, but Amos erupted.

"You've given us no answers. What comfort is it ta tell us we'll languish in the darkness 'only until the day breaks?' When does the day break? Where? How? The words mean nothin'!"

"And what of Phebe?" Simeon added. "Have we any hope of findin' 'er, of savin 'er?!"

Ezra waited long to answer. Amos grew impatient and stormed from the room. Orin watched from a corner. Isolde stared at her lap. Simeon's eyes held Ezra's all the while. Beneath the radiant warmth of the immortals' face, there was a sadness.

"You see yourselves, I think, as very small. You look to me as though I hold infinite power and you hold none. Even now, you forget your glory, your gifts, your names." He sighed and leaned forward in his chair. "Small gifts I can give you, and provisions for your journey, for I have sworn to help you. But even I cannot tell the path of escape from the Shadow. None of the immortals can. It is a path only the Children of the Morning can find, a path only Ram himself could devise."

Simeon slumped in his chair, resting his forehead in his hand as Ezra stood. "There is always hope, Simeon — hope for Phebe, for all of you. Others have found the way. The Shadow could not hold them."

Thirty-Five

As Amos and Simeon loaded the horses' bags with supplies, Ezra pulled Isolde aside.

"Follow me," he said, and motioned her toward a long corridor that ended in a flight of stone steps. The staircase bore back into the wall for some distance before taking a sharp left and climbing steeply upward. Ezra moved swiftly; Isolde had to hurry to keep him in view. Higher and higher they climbed through what seemed like endless stone passageways. Sometimes the stairs would rise for great distances in one direction. At other times, they wound in tight circles.

Within half an hour, Isolde was exhausted. But just when it seemed her strength would fail her, she stepped out onto a landing at the peak of a craggy mountain. Two colossal towers jutted from the mountaintop. They were the highest points of the ancient watchtower, though their tops were broken and tumbled. Isolde's first thought was to look up, to search the sky for some glimpse of the stars as the sons of Burke had done. But overhead was only Shadow.

"Have you the glass?" Ezra asked.

"Aye." Isolde pulled the silver glass from her belt. "But it holds no magic anymore, Ezra. Not fer me, at least."

"For the daughter of Valour? The glass cannot be broken, Isolde, and it is yours by right. If it has failed you, it can only have been because the glass had nothing to show. Try it again. I brought you here, to the heights of the ancient watchtower, to give you the gift of sight."

Carefully, slowly, hardly daring to hope, Isolde lifted the glass to her eye. She winced and pulled back, then tried again, opening her eye gradually as she looked through the glass. Spread out before her was a world she had never seen, could not have imagined. What first caught her attention was the River Meander. The iron-black water shone a sparkling iridescent blue-green. Beyond the river, all the country bloomed with color: deep green leaves and rich brown soil, flowers of bright purple and blazing red and cheerful yellow. There was one thing in particular, though, that filled her with longing. It was the sky. Through the glass, Isolde could see no Shadow in the sky. No fog. No mist. It was clear and bright and wide open. She felt she could fly up into its liquid blue heights for a thousand years and never reach its end. And the sun was suspended in the midst of it: round and red and gold and unspeakably bright.

When she could bear no more, when her eyes had drunk their fill, she lowered the glass and looked to Ezra. "What magic is this?"

"Omega's glass reveals the world behind the veil of darkness, the world stripped of Shadow."

"Did Valour . . . did my people . . . ever see Shiloh in this way?"

"Valour saw only glimpses, and the glass was lost before ever she understood what she had seen."

"She died, then? Here, in the darkness?"

"Yes."

"And will I share her fate?"

"No, Isolde. I think not. But this glass and this gift are not for you alone. Your companions will need you in the days ahead. You go into deep darkness, blackness of darkness. More than ever, you cannot trust what your eyes may show you. Remember the glass." With that, he disappeared down the staircase into the heart of the mountain.

Horses and riders hastened along the stony floor of a narrow canyon, cutting a path to the eastern side of the Black Mountains. Isolde rode Echo, who tossed her mane and whinnied, glad to be moving again. Ahead of her, riding Brand, was Amos, his skin now clear and smooth. Simeon rode Willa at the head of the company. Orin was as yet too weak to travel, and Simeon hated to leave him behind. Were it not for Ezra's gift, he could not have done it.

"For you," Ezra had said, handing Simeon a woman's apron embroidered with the sign of the Star Clan. "It belonged to your mother. The Bright Immortals kept it when they drew you out of the River Meander, in memory of her."

Simeon had only stared back at Ezra, uncomprehending. But slowly, as if in a dream, scenes rushed before him: he saw Jada as she told him the true circumstances of his birth, saw the tiny blanket in Orin's cottage, saw the man himself as he told of his wife's drowning, saw the sign of the Star Clan tattooed on Orin's back as he beat the flames on Caedmon's tunic.

Ezra had smiled as Simeon's eyes grew large and his mouth fell open. "Son of Burke. Son of the Star Clan. Son of Orin."

Now, as he urged Willa around a rocky outcropping and through a narrow ravine, he savored the memory of his reunion with his father. Though nothing of substance would change about his relationship with Orin, Simeon felt somehow *whole* for the first time. And that knowledge gave him strength, even in so dark a place as this.

A night and a day they traveled along the base of the canyon, dreading their first sight of the country that waited on the other side of the mountains. The sound of rushing water grew as they went.

Too soon, the protective walls of the gorge began to sink, and the company was forced into the open. They led the horses up a steep embankment and surveyed their surroundings.

The air was close and wet, and full of the roaring of the mighty river that rushed past, hurrying westward to feed the voracious appetites of Meander and Lost. Mist rose from the ground like steam from a pot. It wrapped the travelers in strange eddies and currents. Ahead, ghastly light from many blue lanterns illuminated the skeletal timbers of a bridge. They all sensed, in a way that made them tremble, that they had never known darkness before this day. "Blackness of darkness," Ezra had called it.

A shriek cut through the mist. "Aaaaagh! It hurts! It hurts my eyes! Throw it in the river!"

They drew their daggers as a ghostly man appeared. He was thin as death and dressed in rags, and his eyes were wild and wide and fully white.

"Put it out! Drown it in the river!" He scratched and clawed at Simeon as he screamed. He was reaching for the lantern, feeling for it. While Amos and Isolde stood by with weapons at the ready, Simeon gaped, unsure of what to do, baffled by the attack of a blind man who fought to destroy a light he could not see.

Finally, Simeon blew into the lantern, extinguishing the light, and immediately the man was calm. He dropped his arms, turned, and, with a queer cock of his head, walked in the direction of the bridge.

They followed the madman, for the river blocked their path, and the bridge appeared to offer the only safe crossing.

A group of huts lay just beyond. Some were lighted with sickly blue fire, though what magic produced the light, none of them could tell. They heard the murmuring of many voices, the plodding of weary feet. Men and women, eyes white and unseeing, paced the well-worn paths that wound through the village. They wandered from hut to hut and back again or circled the huts unceasingly. They were filthy, and their clothes were threadbare, some hanging in shredded flaps from their bodies. And all of them were murmuring, whispering, muttering.

A haggard man made laps around his hut. And while he walked, he spoke one phrase: "Down under the darkness."

An old woman whispered as she shuffled from rock to tree and back, "No road out o' the Shadow, No road out o' the Shadow, No road out o' the Shadow . . ."

More grotesque still were the children. A young boy rocked on his heels, back and forth, back and forth. A little fair-haired girl skipped blindly along a muddy path chanting, "Gone, gone away ta the Hall o' Shadows, Gone, gone away ta the Hall o' Shadows . . ."

Isolde moved in closer, taking the torch from Amos's hand. She saw it first on the shift of a woman who leaned against the wall of her hut. It was embroidered in the hem. Then it appeared in iron, hanging around the neck of a young man. Another of the villagers drew the sign in the mud with a stick, then smudged it out with a wild slash of his arm and drew it again. The sign of the Sun Clan.

"No!" she cried, and covered her face with her hands. These were her people, the dying remnants of a mighty tribe. Here were the sons and daughters of the Sun Clan. At the height of their strength and boldness and vision, they'd been dismissed as mad, and the judgment had lain upon them for a thousand years. Now, in the Village of the Blue Lights, Isolde grieved to find that her people had indeed gone mad. But was it despair that drove them here or some dark curse? She reached out to touch the arm of the fair-haired girl who skipped along the path.

"Child," she said. But the girl pulled herself from Isolde's grip and skipped away, resuming her chant.

"What is this place?" Simeon whispered.

Isolde fought the tears that rose to her eyes. She had clung to the hope that her people had found a way out. To learn of Valour's death in the darkness was a cruel disappointment. To find the rest of the clan here, in this place, was unthinkable.

"'Tis the final home o' the Lost Clan, Simeon . . . my clan."

"Not all o' them, perhaps," he said. "Some may have continued on, may have finished the journey."

"Ta linger so long here . . ." Amos began, peering through the maze of huts. "Are they born this way? Born blind?"

Isolde approached a woman who walked in slow circles, clutching a little baby in her arms. The child blinked empty white eyes and stared at nothing.

"No more," Isolde said. "No more o' this." She touched the silver glass in her belt and stiffened her resolve. "If the Shadow takes me, then so be it. I won't stay here another moment."

They led the horses over the ghastly bridge, into a grove of trees on the south side of the river, leaving the Village of the Blue Lights and the Lost Clan behind them.

Not so very far away, suspended from a tree in a globe of crystal, Phebe waited. Her fingers tapped weakly against the walls of her prison, and her mouth opened in a silent scream. Soon, her hands would be forever stilled, her cries forever silenced. Time was slipping away.

Thirty-Six

Night was falling, if that distinction could be made in this lair of perpetual night, and the mist had grown so thick that they halted not far into the trees on the other side of the river. They spread their blankets, ate from the stores of food Ezra had sent and fell into their own reveries.

Amos rested his head on his right arm. On his left was a leather guard. A new quiver and bow lay on the ground just beside him. These had been his gifts from Ezra, and he was glad of them. He felt more like himself with a guard on his arm and a quiver and bow slung over his shoulder. As his aching muscles relaxed and he moved toward sleep, he mused on Ezra's words.

"Why have you come?" Ezra had asked.

Amos had felt a sinking inside him, like quicksand. "Fer Phebe," he had said.

"Yes, for her. But there is more that you seek, Amos. What is it?"

Amos had searched, digging deep, fearing the pain that would surely accompany the memories of his past. What was it he sought?

What had driven him into the path of darkness? And what was drawing him out of it?

"Amos, as a boy your father told you of Maeve's dreams, of Evander's quest, of the sons of Burke, of stars and sun, and a time before the Shadow fell. And you believed him?"

"Aye."

"You are a true son of Evander, born with courage and strength, born to see beyond the darkness." Ezra's eyes had burned through Amos as he spoke. "When did you forget? When did your eyes cease to really see?"

He had remembered Abner then, lying in his arms in the tangled undergrowth of the Whispering Wood, his lifeblood draining out on the ground. His chest had clenched tight within him, and he had felt he could not breathe for the pain.

"Why him? Why did 'e have ta die?"

Instead of answering the question, Ezra had asked another. "What did your father believe?"

Amos remembered his father's stories: of light and hope and a world beyond. But there was more. Amos thought back to the arguments he'd had with his father over going to the river or hunting in the forest alone. He'd always known that his father had been afraid — afraid for his family, afraid for himself. As much as he had spoken of light, as fiercely as he had clung to that hope, it was the Shadow that held sway over Abner.

Ezra's incandescent face had searched his, perhaps reading his thoughts.

"And your mother? What did she believe?"

Amos had remembered Wynn smoothing his hair and pinching his chin. He'd seen her sitting before the fire with the spindle, rocking and rocking. He had realized then, with a shock, that the memory brought no stabbing pain in his gut. Ezra's water had been the death of the Nogworms, and the last of them, writhing in forgotten corners of his body, had gone.

For the first time, it had come to Amos that his mother had believed herself helpless and vulnerable. When Abner had died, when Amos had failed to protect the flock from the cats, she had been certain of her doom, and she had given up.

"And Phebe?"

What his sister had endured during the years of his absence, Amos could not imagine. But he had recalled her lovely face on the night she was taken. He had heard her voice again, heard her plead with him to remember. And in return, he had snuffed out her last flicker of hope with careless fingers.

"What can I do? How can I save 'er?" he had asked.

"You were born with light, Amos, light that can pierce the Shadow. You have it still, dim though it has been these many years."

Ezra had smiled then, his eyes sparkling. "What do *you* believe?"

There was a foul stench in the air when Amos woke to the sound of Brand's stamping. He could hear Simeon's and Isolde's soft breathing next to him, but he could see nothing at all. The lantern was dark. He listened again, forcing himself to think past the reek that permeated the air. There was the sound of the horses' snorting and stamping. The sound carried farther than he would have thought possible. An echo, perhaps? No. There were other animals stamping in the distance, pawing at the earth. He was sure of it. He could hear the sound of their breathing, of hot breath drawn in and out of many nostrils.

"Sim, Isolde!" he hissed. They stirred and woke.

"What is it?" Simeon asked.

"We have ta get out, away from here. I fear fer the horses," he whispered.

Isolde was first to understand, first to move. Hastily, she stashed her blanket and climbed into Echo's saddle.

"The horses?" Simeon asked.

"Aye," Amos answered. "Hurry!"

He grabbed a torch, kindling it with bright fire. Simeon lit the lantern. They rode, dodging the dark trees that crowded the path of escape. Behind them and beside them the noises grew, as a black tidal wave rushed through the trees, close on their heels. Dark eyes reflected the firelight. Hoof-beats shook the ground. These were the Daegan. They stood taller than stallions, narrow-shouldered and thick-chested. Their coats were black, their manes short, and two spiraling horns jutted out from each head. The light glinted off the horns, their ends like daggers. And as they ran, as they closed in on their prey, they lowered their heads.

The trees of the wood were closing ranks. "Faster!" Simeon shouted.

There was an agonized scream from Brand, and Amos glanced down to see blood spilling from a gaping hole in the horse's hind-quarters as the monster's horn was drawn out. Amos took an arrow from his quiver and shot it deep into the shoulder of the Daegan. The beast only reared up, tossing its great head and preparing for another attack.

Amos cringed as he kicked Brand hard, urging the wounded animal onward. He thought he saw, up ahead, an opening in the trees. Brand surged forward as the Daegan's hooves hit the ground, and they raced for the opening, just a swath of white in a maze of black trees.

Another of the Daegan was closing in on Echo. The flashing black eyes and pointed teeth had come even with Echo's flowing mane when Isolde jerked her leg up and kicked the animal in the face. The toe of her boot gouged the eye out of its socket and sent the creature off its course. But others were nearby, their heads lowered, their great, spiraling horns pointed at the horses.

"We won't make it, Amos. We can't!" Simeon roared.

But Amos's face was fixed on the break in the darkness ahead.

As they closed in on the gap, Amos saw that the light was not an opening in the trees, and his heart sank. They were lost.

"It's a tree!" Simeon shouted suddenly. "A white tree!"

Wild hope rose in them. They pressed the horses, leaning forward, willing the animals to run faster. There was no time to plan, or even to think what they did. As they neared the white tree, its branches lowered, and one by one, Simeon, Amos, and Isolde leaped into the safety of the white bark and shimmering leaves.

For the horses, there was no escape. For Brand, the noble white stallion who had carried both Orin and Amos to safety, and Willa, the tender gray mare who had warned Simeon of the coming of the wolves, and Echo, who had guarded Isolde against attack and carried her over the far reaches of Shiloh, there was only death. It was bloody and brutal, and Isolde wept as black horns punctured the horses' sleek coats and sharp, pointed teeth tore into their flesh.

As the Daegan withdrew, the company was struck by the desperate nature of their situation. Except for the weapons they carried and the glass tucked safely into Isolde's belt, they had nothing. Their food and water was spilled and spoiled in the carnage of the horses. Without their mounts, they could perish from thirst before reaching the end of their quest. And what then?

"What draws you into the heart of the Shadow, travelers?" A single groove of bark opened in the trunk of the white tree.

"We go ta the Hall o' Shadows," Simeon replied. "And we need help."

"The Hall of Shadows?" the voice asked. "You go into grave peril, then. No man returns from the Hall of Shadows."

The branches of the tree shifted in a peculiar way, and the travelers grew uneasy.

"Please," Amos said. "We'll risk any danger ta find it. Will ya help us?"

"How many hang in the Hall of Shadows because of you, Amos, Wielder of Fire? Surely one more does not matter. Surely you would not challenge the Lord of Shadows for the sake of one miserable woman." As the tree spoke, two circles of bark pulled away to reveal glittering green-gold eyes. White branches snaked around the travelers' legs.

"Mordecai!" Amos growled.

"What has become of you, you who were once the fiery arm of the Shadow?" Mordecai's grip tightened with every word. "What do you think awaits you at the end of this road?"

The pain in Amos's legs intensified, the dull pain of bruised muscles giving way to the deep ache of bones pushed almost to the point of breaking.

"There is no *before* the Shadow. There is no *beyond* the Shadow. There is *only* Shadow. And it will feast on you as it has feasted on everything and everyone you love."

He was afraid. Afraid that Mordecai's words were true, afraid that no hope remained for Phebe or Simeon or anyone. By now, the fear was familiar. But others had felt the fear and fought anyway. Others like Evander. And Abner.

Amos wrapped his hands around the branch on either side of his thighs. "Ya said once that wielding fire was not yer gift," he said, channeling all his energy in a desperate effort to free himself. Beneath his palms, the wood darkened to black. Sap bled through his fingers.

Mordecai screamed. It was a burning, cracking sound as of logs splitting under intense heat. "No, Amos. My gift has always been —"

The wood around Amos's legs softened and darkened to deep green. "— adaptability." Mordecai spoke the word just as his shift was complete. Roots and branches disappeared. Only the trunk of the tree and one branch remained. While Simeon and Isolde fell to the ground, Amos found himself in the grip of a monstrous snake.

He held fast, hands gripping as tightly to the sleek scales as they had to the white bark. A thick, muscular loop encircled his chest and squeezed tighter, tighter. He struggled, gasped for air, but he never lost his hold. Soon, the smell of roasting flesh rose to his nostrils. Mordecai's long body twitched and jerked. He raised his head, looming above Amos in the golden light of Phebe's lantern. Long fangs emerged, dripping acid. Mordecai pulled backward, preparing to strike his prey.

At that moment, Simeon pulled the dagger from his belt. He plunged it into the wide, tensed head of the snake. The serpent relaxed its grip, and Amos fell to the ground, crawling quickly out of range. Smooth green scales clouded and darkened, sprouting into feathers. Nose and fangs shrank and hardened into a sharp beak. Mordecai took his favorite form, flapping owl wings and leaping into the air. Isolde sent an arrow whizzing through the dark, but bird and arrow were both lost from sight. Mordecai was gone.

The glass globe was still. All of them were. No wind stirred the branches of the Silent Trees. But within the globes, pale vapors curled around the trophies of the night weavers. Over her empty, staring eyes, Phebe's lashes fluttered, just faintly.

Thirty-Seven

The trees thinned, and the travelers walked out into an open country where rolling slopes collided with jagged outcroppings of black rock. Here and there, cliffs jutted from the ground, their heights obscured by mist; canyons appeared suddenly at their feet, cutting great wounds in the land. The ground was blanketed in foul yellow-green mosses. Malevolent mist swirled around them. The fire that burned in the palm of Amos's hand and the light from Phebe's lantern could not penetrate it.

Isolde walked close on the heels of the men and tried not to think of Echo. She was glad that she had not known what her journey would hold when she left Fleete. Why must the road be so long, so perilous, so disheartening? She thought of the life that would have been hers if she had risked nothing, if she had stayed in her little cottage, in her little village, hidden away. And what sort of life did her lovely sister wake to every morning? She'd promised to return for Rosalyn when she found a way out. In this horror of darkness, that promise was the only thing driving her forward.

They had not traveled long before they were plagued by a parching thirst. Isolde wondered at it again and again. There was no great heat, and they moved at a comfortable pace. She reached out and waved her hand through a current of mist in front of her. It looked wet enough, as if she could cup the moisture in her hands and drink it. But when she withdrew her hand, there were tiny cracks in the skin. The mist, rather than filling up the space it occupied, was feeding on the moisture in the air, draining the life it touched. Isolde grimaced and walked on.

They stepped over small cracks in the ground and leapt over yawning chasms. They rested their legs, walked, rested again. They pushed themselves to their feet and continued their journey. Hour after hour. Step after step. If night turned into day and day into night, if yet another day dawned in the world outside, Isolde would not have known. Time was immaterial, as formless as the mist that circled their weary feet. They sat down to rest on a pile of boulders. How she longed to lie down on those great rocks and sleep, but she refused to give up. Again she rose. Again she walked into the heart of the Shadow.

She began to feel that they had walked in this twilight forever. Her cracked lips and swollen tongue cried out for water. And, though she failed to notice it, her light had dimmed dramatically in the hours or days or weeks since Mordecai's attack. There was hardly enough light to see the place of her next footfall.

Finally, Amos and Simeon sat down, and Isolde slumped to the ground. They sat long in that way, with no thought of getting up again. Isolde thought only of rest, of sleep, of oblivion. Amos spread himself out on the ground. Simeon's chin fell to his chest. Isolde stretched an arm over the moss and rested her head against it. And the world faded away.

Simeon dreamed that the stones around him came alive with legs. They scurried toward him, reached his boots, moved up his trousers. He tried to brush them away. He was frantic. But already his feet had disappeared, wound in webs of darkness. Line upon line, they wrapped him up. The hem of his tunic vanished, then the blade of his dagger. "Show yerselves!" he shouted.

He woke in total darkness. The last flicker of light had faded from their skin. Simeon reached out, groping for the lantern. His fingers closed on it, and he blew feebly into the interior. As always, bright points of light burst into life, circling each other like bees around a hive. He roused the others from sleep and told them of his dream. But they were weary, confused.

"What could it mean?" Isolde asked. "Have ya dreamed o' the Weavers before?"

"No," Simeon answered. "But every dream has been a warnin' or a message o' some kind."

Amos's brow was furrowed in thought. "Ezra said that Olwen gave the gift of magic, did he not? My father . . ." he paused. "Da said it, too, long ago. He said that Man and Woman were great and powerful, that their voices moved the world." He turned to Simeon, "Did anything happen when ya spoke in the dream?"

"No," Simeon replied. "I woke. That's all."

"What o' the glass, Isolde?" Amos said. "Has it anything ta show?" This time there was no mockery in his voice.

She pushed herself up, raised the glass to her eye, and moved it over the surrounding landscape. When she lowered the glass to her lap, her eyes were bright. "I see a broad green country," she said, "and towerin' lines o' trees some ways ahead."

"Does some enchantment lay upon it?" Amos asked. "What does the glass reveal?"

"The world stripped of Shadow," Isolde replied.

Simeon was quiet, thinking on Mordecai's words. *There is no before the Shadow. There is no beyond the Shadow. There is only Shadow.*

He thought of the children, chanting and pacing, in the Village of the Blue Lights. Had the Lost Clan, a thousand years past, braved the Whispering Wood and the Black Mountains only to sit down in the darkness and abandon their quest? Why had they failed? What had they forgotten?

"Leto's curse," Simeon said. "What did she say the Children o' the Morning would forget?"

"Their names, their creator, their gifts," Isolde said.

"Isolde, look at me." Simeon said. "Look at me through the glass!"

She looked at Simeon and raised the glass to her eye. She flinched and dropped it again. "It's too bright. I can't look at ya, Sim."

They had already forgotten their glory. Amos laughed aloud, and there was a blinding flash of light. Their skin lit with brilliant fire, igniting the air around them. They breathed deeply, feeling warmth and energy coursing through them, feeling hope rise in their hearts again. Their weariness and thirst forgotten, they stood and walked shoulder to shoulder into the deepening dark. And the mist fled before them.

The glass had spoken truly. Not far ahead, trees were growing. They were low and scattered at first. Then, they came together into a thick grove that rose up to a great avenue of mighty trees. Gray-white webs draped the branches, weaving them together into dense pavilions of Shadow. The grove was pregnant with movement. They had reached the lair of the night weavers.

Simeon's heart pounded in his chest. These were the loathsome, creeping demons that had spirited away his Phebe. He burned with a desire to crush them all. But the webs stretched in every direction, teeming with legions of invisible enemies.

He stepped into the grove. The ground rustled with the sound of numberless legs skittering over dank weeds. But nothing touched him. Not yet. The night weavers fled from his brightness, moving in another direction instead.

He covered ten paces, twenty, thirty. In another twenty, the grove came to an end in a wall of trees. Thin shafts of light filtered through the branches from the other side of the wall. Simeon made for the light, Amos and Isolde following close behind. Five more paces, then three, and Simeon realized that the shafts of light were disappearing. One by one, the breaks in the trees were being filled. The night weavers were gathering to block their escape.

"Amos, they're comin' together," Simeon shouted, "movin' toward that gap up ahead." Fear washed over him. He faded. Something grazed his shoulder. Something else brushed against his leg.

"Stop," Amos said.

"We can't stop. She's close, Amos!"

"Yer dream, Sim! Remember yer dream!"

It seemed absurd to think that this wicked horde could be moved by the power of his voice. This was the lair of the Shadow. Fear was natural. Fear was reasonable.

Something dropped onto Simeon's shoulder and crawled down his back.

"Show yerselves!" he shouted.

And they did, though Simeon and Amos and Isolde were unprepared for the writhing, twitching mass of legs that appeared. They were everywhere, crawling over one another along the forest floor, scurrying across their webs, dangling from the branches. By their sheer numbers, they could have overwhelmed Shiloh, spinning darkness around their victims by the thousands and carrying them away to the last man.

Fear and revulsion froze Simeon for an instant. Then a fire of righteous anger kindled inside him and he lit up like an inferno. Seen for what they were, the night weavers were a conquerable foe.

Their power lay in secrecy, in mystery. He pulled his dagger from his boot, and fiery light from his arms and his blade burned up the night weavers as if they were dry leaves. They gave way before him, tangles of legs spilling and tripping over one another in a desperate flight.

He smiled, blazing with brilliant light, and slashed through the wall of weavers and webs that blocked their escape. They burst out of the grove into a long, tree-lined lane. Everywhere, crystal globes hung from the branches. Simeon's smile disappeared. The Hall of Shadows.

Thirty-Eight

If a rainstorm of epic proportion had broken in the sky, and if time had stopped just as the first wave of giant raindrops fell in among the trees, it would have looked very much like the watery globes suspended in air, suspended in time, in the Hall of Shadows. The travelers had broken into the lane some halfway down its length. To left and right, the Silent Trees stretched long branches in and up, forming a pointed archway over the lane. The faint luminescence of the globes was the only source of light in that black hall.

They do look like trophies, Amos thought with a shudder as he peered at the lifeless faces behind the glass.

"There are thousands," Simeon breathed. "How are we ta find 'er?"

Isolde picked up a stone and cast it at the nearest globe. Inside, a young boy with blank eyes hovered motionless. The stone hit the crystal and fell to the ground with a disheartening thump. It hadn't made a crack.

"By the gods," she said. "How are we ta free 'er?"

But the men had already gone in search of Phebe. There were so many, *so many* captives: men in trousers and tunics and belts branded with signs from every clan, women with flowing hair and flowing garments, and children. Many children. Small faces that should have been bright with life and hope stared blindly out of glass prisons. It was terrible to behold.

Amos and Simeon had one blessed advantage. Phebe was dressed in white, a color worn in Shiloh only on the rarest and greatest of occasions. In a sea of gray-clad prisoners, she stood out. They found her hanging near the eastern end of the hall.

"Phebe!" Simeon rushed to her, pressing his palms to the glass. The black stain of the river water still marred her lovely shift. Her black hair moved with the motion of the swirling white vapors, and her eyes focused on some invisible point in front of her. Simeon drew his dagger and stabbed at the globe.

"Do somethin' Amos!" he raged. "Ya must undo what you've done!"

Amos touched the glass tenderly. He remembered her little rag doll, the one with the scraps of colored yarn that she played with by the hearth. He remembered how her eyes flashed when he teased her and pulled her hair. He remembered how she greeted him with a hasty embrace whenever he walked through the door. Most of all, he remembered her voice. It was like the sound of bright bells cutting a path through a fog of black memories.

And now her mouth was closed, her voice silent. Her arms hung limp at her sides, and her face was blank. His eyes traced the scar that ran along his sister's cheek. If only the cat's had been the deepest wound she had received. How could he ever free her from this living death?

Amos knew that all the prisoners screamed and fought, pounding the walls of their prisons, when they first came to the Hall of Shadows. He knew that Erebus of the Nether Darkness slowly stopped their cries, slowly bound their hands and feet, until the victims were as lifeless as stone. Phebe looked as still as all the others. He raised both hands to the glass.

"Little nightingale," he whispered. There was the slightest flutter of Phebe's dark lashes, and Amos caught his breath.

"Phebe, ya have ta remember," he said.

But words failed him. He couldn't think what she had to remember. Would memories of Abner and Wynn be enough? Those memories were shadowed with sorrow. And what of her childhood? Of the years haunted and hunted by the Shadow. No. Phebe needed something more, something deeper. She needed to remember what all the Children of the Morning had forgotten.

"Phebe, bright daughter o' the Fire Clan," Amos began. "You were made by the hand of Ram, the First Creator and the Father o' the Immortals."

Phebe blinked.

"You were given gifts of beauty and song and strength and magic, and a glory that shines like the sun."

Her fingers twitched.

"It's there, Phebe . . . the sun. Just beyond the veil o' Shadow." Amos's expression was agonized, his muscles tensed, his fingers gripping the glass. "Da knew it was there. Ma, too. She just . . . forgot."

Amos rested his head against the glass and struck it with his fist. He didn't see Phebe's eyes focus on him, didn't notice her hands touching his through the glass.

A tiny crack appeared in the globe, at the place where their fingers met. Amos felt the subtle shift. He looked up into Phebe's eyes as the crack branched out in a dozen directions, a hundred directions. The Hall of Shadows echoed with the sound of shattering crystal as the globe fell to pieces and its prisoner fell limp into Simeon's arms.

"Phebe?" he asked, laying her down and stroking the hair back from her face.

She sat up and looked about her, at the trees, at the globes, at the motionless prisoners. "This is the place I always feared," she said. For a moment her eyes met Isolde's. Then she turned to Amos. "Are we goin' home?"

The men looked at one another. They had succeeded in freeing Phebe, and that had been the chief end of their quest. But the thought of returning to Emmerich seemed unbearable now. There was nothing for them there. If others had found a way out of this endless night, then surely they must follow. Only one thing blocked their path. Shadow Castle. They sat in the very lane that led to its gate, and the Lord of Shadows waited for them.

"We go ta Emmerich, then?" The light in Isolde's eyes wavered when she asked the question, and she looked to Amos, hoping.

"I don't want ta go back," Amos said. "I mean ta go on." Isolde threw back her head and let out a whoop.

Simeon, meanwhile, felt a pang for Orin. He wished his father had had the strength to come this far. But Ezra was with him. There was still hope that Orin would follow.

"I go as well," Simeon said, looking down at Phebe as he spoke. "If Phebe's willin'."

"I'd follow ya inta any darkness, Simeon," she said, and though her voice wavered, her face was full of love.

Simeon rose and lifted her to her feet, joining Amos and Isolde as they turned their faces to the east, to the last stage of their quest. Very soon they would see death, or they would see life beyond their wildest hope.

"Do ya think we're mad?" Simeon asked, glancing at Amos with a faint smile.

"'Mad as Evander?'" Amos replied. "I hope so, Sim."

On a rocky cliff, the Hall of Shadows came to an abrupt end, offering a sweeping view of the valley and Shadow Castle. It rose up from the heart of the valley in dozens of towers, all tall and pointed, with sharp roofs stabbing at the sky. Blue-gray Shadow stained the castle walls, clinging to them like mildew. It dripped from the towers and clouded the needle-thin windows.

Before any of them had time to speak, before their eyes had even taken in the scene before them, a black gate opened in the center of the castle and out poured the armies of darkness. Wolves and cats emerged in packs, leading ranks onto the floor of the valley. Behind them were the Daegan, black and bucking, and ready for battle. Next came a wave of shifters. Their shapes were indistinct, flickering from one monstrous form to another. Six winged men shot up from the gates and hovered over the assembling army. And one more foe, greater than all the others, was still to be belched from the castle. The dragons. They took flight, one by one. Amos counted ten, twenty, and still they came, blue fire spouting from their nostrils, ragged black wings trailing Shadow behind them.

Every fearsome thing that had ever wounded them or hunted them or held them captive was advancing upon them now. A mighty wave of darkness bore down on four little warriors standing on the edge of the world.

And one dark figure slipped from the shadow of the Silent Trees.

"What did you think awaited you at the end of this road?" Mordecai's words reached Amos's ears as the black dagger dug into his ribs.

Amos gasped and crumpled to the ground. Isolde caught his eye as he fell, and the arrow she had already strung burst into flame. The bow twanged. This time it found its mark, piercing one of Mordecai's green eyes and sending him off in a gust of smoke and wind.

"Amos!" Phebe cried. She was first at his side.

Simeon crouched beside her and tore open Amos's tunic. His chest was branded with the sign of the Wolf. The black dagger protruding from his side bore the same sign.

Phebe tried to staunch the flow of blood with her shift. "No, Amos. No, no, no, no, no!"

"Forgive me," Amos whispered to her.

"No, Amos," she cried. "Please, not you, too!"

Amos coughed. He fought to control his breathing. "Phebe," he managed, "will ya sing fer me?"

"Oh," she moaned. She clasped his hand in hers and looked into his face. And there, at the utmost end, as their enemies filled the valley below, Phebe willed herself to sing over the fading body of the brother she loved.

> Come, little nightingale, rest in the willow
> Sing me a song through the darkening night
> Come as I lay with the shadows my pillow
> And sing me a song o' the light

Isolde knelt opposite Phebe and Simeon and ran a hand over Amos's hair. She wondered if the story could have been different, if Amos could have stood, unwavering, in the face of such brutal opposition. She wondered what it might have been like if the son of Evander and the daughter of Valour could have taken on the Shadow together.

> Come, though the darkness around ya is deepenin'
> Sing, for yer song is a flame burnin' bright
> Come, though the Shadow before ya is creepin'
> And sing me a song o' the light

> Come, for yer music will ring out the clearer
> Brightest when darkness is all but complete

Come when the nightfall would threaten ta take me

Phebe's voice broke. She rested her forehead against Amos's chest and cried bitter tears for the brother she had lost, the mother who'd lost hope, and the father who'd been taken. She wept for the lonely years that followed, and for the sea of heartache they'd all been forced to cross. After a moment, Amos squeezed her hand, and she sat up and struggled on.

Come when the nightfall would threaten ta take me
Show me the path fer my feet

Come, little nightingale, rest in the willow
Sing me a song through the darkening night
Come as I lay with the shadows my pillow
And sing me a song o' the light
Come, sing me a song o' the light

Amos smiled at her as she finished her song, but Simeon shook his head, refusing to accept this, refusing to give in.

"Ya can't go now," Simeon said. "This can't be the end! Ya can't come this far and not see the mornin'!"

Amos looked past Phebe, past Simeon and Isolde. "I see it already," he said.

His blood pooled on the ground beneath him. He looked at Phebe, his eyes twinkling as they had when he was a boy.

"Come out o' the dark," he whispered. "Don't be afraid." His last breath caught in his throat, and he was still.

Phebe hovered over Amos, weeping. Simeon gently tugged Amos's hand from her grasp and laid it across his chest, covering the sign of the Wolf.

"They're comin'!" Isolde called.

The armies were closing in with alarming speed. Wolves and

cats to right and left moved up the slopes with fangs bared and eyes burning. The ground shook with the thundering onslaught of the Daegan. The shifters disappeared and reappeared, taking the shape of every imaginable nightmare. The stargazers flew in on a mad, screaming wind. And behind them were the dragons, born on the breath of hell.

"Isolde, the glass —" Simeon shouted, as he and Phebe tore themselves from Amos's body and turned to face the assault.

One last time, Isolde took the glass from her belt and lifted it to her eye.

"I hardly know ..." she began. "I see no valley, no castle, no cliff's edge. Only green hills rollin' down ta the sea." She lowered the glass and looked at the sheer drop beneath their feet. They could never survive a fall from such a height.

The wind reached them first, nearly knocking them to the ground. Instead of rushing past and on into the heights of the mountains, it turned, wrapping the warriors in a raging whirlwind. Around and around it circled, roaring and screeching. They could do nothing. Nothing but hold their ground. They could see nothing. Nothing but the advancing army.

The wind tore at their clothes. Their limbs shook from the effort of standing upright. There was no turning back now. Either the darkness would take them, or they would step forward, over the cliff's edge, and see what awaited them. They would have to choose between what the glass showed and what their eyes could see.

Simeon gripped Phebe's hand and shouted to Isolde. "Go out ta meet them! Step out!"

"Over the cliff?" Isolde shouted back. But she had heard his words. Already, her eyes were alight with pale blue fire.

The hosts of the Shadow were nearly upon them. They could smell the foul breath of the Daegan, could hear the rushing of the stargazers' wings. There was no more time to consider.

"Phebe?" Simeon held tightly to her hand and looked into

her eyes. What he saw there was trust, and hope. She nodded and turned to face the Shadow.

Against the overwhelming force of the wind, Simeon, Phebe, and Isolde each placed a foot over the edge of the cliff and planted it firmly on the soil of a brand new world.

All at once, the dripping fangs of the wolves and the cats, the great, spiraling horns of the Daegan, the wavering forms of the shifters, the deathly-white skin of the stargazers, the ragged wings of the dragons, even the ghastly towers of Shadow Castle evaporated. And the last whispers of the Shadow blew away like vapor on the wind.

At first, they saw only the black shapes of rocks and scattered trees silhouetted against a gray sky. Then softly, gently, the gray faded to blue. Blue faded to pale green. Green gave way to gold. They watched, captivated. They had only ever seen faint colors fading *into* gray. They had only ever seen light drain *out* of their world. This was altogether new. Beyond the Sea of Forgetfulness, Aurora rose up in a profusion of reds and golds, and the sun broke over the edge of the eastern horizon, loosing rays of golden light like flaming arrows.

Their eyes followed the path of the light, and they turned, their gazes sweeping back over the Black Mountains. Behind them were no iron gates, no blanket of impenetrable Shadow. They had stepped beyond the walls of the world and turned to discover that there were no walls at all. A wild and beautiful country spread out before them, and it pierced their hearts more deeply than any darkness they had ever endured.

Simeon gasped and touched Phebe's face. It was marred no longer. She reached to trace the line where the scar had been and found nothing. And Simeon kissed her as the joyful tears ran down her face.

They turned once more to the east and saw shapes moving on the edge of the sea. It could have been men or immortals. The dead, perhaps, or those who had found the way. They would know soon enough.

The Shadows had fled away at last for Simeon and Phebe and Isolde. They shone bright. Brighter than the sun. And the Children of the Morning ran into the dawn, into the breaking of the day.

Acknowledgments

My deepest thanks:

To my parents, who taught me to love language and story.

To Jon. "I'll walk with you in the shadowlands, 'til the shadows disappear."

To Silas and Lorelei, who are brilliant, glorious.

To Justin, whose questions and ideas helped me shape this world.

To Bud Sorensen, who was my first big fan.

To Jessica Preston, who cheered me through the toughest stages of this journey, and whose instincts are dead on . . . every time.

To Chuck, Aliya, and any of my early readers who gave even the tiniest bit of feedback.

To Phil and Mary, Dale, Peggy, and Denise, who showed me things beyond the Shadow.

To "Him that maketh the seven stars and Orion, and turneth the shadow of death into the morning." (Amos 5:8)

Pronunciation

Amos – AY-muss

Phoebe – FEE-bee

Simeon – SIH-mee-un

Rosalyn – ROZ-uh-lin

Isolde – is-OLD

About the Author

Helena Sorensen believes in the transformative power of words and stories, and in the power of the voices that speak them. Before she became a mom, she studied music, taught English, and dabbled in poetry and songwriting. These days, when she's not playing "royal ball" or "royal feast" with her daughter or doing science experiments with her son, she's hiking with friends at Radnor Lake or talking books with her husband. Of course, she might be at her kitchen table writing fantasy novels. She is the author of The Shiloh Series, including *Shiloh*, *Seeker*, and *Songbird*.

You can read more of Helena's work at www.RabbitRoom.com and www.helenasorensen.com.

Also from
Rabbit Room Press

The Shiloh Series
Book Two: Seeker
Book Three: Songbird

Visit HelenaSorensen.com for details.

RABBIT ROOM
— PRESS —

www.RabbitRoom.com

CPSIA information can be obtained
at www.ICGtesting.com
Printed in the USA
LVHW042026210219
608379LV00002B/12/P